A CLEAN SWEEP

Suncoast Society

Tymber Dalton

SIREN SENSATIONS

Siren Publishing, Inc.
www.SirenPublishing.com

A SIREN PUBLISHING BOOK
IMPRINT: Siren Sensations

A CLEAN SWEEP
Copyright © 2014 by Tymber Dalton

ISBN: 978-1-63258-119-8

First Printing: November 2014

Cover design by Harris Channing
All art and logo copyright © 2014 by Siren Publishing, Inc.

ALL RIGHTS RESERVED: This literary work may not be reproduced or transmitted in any form or by any means, including electronic or photographic reproduction, in whole or in part, without express written permission.

All characters and events in this book are fictitious. Any resemblance to actual persons living or dead is strictly coincidental.

Printed in the U.S.A.

PUBLISHER
Siren Publishing, Inc.
www.SirenPublishing.com

DEDICATION

For Sir. Because He's always helpin'.

AUTHOR'S NOTE

While the books in the Suncoast Society series are stand-alone works that may be read independently of each other, the recommended reading order to avoid spoilers is as follows:

1. *Safe Harbor*
2. *Cardinal's Rule*
3. *Domme by Default*
4. *The Reluctant Dom*
5. *The Denim Dom*
6. *Pinch Me*
7. *Broken Toy*
8. *A Clean Sweep*

Many of the minor characters who appear in this book also make appearances in—or are featured in—other books in the Suncoast Society series. Purson Gibraltar, who makes a cameo appearance in this book, can also be found in my Good Will Ghost Hunting series. All titles are available from Siren-BookStrand.

A CLEAN SWEEP

Suncoast Society

TYMBER DALTON
Copyright © 2014

Chapter One

Wednesday morning, barely five o'clock Spokane time, Essline Barrone stared at the cheap push-button phone in her hand. She could hear the dial tone droning on since her mom had hung up, but she just couldn't process the news.

Dad…dead?

It didn't seem possible. Edgar Barrone wasn't someone who died. He was the man who *gave* heart attacks.

He didn't die *from* them.

She finally realized the receiver was buzzing at her and hung it up. It was only pure chance her mom had reached her on the landline in the first place. Normally, they kept the phone unplugged and checked the voice mail once a week. People who needed to get in touch with her or her roommate, Amy, had their cell numbers. They only used the landline on the rare occasions they needed it. It came free with their cable and Internet package, or they wouldn't have had it at all.

Essie's parents were *not* people she gave her cell number to. Unfortunately, her cell phone had taken a swim in the toilet the previous day, and she'd used the landline to call Verizon to find out about a replacement that evening. She'd forgotten to turn the ringer off and it had awakened her from a sound sleep.

She heavily sat on the couch as shock settled in her system, nearly physically weighing her down.

Dead.

It didn't seem possible.

She hadn't talked to her mother in over five years. Not that she'd wanted it that way, but Edgar Barrone ruled his house with an iron fist.

It was one of the things she'd been happy to escape when she left home for college the day after she turned eighteen, almost three months after graduation. She hadn't set foot on their property just outside of Sarasota in the sixteen years since that day. She'd last seen her parents at a cousin's wedding in Tampa six years earlier. Her mom had looked tired and sad then, even more so than Essie remembered.

When her father started in on her mom about something stupid at the reception, Essie had stood up to him, for her.

That had earned her years of silence from her father, and only cards at the holidays and on her birthdays from her mother.

Maybe now I can have a relationship with Mom again.

She felt horrible about the thought. Then on the heels of that, angry that her father had put her in this position in the first place.

Amy walked through, looking bleary and half asleep. "Was that the phone?" She stopped when she got a look at Essie. "What's wrong?"

"That was my mom on the phone." She looked up at Amy, who'd also been her college roommate, and was her best friend. Amy Lionel and her sweet, welcoming family were the only reasons she'd moved out to Spokane after graduation.

Well, that, and she'd wanted a fresh start, a clean sweep far away from her angry, dysfunctional father.

"What's wrong?"

"Dad's dead." The words still felt foreign in her brain, much less coming from her mouth.

Amy gasped. "Oh, no!" She rushed over and hugged her. "I'm so sorry! What happened?"

"Mom found him this morning. They say it looks like he died of a heart attack or something."

Questions spun through Essie's mind. Her mom had been skim on the details, but Essie suspected the story was worse than what her mom had told her.

I found your father on the floor.

It couldn't have been *that* simple.

Not if the house was as bad as she remembered it. And chances were, in the sixteen years since Essie had left home, it was probably worse.

Much worse.

* * * *

Essie had already called her boss to arrange two weeks of vacation time, made her airline and rental car reservations, and had been gathering things to pack when the second phone call came through on their seldom-used landline.

The man's voice sounded slightly officious and vaguely accusatory. "Is this Essline Barrone?"

Her fingers tightened around the receiver. "Yes?"

"My name is Inspector Jack Davis. I'm with the Florida Department of Children and Families, Adult Protective Services. I need to talk with you about your mother. She listed you as her next of kin and gave me your contact information…"

Twenty minutes later, Essie was sitting on the couch, staring at the phone, stunned.

Again.

Yes, the day could get worse.

Much worse.

After explaining she'd been estranged from her parents because of her father's actions, the inspector's tone and approach had softened a little. It didn't change the fact that the house would be condemned by Sarasota County if they didn't get it cleaned out and repairs made immediately.

From the way he described it, she knew it had to be bad. Likely even worse than he described, but she didn't want to think about that now.

For now, her mom was staying across the street, at a friend's house, so they wouldn't take her into protective custody.

Thirty days.

What the hell *am I supposed to do?*

She didn't want her mother to be homeless. She knew the house was paid off, but how much would it need in repairs when they got the mountains of utter crap her dad had hoarded over the years shoveled out of it?

She quickly did a mental rundown of her own finances. She wasn't rich by any stretch of the imagination, but she did have a small and growing nest egg in her savings. She was a vet tech, luckily with a very good relationship with her boss. He would give her unpaid time off if she needed it, in addition to her paid vacation time. She could also tap into another two weeks of paid vacation she'd rolled over from the year before.

Amy returned to the living room, fresh from the shower. Her sleep had been blown, too, a fact for which Essie felt vaguely guilty. Now awake, Amy had started getting ready to drive Essie to the airport while Essie packed.

"*Now* what?" Amy asked. "You have that look again."

Essie tried to think about how to say it. Amy had never been to her parents' house.

No one had ever been to her parents' house when Essie was growing up. No friends, no relatives. If there was a repair her father couldn't make himself, it stayed broken or he replaced the item.

She'd gone out of her way not to describe her dad to most people, just leaving it at they had a contentious relationship and were estranged from each other.

Only Amy knew she'd grown up the child of a hoarder, and of a woman who felt too weak to stop him.

Essie finally settled on just relaying her conversation with the inspector to Amy. Amy, her best friend and roommate, who saw her every day and literally knew her better than anyone else. If Essie couldn't tell her, she couldn't tell anyone.

When she finished telling it, Amy walked over and sat next to her on the couch, draping an arm around her shoulders and holding her close. "Are you going to be okay?" she asked. "I know you bought the ticket already, but your mom didn't ask you to come home. You don't have to go. You don't owe the man shit."

Essie rested her head against her friend's shoulder. "I know. I kind of need to. I can't leave her to deal with all of that alone."

"She made her choices over the years. She's an adult. You gave her plenty of chances."

"Yeah, but I couldn't live with the guilt if I abandoned her now."

"Okay. Remember to call me if it gets too rough. No matter how late or early, I'm here for you."

"I know." Amy was an ER nurse, used to dealing with people at their worst. Either one of them could have afforded to live alone, but since Essie didn't mind when Amy's boyfriend Pete stayed over, and they'd just sort of grown into the habit of living together, they found it easier to be roommates.

It wasn't like Essie had a man in her life. She'd tried.

Unfortunately, the ghosts in her head were stronger and louder than any logic that tried to break through.

Amy easily tolerated Essie's spartan habits. Essie had learned how to compromise with Amy, now certain her friend's decorating and housekeeping style would never come close to her father's hoarding ways. Amy was laid back and flexible compared to Essie's rigidly structured, in-control nature. Amy taught Essie how to have carefree fun without sending herself into an anxiety attack over it.

It was an arrangement that worked for both of them.

And Essie didn't have to explain herself to Amy, explain why she refused to buy a printed book if it was available in electronic format.

Why she never bought DVDs or music CDs, and instead bought digital.

Why she used an app on her iPad that utilized the camera to scan paperwork, unless it was something like a car title for which she had to keep the original, which she then saved on redundant backup sources before shredding and disposing of the paper copies.

Why she always went for the paperless billing option, and frequently refused to deal with companies who wouldn't offer paperless.

Why she never brought new articles of clothing into her room without getting rid of at least the equivalent—or more—pieces at the same time.

Why she preferred not using paper plates, and making sure the sink never had a dirty dish in it.

Why she preferred to go to the store more than once a week, rather than stocking up extra items.

Why the only "clutter" she allowed in the kitchen were the magnets on the refrigerator.

Why they had the cleanest trash and recycling bins in the apartment building.

Why she kept a small, twelve-volt vacuum in her car's trunk and used it nearly every day.

Essie drew in a breath and let out a long sigh. "This is *really* going to suck," she softly said.

Amy nodded. "Probably. In more ways than one."

* * * *

At the start of his day, Mark Collins was the first one into the office. He was just getting ready to sit down behind the double-sided desk he shared with his brother, Josh, when the office phone rang.

Juggling his coffee and his laptop case, he managed to set both of them down without dropping either, and still grabbed the phone before it stopped ringing.

Yay, me. "Collins Cleaning Management. Mark Collins, speaking."

"Hey, Mark? It's Jack."

His heart sinking, Mark was already reaching for a notepad and a pen. They'd worked with Jack several times over the past few years.

It was never good when they did. Not because of Jack himself. He was a nice guy.

But because of the situation requiring Jack's involvement in the first place.

"What do we have?" Mark asked.

Jack had been busy that morning for several hours already. As he read off the particulars, Mark sipped his coffee and noted them. An elderly woman called 911 early that morning to report she'd found her husband unresponsive on the kitchen floor.

When EMTs arrived, the man not only had no vital signs, but had likely been dead for several hours, based on his body temp and rigidity.

And they'd had to climb through mountains of stuff, as well as excavate a path, to get to the patient and remove the body from the home.

They called the medical examiner's office, as well as the sheriff's office.

Who had then called in Jack Davis.

"She's safe, though?" Mark asked when Jack finished the rundown.

"Yeah. She's across the street with some neighbors. I talked to the daughter already. She's flying in today from Spokane. Apparently her cell took a swim, but she gave me that number anyway and said she'd have a replacement this morning before she caught her flight to Tampa." He read the number off to Mark. "Her name's Essline Barrone."

That name struck a bell, but at first he wasn't sure why. *Wait, that was the family's name on* Everybody Loves Raymond, *that TV show.* "How'd she sound?"

"Shell-shocked, naturally. She's been estranged from them for years."

"Damn." He took another sip of coffee. "Do you suggest waiting for the daughter before I talk to the wife?"

Jack let out a noise on the other end of the line that sounded like a sigh. "I probably would. From the way Corrine Barrone talked, her husband was the hoarder, but she seems pretty stressed out herself right now. Understandably so."

That was a relief. If the hoarder was the one still alive, it usually meant they only had a fifty-fifty chance, if that, of successfully saving the home. If it was a loved one who could let go of the clutter, their success rate was closer to one hundred percent.

"I'll try calling the daughter."

"Good luck with this." Jack read him off a case number. "Let me know if they refuse your services, and please keep me posted if they hire you."

"Thanks. Will do." Mark hung up and stared at the information he'd written on the paper. Sometimes, families hired them. Sometimes, they couldn't afford to hire them. Sometimes, they hired them on as consultants at a reduced cost, and family and friends and even fellow churchgoers pitched in for the sweat equity part of things. It fortunately wasn't the largest part of their business. Their main business was commercial and rental property cleaning services and disaster recovery.

But when one of their own aunts had been exposed as a hoarder eight years earlier after she had a mild stroke and had been rushed to the hospital, they suddenly found themselves in the hoarder recovery business as well. They averaged fifteen major cases a year with full involvement, and another fifteen to twenty where they were consultants working in some capacity with the family.

They were even featured in several episodes per season of a show on gO! Network. A production company out of Tampa contributed episodes to *Clean Turnaround*, that network's popular answer to *Hoarding: Buried Alive*. In fact, Purson Gibraltar, one of the production company's producers and costar of another show on the network, had called Mark over a week ago to check in and see if they had any jobs lined up they could film.

The family's name still rang a bell, though. And it was bugging the crap out of him.

Josh walked in, his own laptop case slung over his shoulder and a travel mug of coffee in hand. "You're in my spot," he joked.

"Bite me."

He pulled up short. "What's wrong?"

Mark held out the legal pad.

Josh took it and frowned as he read through the notes. "Dammit," he muttered. He handed it back to Mark. "I guess we're going to be on TV again."

"If they agree to it," Mark said.

Josh sat in the chair in front of the desk, setting his laptop on the floor between his feet. "I'm really beginning to wish we'd never started doing the TV show. It's sort of like we signed a deal with the Devil himself."

Fortunately, they didn't have much screen time. The network had their own team of "experts" who usually handled the clients. Most of what they did was provide the actual cleanup and related logistical services. Of the three of them, Ted got the most screen time, which was usually less than a few minutes per episode.

That was fine with Mark and Josh.

Mark tossed the notepad onto the desk. "Yeah, I know. Every time an episode airs, we get another shit-ton of calls."

It wasn't that they didn't enjoy helping people, because they did. But that wasn't where they made money.

If it wasn't for the royalties and stipends they earned from the show itself, they'd actually lose money on nearly every hoarding call where they provided more than just consulting services. They couldn't bring themselves to charge customers more than they could afford. They would state a set cost, and if customers could pay it, fine, and if not, they worked with them to help make it work and get as much of the job done as the client would let them.

And it emotionally drained all three of them. Especially Ted, who ended up quitting the practice he'd worked at as a counselor. He came to work with them as a full-time advisor and counselor, both on the show and privately, specializing in clients with hoarding disorders.

"Did you tell Ted?" Josh asked.

"I don't think he's home yet. Remember, he was up at Sully's this weekend. He was going out fishing on the boat with them."

"Oh, yeah. I forgot." He rubbed at his temple. "Sorry. I knew that. That's why they all weren't at the club Saturday night."

"Duh." Mark leaned back with his coffee again. "I guess when our contract comes up for renewal with the network, the three of us need to sit down and decide if we want to do this again."

Despite the emotional toll, Ted especially liked helping people, liked the way the network handled the editing of the episodes to be as respectful to the clients as possible while still showing the process. Liked it when they got e-mails saying that someone's relative finally reached out for help because of what they'd seen on the show.

Mark and Josh agreed with him there, but it was still a pain in the ass.

The door opened and their office manager, Tracy Porter, walked in. She and Mark had gone to high school together, and he was best friends with her husband.

She pulled up short. "Oh, don't tell me. Another episode has revealed itself."

Mark and Josh shared a look. "Dang, she's good," Josh said.

"That's why we pay her the big bucks," Mark joked.

She set her things down on her desk and walked over, her hand out, fingers waggling. "Gimme."

Mark handed over the notepad. She chewed her bottom lip as she read through his notes before handing them back. "Wow," she quietly said. "I always hate it when a death triggers it. Extra layer of epic fail for the family to deal with."

She knew as well as they did that it was easier for the process when the person doing the hoarding willingly wanted to change. It compounded the tragedy when something like a death forced the issue.

"Yeah," Mark said. "I know."

Tracy returned to her desk and powered up her computer.

"I wish I could figure out why the name sounds so familiar," Mark said again. "It's driving me crazy."

"*Everybody Loves Raymond*," Josh said. "That was the family's name."

Tracy didn't look up from her computer. "What was the daughter's first name again?"

Mark looked at the page. "Essline."

She *tsked* and shook her head at him. "Idiot," she teased. "Essie. How could you forget *her*? We went to school with her. She was in my English class sophomore year. We all went out to the movies together one day senior year. You were panting over her. And you spent the better part of a year pining for her."

He froze, staring at her name. "*Essie?*" He stared at his notes again. "Holy crap," he muttered. Now it hit him.

How could I have forgotten her?

"Yeah." Tracy swiveled her office chair to face him, concern in her expression. "We don't have to take the case if you don't want to," she gently said.

His notes seemed to scream at him, the black ink on lined, pale yellow paper in his face like DayGlo neon.

"No," he quietly said. "We have to. If they'll let us."

Chapter Two

Essie found herself sitting in the Starbucks inside the gate area at Spokane International a little before ten that morning. She still had an hour before her flight. Amy had taken her by the Verizon store first, so Essie could replace her phone. Then Amy had dropped her at the airport on her way to work.

She rubbed her finger up and down up the outside of her venti order of Pike's Peak—black—staring at her bare, neatly filed nail as she dragged it across the cup's smooth surface.

Just the thought of having to step inside that house again sent an itchy, crawling sensation wriggling up and down her spine.

The good news was, her mother was safe. Essie had called her at the friend's house once she'd gotten her replacement cell phone. She'd given her mom the number, as well as told her approximately when she'd arrive.

The bad news was, as Essie recalled the conversation with the inspector, her mother would lose her home to condemnation unless they got it cleaned out. Worse, the county could possibly have her committed, seizing her assets to pay for her care, if Essie didn't step in and do something.

Why should it be up to me *to do something?*

Her father didn't want her help while he was alive, and her mother never stood up to him despite her quietly siding with Essie.

Still, something inside her couldn't stand by and not at least reach out once more. One more time.

One last attempt to reconnect.

Now that Edgar Barrone no longer ran the show.

But it was going to suck. Big-time. And she knew it.

After she finished her coffee, she threw the cup away, shouldered her carry-on, and headed for the gate area. For the first time in her adult life, she regretted moving away from Florida.

If I'd stayed there, I could have driven home. Been there this morning for Mom. Or maybe forced Dad to get some help before it came to this.

As she settled into one of the chairs at the gate area and dug her Kindle out of her bag, Essie tried to shove that thought out of her head. This wasn't her fault, and logically she knew that.

I'm not the first estranged adult child to move far from home.

Hell, if it hadn't been for her stellar grades in high school, she wouldn't have been able to attend school at UF in Gainesville, earning a full-ride scholarship, including housing.

And college in Gainesville had been a blessed relief. Freedom. Control.

A dorm room, shared with Amy, which was always neat and tidy and company-ready.

Amy's grandparents had retired to Jacksonville from Washington state several years earlier. She'd actually accrued enough high school credits she could have graduated early, but opted to move in with them for her senior year, earning her residency status and a lower tuition rate at UF, her school of choice.

Before Essie lost herself in the erotic ménage romance she was currently reading, she glanced at her new cell phone and realized it was practically dead already. The battery had been less than half-charged when it came out of the box.

Moving to a seat at one of the workstation counters, she switched the phone off and hooked it to the charger before plugging it in. Her mom had promised to call and leave a voice mail if she had to call before Essie arrived in Florida. By the time her flight was called to begin boarding, the phone had reached full charge.

She took a deep breath as she queued to board. She tried to stay positive, to think good thoughts.

This will be okay. I will get my mom back.

Even as the ticket agent scanned Essie's boarding pass before she could step onto the Jetway, Essie said a silent prayer to a god she didn't believe in that those words would come true.

* * * *

With the time difference, it was after eight o'clock that muggy May evening when Essie stepped out of the Tampa International terminal in search of the rental car counter. So much had changed since she'd last been there, including the airport itself. Purple light painted the landscape as she finally got her rental car pointed west over the Howard Frankland Bridge across Tampa Bay. She'd had a voice mail when she powered up her phone again upon getting in the car, but didn't recognize the number so she didn't play it.

She pulled over at the northern rest area on the Sunshine Skyway Bridge to use the restroom and settle her nerves. After she was back in the car, she played the message.

"Hi, Essie. I don't know if you remember me, but it's Mark Collins. We, uh, went to school together. Jack Davis called me in on, uh, the case with your mom. I know you're probably in the air now, but please call me when you get this, even if it's late. I'd like to discuss the options with you. Our company specializes in situations like this."

He hesitated. *"I'm really sorry about your father. I wish this was under better circumstances."* He listed two phone numbers, one matching the one on the caller ID. *"That's the office and my personal cell. Please, even if it's late when you get in, call me, okay? I'll be up 'til at least midnight. If nothing else, I'd like to know if there's anything I can do for you as a friend."*

She saved the message and noted his phone numbers in her contacts, her heart in her throat.

Remember him?

Hell, she never could *forget* him. Him, or his two hunkalicious older brothers. In high school, she'd mistakenly thought she could have something resembling a normal life if she devoted herself to studying as much as she could at the library or went out with friends. She'd secretly liked Mark from afar since her sophomore year, eventually meeting him through her friend and classmate, Tracy. And then they'd gone to a movie together one night, a bunch of them.

She'd had the time of her life.

When her father had insisted on her bringing Mark home to meet them before he'd let her go out with him again, she'd taken the coward's way out and told Mark she couldn't see him again.

There was no way in hell she was bringing *anyone* home to her house. The last thing she wanted was for her secret to get out. As a teenager, she'd been terrified of being kicked out of the only home she had, as disgusting as it was. Her room, and the bathroom she and her mom used, were the only functional rooms in the house. The kitchen was barely useable.

Her father had filled the rest of the house with junk, stuff he got everywhere, some of it bought at yard sales or flea markets or found on the side of the road.

The only good thing she could say about her dad was he had provided a roof over her head, food on the table, and clothes on her back. As she'd grown older and realized none of her friends lived the way they did, and began to understand why her parents, especially her mother, never allowed anyone over to the house, it made sense.

At least he hadn't fought her and her mom about throwing away obvious garbage, so they didn't have insects and rodents sharing the house with them. There were countless times she'd come home from school to find her dad had tried to "store" stuff in her room. She'd immediately throw it away, or move it into another room. It happened to the point she'd begged her mom to allow her to put a lock on her door.

Which her father had overruled.

Of course.

I bet I can't even get into my old room now.

She'd done a good job over the past sixteen years of avoiding the "what if" train of thought. First she had college and a part-time job to distract her. When she moved to Spokane after graduating from college, she had a full-time job to distract her. Amy had introduced her to her friends out there, and she'd basically been adopted by the whole Lionel clan.

She'd dated off and on, but had never found a guy she could be with long enough to either make it past her exacting standards, or who would put up with her control freak ways.

She was also weird in that she was the only vet tech at the animal hospital without any pets. She loved animals.

But she didn't feel ready for pets. For the responsibility of them.

For the emotional investment they required.

Her secret fear that something inside her might snap and instead of one cat, she'd end up with thirty of them.

As she stared at her phone, she made her decision. She'd wait to call Mark Collins until after she saw her mom.

Switching her phone to map mode, she punched in the address of her parents' house and pointed the car south again. Everything, including the rest of her life, would be on hold until she got to her mom and assessed the situation she had to deal with.

* * * *

All morning, Mark tried to focus on his work and not on the ghosts of what might have been. When lunchtime rolled around and he realized how obsessively he was checking his cell phone for missed calls, or how his heart started thumping when the office phone rang, he realized he needed to get out of the office.

He was heading for the front door when Josh called out to him. "Going to lunch?"

"Yeah, but—"

"Hang on. I'll go with you."

It wasn't really what Mark had wanted, but he found himself waiting for his older brother anyway. Ted still hadn't come in yet, wouldn't be there until later in the day.

They took Mark's car and went to a small family-owned pizza joint that they frequented a couple of blocks from their office. It was only May, and already heat shimmers sizzled off the pavement, bouncing Sarasota sunshine back at them from the ground as they crossed the blacktop parking lot and walked into the air-conditioned restaurant.

"You've been distracted all morning," Josh said.

Josh was only two years older than his own thirty-four, with Ted two years older than Josh. Both divorced, he and Josh shared a house. Ted, also divorced, had a small apartment near their office.

"A little," Mark admitted.

"Well?"

Mark played with the paper wrapper for his straw. "I keep thinking about Essie Barrone."

"Oh, boy. I was afraid of that."

"Don't give me any crap."

"You were in high school, dude. That was, what, sixteen years ago?"

"Yeah. I know."

Josh shook his head. "I thought you quit thinking about her when you met Carolyn."

"I did. Until today."

"Sheesh, you only went out once, and then she dumped you."

"I'm wondering now if there was more to it." At the time, Essie had tearfully insisted it wasn't him, that he hadn't done anything wrong, but she couldn't get into the reasons why she couldn't see him again.

Maybe the reason had been what he'd stumbled over this morning.

"She's probably married," Josh said.

"Probably." *It would be my dumb luck if she is.* "But are ya helping?"

"I'm trying to." He stared at Mark. "Her dad just died."

"I know."

Josh sat back in his side of the booth, slowly shaking his head and staring at him. After a moment, he broke his silence. "Wow. *Really?* Ted will have a damn field day with this."

"Not if you don't fricking tell him," Mark grumbled.

"You're not going to go all emo on us now, are you? I already talked to Purson and gave him a heads-up about the lead."

Mark inwardly groaned. Yes, they had a contract with the network for a total of thirty episodes, which at their current rate of hoarding cases, and at the current percentage of people who agreed to be filmed, would take them about another eighteen months or so to fulfill.

If the people agreed to be filmed. Many of them didn't.

Frankly, he didn't want Essie Barrone's pain splattered all over TV screens for people to revel in. She was different.

And this was personal.

At the time, his two older brothers had busted his balls about moping around for months after Essie ended things between them. Then in college he'd met Carolyn and eventually forgot about Essie.

Then his nasty divorce four years ago had been the focus of his life for nearly a year, and he hadn't thought about much other than work since then despite his friends trying to fix him up time and again with women.

Josh pulled out his iPhone and thumbed through it. "Tracy typed up the notes from the call already," he said, opening the e-mail with the document file attached. She'd cc'd all three of them.

Mark watched his brother's expression as Josh frowned. "What?"

"That address," Josh said. "Of the Barrone house. That's really close to Ross and Loren's house, isn't it?"

"What?" Mark pulled out his phone, but Josh was faster with the Google-fu.

"It is. Look." Josh turned his phone around to show Mark. On it, the maps feature, with a pin in place. "It's right across the street from them."

Mark took the phone from him and zoomed in. "Sonofabitch. I wonder if they know the family?"

"Who knows." Josh took the phone back. "They've only lived there a few years. I don't remember seeing anything last time we were over there, though."

No, as best he could remember, none the houses on Ross and Loren's street, while some of the yards looked a little scraggly in places, had appeared like a hoarder lived there.

"Well, if it's only the inside, maybe that makes our job easier," Mark said.

Josh arched an eyebrow at him. "And how long have we done this? You know as well as I do what kinds of secrets can lurk behind closed doors. And not just hoarders."

Josh picked up his glass of tea and took a sip. "Look at *us*, for example." He grinned. "Just three harmless brothers running a cleaning business. What could possibly be wrong with *that*?" He gave Mark a look of mock horror.

Mark tossed the balled-up straw wrapper at him. "Shut up," he mumbled.

Josh dropped his voice and leaned in, his tone changing from ball-busting to concerned. "Look, all three of us learned the hard way that it sucks to fish in the wrong pond. If nothing else, even if she is single and interested, don't settle for less than what's going to make you happy just because there's a teenaged boy locked in there wishing things had turned out differently and that the Kraken hadn't taken you to the cleaners. Ha."

The Kraken was one of the nicer nicknames his brothers had for Carolyn, who'd nearly succeeded in her quest to make him liquidate his share of the business. Until the brothers pooled their money for a better attorney, who proved she'd not only had nothing to do with the business, but that it had been Mark's before they met.

And Mark hated to admit it, but Josh was right.

For all three of them, dating and marrying vanilla women had just not worked out well.

As in, it had ended in miserable divorces for all three of them.

Josh tapped the table in front of him. "We've been through this before. Even Tony told us that. Don't settle. Life is too short to settle if it won't make you happy in the end."

Mark slumped back in the booth. "I know," he muttered. "I know."

He knew it. His brain had the message chiseled in granite in huge letters.

His heart, however, still softly pleaded for one more chance.

Chapter Three

Essie was glad the exit was clearly labeled, because when she turned off I-75 onto Bee Ridge Road, she didn't recognize anything. It felt more like sixty years had passed instead of sixteen.

Heading east in the dark, she tried to make things out with just the street lamps and lit store signs to guide her. So much had changed.

Well, I guess with Dad gone, everything's changed.

She didn't know if it made her a horrible person or not, but she hadn't cried yet. She'd loved her father despite what he was, but somehow she couldn't bring herself to shed tears for him.

She didn't know if that would change when she finally reached her mom or not. For right now, she knew she needed to be strong and hold her emotions back. For her mom, if nothing else. The next days—and likely weeks—would no doubt present plenty of opportunities for tears. And a fair amount of silently swearing at her father.

And I still have to call Mark back.

No doubt about it, she wasn't relishing the thought of *that*. She felt horrible, in retrospect, for ending things with him before they'd even had a chance to start. It didn't matter that they'd been teenagers. She still felt guilty over it.

Especially since she hadn't wanted to end it, but she'd panicked at the thought of bringing anyone over to their house.

He's probably happily married to a gorgeous wife with a whole minivan full of perfectly adorable kids by now. Would serve me right.

Finally, she reached her old neighborhood. Slightly rural, the middle-class neighborhood in unincorporated Sarasota County was mostly comprised of houses built in the late '60s and early '70s, each with huge yards, front and back.

She pulled into the driveway, behind an ancient Dodge pickup truck she recognized as her dad's, and a small Toyota sedan she suspected was her mom's.

I can't believe he's still driv—drove *that thing.*

That a peek inside the truck's cab revealed a passenger compartment with barely any room for the driver confirmed her suspicion.

The Toyota was neat and tidy, clean, although it looked like it was several years old.

At least one thing her mom had been able to hold her ground against, apparently.

Across the street, an outside light came on. The front door opened, light spilling out onto the lawn. Essie punched the lock button on the rental car's key fob and headed in that direction.

Her mom met her on the front walk, tears running down her cheeks. At least she looked healthy, if not thinner and more frail than she remembered, and her hair had a lot more grey in it.

She didn't think twice about wrapping her arms around her mom and hugging her as Ross and Loren Connelly stepped out behind her. She'd never met them before, and only knew their names because her mom had told her on the phone that morning.

"You must be Essie," he said. "Nice to finally get to meet you. We've heard a lot about you."

Considering she hadn't talked to her mom in over five years, Essie wondered how much her mom had told them, and how accurate it was. "Thanks for letting her stay with you guys today. I'll get us a hotel room and—"

"No," Ross quietly said. "We have two guest rooms. You're welcome to stay with us. As long as you need them, but at least for tonight. We insist."

Essie felt too tired and too emotionally wrung out to argue. Besides, his firm tone really didn't brook any resistance. Normally that might piss her off, but from the concerned expressions both he and his wife wore, Essie was in anything but an arguing mood. "Thank you again."

He smiled and stuck out his hand. "Ross Connelly. My wife, Loren."

His wife also shook with Essie. "Nice to meet you," Loren said.

Essie looked across the street. "How bad is it?"

"Honey," her mom started, "we don't need to—"

Ross gently cut her off. "Loren, why don't you and Corrine go back inside? I'll help Essie get her luggage and we'll be back in a few minutes."

Loren immediately draped an arm around Essie's mom's shoulders and led her inside their home.

"Thank you," Essie said.

"You say that now," he said, pulling a key from his pocket. "You haven't seen the inside yet. It's bad."

He led the way across the quiet street. "Fortunately, I've done work for the county code inspector who came by this morning. Technically he should have slapped a red tag on the front door and had the power shut off as a fire hazard, but I promised him we wouldn't let her come back here by herself, and that you were flying in and needed a chance to make arrangements to get it cleaned out. So he wrote a warning ticket with a thirty-day mandatory deadline for reinspection."

Her stomach tightening, she noticed he bypassed the front door and angled his path toward to the side garage door. Now other people had been inconvenienced, put their own necks on the line, all because of her father and his actions.

She pointed at the front door before they rounded the corner of the garage. "Do I want to know?"

"The front door isn't accessible from the inside."

She groaned. When she'd left home, while there was a path through the hallway and foyer, you could still come and go through the front door.

He unlocked the side door and reached in, finally finding a light switch. "How long's it been since you've been inside?"

"Sixteen years," she muttered. "Since I left home."

"Then maybe I'd better go first."

They had to pick their way single file along a narrow path that wound through floor-to-ceiling junk from the side door to the utility room door. Inside the utility room, the washer and dryer were barely accessible.

Yea, though I walk through the valley of the shadow of death…

Somehow she suppressed the nervous giggle that wanted to burp through.

"I walked over this morning when the ambulance showed up," he said, interrupting her snarky and what would have been sacrilegious thoughts, if she wasn't a nonbeliever. "I saw them keeping your mom outside, and I was worried about her. By law, the paramedics had to call in the sheriff's office and county inspector. Only because Loren and I stepped up did it keep them from taking her into protective custody as an endangered senior."

She could see why. He found the light switch inside the kitchen doorway. What she saw when she followed him into the kitchen pulled the breath from her lungs.

What used to be a spacious open counter looking out over a dining room area was a solid wall of…stuff. Fortunately, it looked like her mom had still held her own in keeping the kitchen functional, because the sink was empty, the stovetop clean, but even the kitchen floor had paths through stuff where the creep had begun. It didn't appear to be outright garbage by the traditional sense of the word, which relieved her. But it was still a mess.

There were two chairs at a mostly buried table in the corner of the kitchen, with just enough space for two plates.

Her eyes couldn't settle anywhere or on any one thing. It was not only far worse than when she'd left, it was far worse than she'd imagined it would be, even after her discussion with the inspector. A small path led out of the kitchen and through the dining room area. Another led down what should have been a hallway toward the smaller bedrooms.

"She found him here on the kitchen floor," he quietly said. "He'd been dead for several hours. Your mom said she sleeps on the couch in the living room because he's cluttered their bedroom so much, there's only room for one person in their bed. I didn't make it that far inside. I only made it in here to get her purse for her from the counter because her meds were in it. I had Loren take her out this afternoon to buy her some toiletries and a couple of changes of clothes to get her by."

Up, on top of the fridge, it was packed solid with boxes and…stuff. There was no rhyme or reason to any of it. Stacks of magazines and newspapers littered the kitchen floor, some of which had been scattered, likely by the paramedics and others. The counter was another meticulously arranged wall of boxes, plastic storage tubs, and carefully piled piles of…stuff. Crap. Junk. Clothes, yard sale finds, things that she had no idea what they were or if they were even worth anything.

"Holy crap."

The air felt stuffy, suffocating. She wasn't aware she'd started to faint until she realized there was a roaring noise in her ears and Ross had grabbed her, helping her down into one of the chairs and having to knock over another pile of magazines to do so.

"Are you all right?"

"No," she whispered. "How the *fuck* am I supposed to deal with this?" she said, hoping her language didn't shock him. "It'd take me a month just to clear out the kitchen and garage. I…I can't even imagine where I should start or what to do."

"We have some friends who have a cleaning contracting company. They specialize in this kind of thing. I can have you talk to them, if you'd like."

She focused on trying to drag air into her lungs. "I had a voice mail from…someone I need to call back. Tonight, apparently."

"Was it one of the Collins brothers?"

Her attention sharply focused on him. "You know them?"

"They're friends of ours."

She nodded. "I went to school with Mark. I guess the inspector from Children and Families called him."

"They're good."

Her new phone was in her pocket. "He said I could call him back tonight, even if it's late."

"I'm sure he means it."

Breathe. She had to keep reminding herself to do that. "How much and what kind of repairs does the house need?"

"One of the toilets doesn't work and hasn't for years, so they haven't used that bathroom. It's apparently not accessible anymore."

"Because of all this stuff." Everywhere. Some dusty cobwebs had been strung along the tops of some of the crap in the dining room, stuff that literally seemed to stretch nearly all the way up to the ceiling in many places.

"Yeah. And she thinks there's a roof leak in the master bedroom, because there's water spots on the ceiling, but she says that only started a few weeks ago."

Essie let out a snort. "Well, isn't *that* convenient, that it waited." To her right, on top of the pile of stuff on the table, lay several small, pink Dora the Explorer T-shirts, children's sizes.

She didn't have any kids. She was their only child. So who the shirts were for, she had no idea.

"Your mom said your dad was the hoarder."

Essie nodded. "Yeah," she quietly said. "It's sort of why I busted my ass to get a scholarship and never came back after I left for college."

"I take it you're—"

"*Not*," she firmly said, the nearly hysterical giggle burping through. "*Definitely* not." She thought about her bedroom at the Spokane apartment, which would make a carefully staged IKEA display look like a hoarded mess by comparison.

She desperately wished she was there instead of here.

"Okay," he said. "I have a lot of mutual friends with Mark and his brothers. We'll help pitch in. Whatever your mom needs. But you're her daughter. She's going to look to you for guidance here. So I need you to tell me what you want to do, and I'll throw my full weight and effort behind it to help you. We really like your mom. She's been so sweet to us ever since we moved in. I wondered if there wasn't a problem when she never invited us over, and wouldn't even open the front door for anyone."

"Oh, there's a freaking problem, all right." She looked at a Target bag on the floor next to the table. Inside lay several new plastic dog food bowls, each with orange clearance stickers on them marking them down to the whopping bargain of only one dollar each.

Her stomach sank. "Please tell me they don't have any animals."

"No. Your mom said they don't."

"Oh, thank god. I don't think I could deal with that."

"She said you're a vet tech, but I kind of get the impression she didn't have recent news on you."

She felt the tears rolling down her cheeks. Overwhelmed, she confided in him. "Yeah. Dad and I got into it at my cousin's wedding about six years ago. He was being a jerk to her and I finally called him out on it. I think he forbid her from talking to me after that."

"Ah." He let out a sigh. "From the differences in your mom's car and your dad's truck, it wasn't hard for us to connect the dots."

She snorted. "Ya think?" Immediately, she regretted her tone. "I'm sorry. I'm…just…this…everything…" She looked around again, feeling like the mountains of crap were crushing her shoulders.

He knelt in front of her and took her hands in his. She didn't get a flirty feeling from him. She wasn't sure how old he was, probably late forties or early fifties, but she felt almost a fatherly vibe.

A *good* fatherly vibe.

"Call Mark," he gently said. "Right now. If you want to do it alone, I'll step outside and wait for you. Or I can call him for you."

"The rest of the house is this bad or worse?" Frankly, she didn't have the mental or physical energy to go explore at that moment.

"I think so. From what she said."

Letting out a defeated sigh, she nodded. "Please stay."

He squeezed her hands. "Okay. You've got his number? If not, it's in my phone."

"I've got it, thanks."

He released her hands and rose, stepping back as best he could so she could dig her phone out of her pocket. Pulling the numbers up from her contacts, she dialed Mark's cell.

* * * *

Mark was sitting up in bed, half ignoring the TV where a crime drama droned on, and half ignoring the iPad in his lap where he was trying to clear out his e-mail. While he'd been hoping Essie would call him back, he was beginning to think she wouldn't, considering it was after nine o'clock.

Maybe she'll call tomorrow.

He'd just picked up his phone to look at it when it rang in his hand, startling him and nearly causing him to drop it as he fumbled it and finally hit the green button to answer the call.

"Hello?"

She still sounded the same as he remembered. "Um, hi, is this Mark?"

"Yeah. Essie?"

"Yeah."

He started to ask how she was, then mentally kicked himself. She was obviously horrible considering what had just happened. "Um, glad you got my message." *Lame.*

"Is it too late to talk? I can call back in the morning."

He desperately didn't want that. Despite what he knew his dating preferences were, he selfishly wanted to talk to her right now, right this minute, for as long as he could keep her on the line. "No, it's fine, seriously." He punched the home button on his iPad and called up the document file Tracy had typed for them. "I'm really sorry about your dad."

"Thanks. I...I haven't even thought about that part yet. I just got here a few minutes ago. Mom's across the street. The neighbors are really great. The Connellys. They say they know you."

Connellys? Then it hit him. "Oh, yeah. Ross and Loren." No doubt the couple hadn't revealed exactly how they knew Mark and his brothers.

"Ross is here with me right now. I wanted to see how bad it was before I talked with Mom about anything else."

And thus they had arrived at the crux of their conversation. "I don't want to overwhelm you tonight. If it's not a good time to talk, we can do this tomorrow."

"I don't think there will be a good time to talk until this...*disaster* is cleaned up. I'll be honest, I don't know what Mom's finances are, and I can't afford tens of thousands of dollars for this."

"Don't worry about it," he said. "We can deal with all that tomorrow. We will help you, I promise. Even if she can't pay for it, even if you can't pay for it. We *will* help you."

She sounded choked up. "Thank you. I–I'm just..." A little sound like a sniffle. "I'm in shock, I guess."

"I know losing your dad was—"

"Not even that!" Now she sounded angry. "I can't believe he'd do this to her. That she'd *let* him do this to her. I told her years ago, if she ever wanted to leave and come live with me that she was welcomed to do it and she wouldn't."

He expected Essie to run through the full gamut of emotions many times over during the process. And he was certain of one thing.

If she'd let him, he'd be there by her side through it all, even if all he could do was be a friend to her.

"Is your husband going to come help?"

Now that sound was definitely a snort. "I don't have one of those. Or a boyfriend. It's just me and Mom. And my best friend Amy, I'm not about to ask her to drop her life and fly out here for this. This isn't her mess to clean up. It shouldn't even be mine, but I can't let my mom do this alone."

"Do you think your mom will be open to us handling it for her?"

"Yeah. And she'll have no choice. I won't let her *not* handle it."

He knew from experience that wouldn't work. Her mom had to want it. "But she is the homeowner?"

"Yeah, she is now. This was Dad's mess, not hers. Believe me, she'll be all for getting it cleaned out."

He hoped she was right. It was what Jack had also told him, but Mark didn't want to count on that until the process was underway and they saw firsthand that Essie's mom was on board with it. "Okay. Look, let me meet you in the morning and talk. Is nine okay?"

"Yeah. Hold on. Tell Ross, please."

There was a moment as she passed the phone over. "Hey, Mark?"

A little disappointment filled him. He'd wanted to keep talking to her. "Yeah."

Mark confirmed the time, and Ross agreed he'd be there at the house, with Loren, to provide emotional support to mother and daughter.

When Mark hung up, he stared at the phone. He knew he was already on thin ice, but the fact that Essie was single wouldn't leave his brain now that it had dug its talons deep into him.

She's not married, and not involved.

Maybe I have a chance.

Maybe she's not kinky.

But maybe she is.

He didn't want to take advantage of her when she was emotionally vulnerable. But inside him, the teenaged boy who'd always wished they could have had a chance, a gut instinct it would have worked out all right, wanted to go for it and quit being afraid.

Wanted to quit settling.

He'd dated off and on since his divorce, falling in with Josh's friends, who he'd accidentally discovered all frequented the same private social club.

A BDSM club, to be precise.

While at first shocked, once he'd let go of his preconceived notions, he realized for the first time in his adult life he felt like he was right where he belonged. He wanted someone strong as a partner, who'd let him take care of her, a woman who could tell the world to go fuck itself while giving herself to him.

He and his brothers had all ended up members of the club. Once, two years earlier, they'd all even dated the same woman, who was looking for far more of a kinky experience than they were willing to give. He wouldn't deny it'd been fun with the three of them blowing her mind at the same time in bed. It gave them all a tantalizing taste of how good a poly arrangement might be for them.

Unfortunately, they didn't have the stomach for the level of edge play she'd enjoyed, like needles and cutting. They had all parted friends after a few months and still saw her from time to time at events or the private club they were all members of.

And yes, Josh was right that he couldn't settle. Even if lightning did strike and Essie and he had a chance, if she wasn't open to their lifestyle, it'd never work in the long term.

A slightly loud and obnoxious car commercial blipped across his brain from the TV and rudely yanked him out of his rapidly unfolding poly fantasy.

Her dad just freaking died and you're having dirty thoughts about her. Nice, asshole. Fucking classy. Keep it in your pants.

He put his iPad and phone on their chargers, shut off the TV, and tried to go to sleep without thinking about the things he'd really like to do with Essie.

Chapter Four

Ross shut off the lights and they walked outside, locking the side door behind them. Essie stopped in the driveway, next to her rental car, and rested her hands against the doorframe. With her head hung down, she tried to suck the clean night air into her lungs and drive out any last vestiges of the musty air she'd breathed in the house.

This was sooo much worse than she'd imagined.

"Where are your bags?" he asked.

"In the trunk," she muttered, still reeling. "Oooh my god." She burst into tears, letting Ross gently turn her and hold her as she cried.

"It's okay," he calmly said. "We'll take care of this."

"No offense, but that's easy for you to say," she sobbed. "I'm all alone here. I'm the only person she's got now, and I'm a damn basket case. I have no idea what the hell to do next. I don't have anyone to lean on, and how am I supposed to be strong for her when I don't even know how to be strong for *me*?"

"I meant it." He tipped her face up so she had to look him in the eyes. "*We* will take care of this. All of us, helping you. We have a pretty great group of friends, and between us, we know a lot of people."

"I can't impose on you all like this. This isn't your problem."

He smiled. "You're not understanding me. I'm not asking you if we can help you. I'm *telling* you we are *going* to help you. The proper response, and the only one I'll accept, is 'thank you.'"

Under normal circumstances, something like that would bristle her and make her lash out. But just like him telling her they would be staying with him and his wife, she found she didn't have the energy to fight.

Didn't have the desire to overrule him.

She nodded. "Okay. Thank you."

He hugged her and released her, taking the car keys from her and opening the trunk to get her bags. As she followed him back across the street to his house, she turned and looked. Yeah, the grass was scraggly in a few places, but it wasn't any worse than any of the neighbors. The house didn't stand out. The curtains were drawn in the windows along the front of the house, but it was nighttime.

No one had known the nightmare hiding behind the average-looking façade.

With a ragged sigh, she continued on behind Ross.

She was relieved to see their house, while tastefully decorated and bearing a lived-in feeling, was neat, tidy, clean, and non-cluttered.

Her mom sat with Loren on the sofa, her eyes red from crying.

Essie put down her carry-on and walked over to her mom to sit next to her on the couch while Ross continued on through the house with her suitcases.

She wrapped her arms around her. "I love you, Mom," she said.

"I love you, too, sweetie."

"We need to talk."

Her mom nodded. "I know."

"This is going to be difficult if you don't work with me. We have some things we need to discuss. For starters, funeral arran—"

"I want him cremated," she said, blowing her nose in a tissue Loren handed her. "He kept saying he wanted a burial plot, but he never bought one. And it's cheaper. No service. I don't want that. I can't deal with a service, and I don't want one."

The question Essie desperately didn't want to ask and knew she had to. "What is your financial situation like?"

Her mom sniffled before pulling out a smartphone, which surprised Essie. A few taps later, and she'd logged into a banking app. She turned the phone around to show Essie. "He didn't know I opened other accounts years ago. I had to. I didn't know what he'd waste our money on. I only showed him the one account. There's about eight thousand in that one still, and it's at a different bank. Those three there are in my name only."

Essie breathed a sigh of relief. At least her mom had some backbone left. Her mom had over fifty grand in the three different accounts in her name. With the joint account, that brought the total up to about fifty-eight thousand.

"Okay," Essie said. "That's good. We won't have to worry about probate or anything with those accounts."

She'd worry about her mom's future living expenses later. At least tonight it took a little of the pressure off Essie, that she wouldn't have to juggle too hard and fast with her own finances to get things moving. She also learned that her mom still worked part time, and received a pension from being a retired 911 dispatcher for the county. She wouldn't be eligible for social security for another couple of years yet.

"The other account is a joint account," her mom said. "I should be able to withdraw that money. And I have a 401k that's not part of any of those."

Essie choked back the relieved tears threatening to break through. "Do you know who you want to handle the cremation?"

"Are you okay with a cremation?" her mom asked her.

One less thing Dad can hoard, and one final fuck-you at him? Suuurre.

But she didn't say that. "I'm fine with that, Mom."

"Loren and Ross gave me a name of a place. I already called them to get a price. They said it would be less than two thousand dollars total if we're not having a service."

Essie's mental tally clicked down a little on the financials.

Fifty-six grand.

Ross returned and sat in a chair across from the couch. "Corrine, remember the friend of ours we talked with you about earlier?" Ross asked her. "The one who runs the cleaning service?"

Her mom nodded.

"Essie talked with him on the phone. He'll be over in the morning to meet with you both."

"I want it allll gone," her mom said, spreading her arms out in front of her for emphasis. "If they can help me dig out my clothes and family pictures and stuff, that's it."

Essie shared a glance with Ross. "Mom, I remember a china cabinet in the dining room."

Loren handed Essie's mom another tissue. She nodded as she blew her nose again. "My mother's china. Yes, things like that, I suppose, I want those saved. But the…*garbage*. All that…*shit*! I want it gone!"

Yay, Mom!

Essie didn't cheer that out loud, though. She hugged her mom again, knowing for her mom to swear it meant she was really upset. "I know this isn't easy on you."

"Oh, honey, this is a lot easier than you can possibly imagine." She blew her nose. "I loved your father. And I know he wasn't the easiest man to live with. And I love you for offering to let me come live with you, but when I took my vows, I meant them. For better and for worse."

It couldn't get much more *worse.* "I know, Mom." It wasn't the first time they'd had this conversation.

"I'm sure I'm going to cry a lot as we do this. But I want my life back. I want to be able to invite people over. Do you know how long it's been since I've been able to have people into my house? It was almost a…a *relief* this morning to go out there and see him lying there. And maybe it makes me a horrible wife for thinking it, but I'm not going to waste another minute of my life."

Warning bells started going off in Essie's brain. Maybe her mom wasn't doing as well as she was saying she was.

She gently patted her mom's back. "It's okay."

"No, it's *not* okay!" Corrine shouted, making the other three jump with the force and volume of her voice. "It's *not* okay what he's done to us! He was a selfish, stubborn man who wasted his life on this...*crap!*" She burst into tears again. "It was more important to him than we were, and that's not right."

Confused and uncertain, Essie embraced her again as Loren pressed more tissues into the older woman's hand. Essie met Loren's gaze this time. The other woman offered an apologetic expression and a confused shrug.

Great.

"Corrine," Ross said, "I think it's time you went to bed. You promised us that when Essie got here, you'd go to bed. You've had a very long, very stressful day. You need your rest."

There was that tone again. The one that Essie was more than willing to give a pass to tonight. Firm and brooking no argument, and yet gentle, the proverbial velvet-coated iron fist.

The way a father should be.

If they have kids, they're lucky kids to have a dad like him.

But her mom nodded as she calmed down a little. "Thank you both," she said. "I can't tell you how much."

After a round of good night hugs, her mom headed down the hallway.

Once they heard a bedroom door close, Essie let out a tense breath.

"Holy crap," she muttered.

"She's been like that off and on all day," Loren softly said. "I think part of her is relieved he's gone, and I don't mean that to sound horrible."

"No, I get it, believe me. I just can't thank you two enough for everything."

"I'd rather you both stay here with us," Ross said. "I think we haven't begun to plumb the depths of her emotions yet." He arched an eyebrow at her. "Or yours, quite frankly. If you're staying here, you both can retreat here for a safe space if you get overwhelmed during the process. And we won't have to go far if we need to ask questions or opinions. But are you going to be able to handle this? I'm willing to take point if you need me to. Just say the word."

"No, I need to do this. I *can* do this. I remember when I was really little, the house used to be clean. Mom kept up with things."

"I saw on one of those TV shows about hoarding that sometimes there's a triggering event," Loren said. "Was there something like that for your dad?"

Essie nodded. "His parents and his mother's mother died in a fire. It was the house he grew up in up north. I was really little, only two or three. But I remember Mom once saying that seemed to change him for the worse. His father was a hoarder, Mom said."

"That could do it," Ross said.

"She said before that happened, she could go behind him and toss stuff out. But it was like once the fire happened, he got worse, would fight her, get really mad if she tried to clean up. Eventually it got to the point where she was working so much, and taking care of me, that it was easier to drop the battle and just give in."

"We didn't speak much," Ross said, "but he struck me as a very stubborn man."

"*That* is an understatement," Essie said.

They all fell silent when they heard a door open again. Her mom reappeared. "Oh, I forgot," she said when she returned to the living room. "I have a life insurance policy on your father."

Essie hadn't even thought that far. "You do?"

"Yes. We each did. One hundred thousand dollars."

Essie's mental tally clicked up again, more relief pouring in.

"That's good, Mom. We'll talk about that in the morning."

She nodded and returned to her bedroom again, the door closing behind her.

Essie heavily sat back on the sofa, her head in her hands. "Holy shit. Oh, sorry," she added. "I just…Please stop the roller coaster."

Ross and Loren flanked her on the couch. "We'll let Mark tell us what the next step is when he gets here in the morning. Right now, let Loren show you to your room. You look like you need rest."

"Thank you."

She got up and grabbed her carry-on, following Loren down the hall.

"That's your mom's room," Loren softly said, pointing at a closed door as they passed. "This one's yours. You share a bathroom with her." She pointed to a closed door. "There's extra towels and everything in there. Please, make yourself at home. Help yourself to anything in the kitchen cabinets or the fridge."

"Thank you." Essie gave her another hug before Loren left the room, closing the door behind her.

Ross had left her suitcases on the bed for her. She thought maybe the room did double duty as a home office or craft room, because the bed was a fold-down Murphy bed that looked like it was normally a sofa. When she sat on it, however, she realized it was a high-end mattress, every bit as comfortable as her own bed at home.

Her phone vibrated in her pocket, a text message from Amy.

You okay?

She sat on the bed and thought about how to text her back.

I don't know how I am.

Amy texted her right back.

You need to talk? I can take a break.

That was right, while she was here dealing with the fall-out of her father's several decades of bad choices and stubborn behavior, there was a real world still spinning on around out there.

A world she'd never missed as much as she did right that minute.

No, that's okay. I'm exhausted and need to grab a shower.

What she didn't add was that she felt like crawling into a hole and pulling the dirt back over her.

Chapter Five

Essie spent a restless night tossing and turning, her brain spinning despite the relief of knowing her mom had her finances handled for the immediate future.

Does it make me a horrible person that I'm not sorry he's gone?

If she truly dug deep, she knew she loved her father. When she was little, they did things together. He took her places, shared his love of learning with her. But as she grew older, saw how her friends lived and how drastically different it was from how they lived, she felt a visible gulf widen between them. Her resentment over his actions didn't help.

As she kept her room clean, learning to do purges of toys and clothes when he wasn't around to scoop them up and take them out to the garage, she felt less and less charitable toward him, and even somewhat angry at her mother for not standing up to him more.

When do I get to grieve? Or can I, after all these years?

Yes, as an adult, she understood her father had likely suffered from a mental health disorder, possibly a form of OCD triggered by the horrific loss of his own parents.

It didn't mean it made her look back on her childhood with a different, less critical eye.

She couldn't do that.

When was the last time he told me he loved me?

She couldn't remember. Before she left home, certainly.

It was different with her mom. Essie understood, to a certain extent, why her mom remained with him. And she could forgive the years of silence from her.

But at least Mom's alive to explain herself.

And, somehow, had managed to wrangle control of their finances away from her father.

Essie knew she still needed to have a more detailed conversation with her mom about that topic. Before she moved away from home, she remembered her dad being in charge of the money.

Mom obviously has more of a backbone than I gave her credit for all of these years.

It was only six o'clock, and she knew any further attempts at sleep would be impossible, but she didn't want to get up and disturb the household. She didn't know how early the Connellys normally arose, and she felt badly enough as it was for disrupting their lives, no matter what they said to the contrary.

Did she have friends who would go to bat for her like this? Well, she had Amy, and Amy's family, who were like an adopted family to her. She had some friends, not as close as Amy, but still friends. Coworkers she cared about.

But, with the exception of Amy and her family, would any of them step up to bat for her like these nice people had for her mom? Would they shoulder the responsibility and risk and get involved?

She didn't know, and that saddened her. She'd like to think they might, but she wasn't even sure, other than Amy and her family.

What does that say about me*?*

Finally, a little after six thirty, she got out of bed and took a shower, despite having had one before going to bed. She wanted the time to think and wake up. When she emerged, she smelled coffee brewing.

Oh, thank god.

She didn't just drink coffee in the morning, she *needed* coffee in the morning. And according to her body clock, it wasn't even quite four o'clock in the morning yet, exacerbating her "not a morning person" problem.

I wonder how long it'll take me to adjust to Florida time?

Then again, if her mom was still as gung ho to clean out the house this morning as she was last night, maybe they could expedite the process and she could return to Spokane sooner rather than later.

On the heels of that, she felt like a royal shit of a daughter for thinking only about herself. There weren't many places in the contiguous forty-eight states she could go that were farther away from her mom's Sarasota home than Spokane.

Seattle, maybe.

Then again, with her father out of the way, maybe now her mom could call her whenever she felt like it.

She pulled on shorts and a T-shirt and made her way out to the kitchen where Loren, wearing a bathrobe, stood at the counter.

"Coooffeee," Essie moaned.

Loren gave her a smile. "In this house? Abso-friggin-lutely. Si— Ross needs it worse than I do."

It had sounded like Loren had started to say something else before saying her husband's name. She let it go, too tired and overwhelmed to even think about it. "Thanks again for letting us stay here. I can't tell you how much I appreciate everything you're doing for my mom."

"It's okay," Loren assured her. "We like having guests over. We don't have any kids or close family, just a lot of good friends."

"Considering the kind of family my dad was, maybe friends are better," she muttered. Heat filled her face. "Sorry. I guess you think I'm a pretty horrible daughter."

"No, not at all. Ross was estranged from his father. Fortunately, they reconciled right before he died, but I get it, believe me. And Ross and I share your view. You can pick your friends, even if you can't pick your family."

The man himself joined them in the kitchen a few minutes later, his hair damp from the shower and also dressed in shorts and a T-shirt. "Good morning. Did you sleep well?"

"The bed was great, thank you."

He smiled. "Not exactly what I asked, but then again I know it's a stressful time for you."

She felt more heat in her face. Why he flustered her, she had no idea. She hadn't felt like this since college, when one of her professors, whom she adored, made her feel like he was running intellectual circles around her without even breaking a sweat.

And it totally wasn't anything romantic. It was…

Well, like the kind of dynamic she wished she'd had with her own father. Someone with whom she could lay her burden down for a few minutes, who would watch her back for her and step in and give her a break.

Someone to lean on who she wasn't afraid of breaking under the weight of her problems.

Who am I kidding? I need to suck it up and deal with it.

A little after seven o'clock, they were all sipping their coffee when her mom's bedroom door opened. She was wearing what looked like a brand-new pair of pajamas when she walked into the kitchen.

Essie put down her coffee mug and went to her, hugging her. "Hey, good morning."

Her mom offered her up a tearful smile. "I was afraid I'd wake up this morning and dreamed you got here last night."

"No dream." *Just a fucking nightmare.* "I'm really here."

"Would you like some coffee, Corrine?" Loren offered.

"Yes, please. What time is that man coming this morning?"

"Nine o'clock," Ross told her. "Mark. He's a friend of ours. He's going to sit down with you and Essie and detail everything that has to happen to get you back into your home."

"I want it all gone. Just…gone."

"You can tell him that yourself when he gets here," Ross assured her.

"There's not much I want to keep. Just my clothes, the dishes, some of the furniture."

"We know," Essie said. "It's okay. We'll deal with that with him. I'll be there to help you."

"You know, I've seen those TV shows where they go into houses, and I used to dream about calling them and asking them to come help me with your father. But I knew he would never have allowed it. He would have thrown them off the property."

Now Essie felt even worse. Maybe she shouldn't have abandoned her mom. If she'd been closer, maybe she could have helped work on him for her, gotten him the mental health assistance he so obviously needed.

"Can they get rid of his truck, too?" her mom asked.

Ross nodded. "I'm sure we can."

"It still runs. I'll give it away to them." She let out a barking laugh. "One of the few things I can find are the car titles. I kept that stuff in my little filing cabinet."

"Mom, can I ask you a stupid question?"

"Sure."

"How did you get the money away from him? I remember Dad doing all that."

She smiled, but it looked sad. "A couple of months after you left for college, he forgot to pay FPL. He lost the bill. It cost us money to get the electricity turned back on, of course. Then he did it the next month. The third month in a row, I finally stood up to him and told him we couldn't afford for him to keep doing that. So I said either he let me handle all the money and the bills, and I'd give him a cash allowance every week, otherwise he would come home from work one day and every bit of trash in the house would be gone."

"Wow."

"Wow exactly. He caved. I'd already set up one of the other accounts by then. I told him the big check I wrote out of the joint account every month was for free money orders to pay all the bills at one time at one of those check cashing places."

She reached over and ripped a piece of paper towel off the roll hanging from under the cabinet and dabbed at her eyes. "He believed me. He never looked at the bank statements once I took over the bills, and I gave him his cash allowance every week. I made him think we were a lot poorer than we really were."

It was as if she deflated. "I feel horrible I lied to him about our money, but I was afraid if he knew how much money we really had that he'd go spend it on more of that…crap."

She waved her hand toward the front of the house, but her meaning was clear. She meant the massive undertaking across the street. "At least the mortgage is paid off, and I make enough between my pension and my part-time job that I have more than enough money to cover my monthly bills. But my greatest fear was if he blew through all our money and then I'd be left with a mountain of garbage *and* a mountain of debt."

When she burst into tears again, Essie held her close, awash in a sea of conflicting emotions and feeling like she was close to drowning herself.

* * * *

By the time nine o'clock rolled around, her mom had grabbed a shower and dressed and they'd all had breakfast. Her mom vacillated between tearful and laughing, sometimes from one second to the next. Essie wasn't sure if that was normal or not, and knew she'd need to text Amy with the question.

Essie was used to dealing with grief in terms of clients losing their furbabies to age, illness, or accident. She hated that part of her job with a passion, made even worse by not having a pet of her own to go home to and cuddle after work.

But she loved the rest of it, loved the animals, loved the people. Well, usually loved the people.

A few minutes after nine, a truck pulled into the driveway with Collins Cleaning Management logos on the sides. Essie held her breath as she followed Ross, Loren, and her mom out the front door and watched as a missed opportunity from her past stepped back into her life.

* * * *

Mark's eyes were drawn to Essie immediately. Standing behind Ross and Loren and an older woman he suspected was Corrine Barrone, Essie looked like she hadn't changed at all.

Scratch that, she was even prettier than in high school. She wore her brown hair longer now, pulled into a ponytail on the back of her head, no makeup, and her brown eyes bearing a sadness he wished he could fix for her.

Play it cool. Stay casual. Don't be an asshat.

It was difficult to remember her father had just died and her mom was facing losing her home when all he wanted to do was ask her over to his house for dinner that night.

"Hey, Mark," Ross said, shaking hands with him. "Thanks for coming out this morning."

Their eyes met briefly. He'd seen Ross and Loren two weeks earlier, at the last munch their BDSM group held. "No problem."

"This is Corrine Barrone, and her daughter, Essie."

Now Mark's gaze met and held Essie's, even while he was shaking hands with her mother. When he shook with Essie, he offered her a smile he hoped didn't come off as creepy and manic. "It's nice to see you again. I'm sorry about the circumstances."

Her brief flicker of a smile in return bore so much sadness that it nearly broke his heart. "Thanks," she softly said.

He couldn't help it. It'd been so long, and all those feelings he'd had as a teenager rushed back into his heart and soul despite his brain trying to apply the logic brakes.

"Did you want to head over there now?" Ross asked.

"Not yet," Mark said. "Let's sit down and talk first before we do that."

Once they were inside the Connellys' home and situated at their dining room table, Mark pulled out his iPad and got started. It was difficult for him to do what he normally did, speak how he normally spoke. This was different.

This was personal.

"Okay," he said. "Let me give you an overview of the process, for starters." He detailed what they did, what they handled, how they did it. That they were welcomed to bring in friends and family if they wanted to help with the cleanout, but those friends and family needed to be willing to sign liability waivers and follow the orders of the crew managers.

Then he got to the part of it he didn't want to discuss, and wanted to gloss over as quickly as possible. "We've also got a contract with gO! Network for a show they film. You are under no obligation to agree to crews coming and filming. Some people do, because then the network will underwrite a minimum of half of the expenses, but I can tell them that you don't want—"

"Yes," Corrine Barrone said with a firm nod of her head.

Relief filled him. "Good, I'll tell them we won't need their film crew for this."

"No, I meant yes to filming it," Corrine said.

Essie looked shocked. "Um, Mom, are you sure that's a good idea?"

She stared at her daughter. "He said they'd underwrite at least half the expenses, right?" The older woman turned back to him. "Isn't that what you said?"

"Well, yes, but—"

"Bottom line, how much are we looking at, minimum, if we don't film?"

He had to admit her forthright approach caught him off guard. "Well, without seeing the house, it's hard to say. But since there doesn't appear to be any major biological hazard involved other than dust, likely a base cost of ten to twelve thousand dollars, with possibly—"

"Alrighty then," Corrine said. "Yes to the filming. What else? Where do I sign?"

Mark's gaze met Essie's. She didn't look happy about this decision. "You don't have to decide that right this minute," he told the older woman.

"There's nothing to decide. This was my husband's mess, *not* mine. I want it out of there. If it means they can help pay for some of the costs, I'm all right with that. I'm tired of having to hide my life."

She grabbed her daughter's hand. "I have my daughter back. That's all I care about now. If putting this on TV can help someone else, and it can help pay for it, let's do it."

"Are you sure you want to do this?" Essie asked her.

"Absolutely. How soon can we start? Can we get this started today or tomorrow?"

He was in uncharted waters. Normally the process was the producer and their people met with the family and discussed things with them before initial filming started. Ted closely worked with the family, assessing the best way to proceed. Then they got the arrangements put together, and the crew assembled. Usually it took a couple of weeks, unless there were children involved and it needed to happen sooner to keep parents from losing custody. Or an animal hoarding case.

"We can't get the cleanout started today," Mark explained. "I need to coordinate with the production crew and assemble a team."

"I already made some calls this morning," Ross said. "I can have fifteen volunteers here in the morning to help start the process if you can get the waste containers brought in. Even more on Saturday and Sunday."

"And," Corrine continued, "if you can't arrange for a charity to take the stuff that's worth anything, I'm fine with you tossing that, too."

Essie looked uncomfortable. "How are *you* with all this?" Mark asked her.

Essie shrugged. "It's her house," she said quietly. "She's in charge of this."

"Are you all right with people coming in and cleaning it out?" Mark asked.

Essie let out a barking laugh. "Yeah. I don't want Mom to lose anything she wants to keep, like her clothes or family keepsakes, or pictures and stuff. As long as the people will help sort through all that, yeah, I'm good with it. I know I can't help her do this without a lot of help behind us. It's just too overwhelming. If she's okay with it being filmed, fine. I personally don't want to be on TV, so as long as I don't have to say a lot, whatever."

"Well, they usually film scenes of the family talking with their counselors for the show."

"If Mom's okay with them cleaning it out, why do we even need to do that?"

He knew they were putting the cart before the horse. "They have a formula they follow for the show, but nothing's set in stone. I'll let the producer know we need him down here ASAP to talk with him. I'm not going to push you into doing the show if you're not comfortable with it. We can say no to the filming, and if the expense is an issue, we'll work with you to get the costs down as low as possible and work out something."

"I want to do the filming," Corrine said.

"I'll do whatever Mom wants to do," Essie said, the set to her shoulders telegraphing to him that she wasn't happy with that idea at all. "If she wants to film, I guess we're filming."

He wasn't the counselor, though. That was Ted. And he suspected he needed to get Ted here sooner rather than later.

He went through some more things with them before shutting down his iPad. "Let's go take a look at the house then," he said. "I need to see what we're dealing with before we go any farther."

Chapter Six

Ross led the way, Mark following, Essie behind him, and Loren and Corrine bringing up the rear. Mark's memory had been right—the outside didn't look too bad.

"Can I walk around and take a look at the backyard real fast?" Mark asked Corrine.

"Oh, sure," she said. "It's not the greatest, though."

He opened the gate on the wooden stockade fence and breathed a sigh of relief. The expanse of backyard, while knee-high in weeds in some places, was clear of debris and garbage except for a tiny pile of branches in one far corner.

From behind him, Corrine spoke up. "I told him if he put anything outside, it would disappear," she said.

He looked at her, catching her firm nod. "The first few times he tried it, I did it. He stopped doing it. I don't know if that ended up being good or not, because then all that crap came inside. But at least outside we didn't totally look like white trash."

The screened-in porch sat empty except for a cheap set of plastic chairs and a table. "On nice nights, I come out here and eat at the table, or read," she said.

The sliding glass doors leading to it from the house were covered by vertical blinds that were pressed against the glass in an unusual way.

"You can't get to the sliders from inside," Corrine said. "He has too much crap piled in the way. I'd have to walk out and around from the side garage door."

Corrine crossed her arms over her chest, Essie draping an arm around her mom's shoulders and pulling her close. "I want my life back," Corrine softly said, sounding close to tears. "I loved him, and I paid my dues. I was a good wife. I never cheated on him, I didn't leave him, and I tried to take as good of care of him as I could. But dammit, it's *my* life now."

Then her tears flowed. Mark realized Loren was holding a small box of tissues. She pulled one from it and pressed it into Corrine's hand.

"Who does your yard work?" he asked.

"I've been paying the son of our neighbors next door to mow the front when he mows theirs. Once a month, I have him come back here and mow."

"We can use the backyard for one of the staging areas," Mark said. "We can bring things out through the back sliders and have one of the waste containers placed close to the gate if we can move the vehicles. That will speed things up, being able to move stuff out of the front and back doors."

Corrine nodded even as she sniffled. "Good. The faster, the better."

"I'll bring my mower over here this afternoon," Ross offered. I'll get it cleaned up."

"Perfect," Mark said.

"I'll help," Essie said.

"Ross, can you get the house unlocked?" Mark asked. "I need to make a quick call."

"Sure." He led the women through the gate while Mark pulled out his phone and hit the speed-dial number for Ted.

His older brother answered on the third ring. "Where are you?" Ted asked by way of greeting.

"Listen, I'm at the Barrone house." He quickly detailed what was going on. "I need you out here today. We need to expedite this case."

Ted paused. "Expedite it because you still have a thing for her? Josh and I already talked this morning."

Dammit.

He was going to beat the snot out of Josh. "Expedited because Essie lives in Spokane, and because Corrine Barrone wants it expedited. This isn't the typical case of having to fight a hoarder to clean it out. She's the surviving spouse, and she wants it cleaned out as soon as possible. Can you please call Purson and see if we can get him down here today to talk to them? And have Josh arrange for trash containers to be delivered ASAP. The biggest ones."

Ted let out one of those aggravated grunts Mark knew all too well. "Is this going to be a problem for you?" he asked. "I remember what you were like over her."

"Dammit, I'm not in high school anymore."

"Just remember that. We'll be there at two." Then Ted hung up on him.

Asshole. For a counselor, sometimes Ted could be too much of an annoying older brother to him and Josh.

He pocketed his phone and followed Ross and the women.

When he reached the garage side door, he tried to keep his mind firmly rooted in the professional end of things, but it was difficult. He could hear them talking from somewhere inside the narrow canyon running from the doorway into the dark recesses of the choked garage.

Fortunately, he didn't smell any rotting food or animal waste odors.

He hated the cases where animals were involved. He loved animals, and hated to see what happened in many cases of hoarders who had pets. Or, worse, who were animal hoarders. Or even cases where hoarders ended up with rodent and insect infestations.

Picking his way carefully toward the sounds of the voices, he finally found himself in the kitchen area. Carefully schooling his expression, he took a moment to look around with a professional eye to details. Poor Essie appeared close to tears, while Corrine just looked angry.

"Gone," Corrine said, waving her hands around. "I want. It. Gone. A clean sweep."

The kitchen, at least, was marginally functional, so that was a good sign. "May I?" he asked Corrine as he pointed at the fridge.

She nodded and waved her hands again. "Whatever you need to do, do it. I don't care."

He noticed a wedge-shaped area in front of the fridge door that was free of stacks of magazines and newspapers. Holding his breath as he opened the fridge, he was again relieved to see that not only did it work, it was relatively clean and not packed with old and expired food.

This was the first time in months that he'd opened a fridge in a hoarder's house and not gagged at the smell, or a cloud of flies escaped when he did.

"I clean it out every week," she said. "Another of the small battles I won. The first time I caught him trying to bring garbage back into the house, I told him he'd come home from work to find an empty house."

The inevitable tears. Loren pressed another tissue into Corrine's hand. "I hate that I had to be like that, but I didn't have the energy to fight him any other way. I wish I could have been stronger. I finally gave in and only fought the battles I knew I could win."

From what he was seeing, it was definitely what they would consider a Stage 4 situation, even a borderline Stage 5. Working in their favor was the fact that the house, like so many in their area, had a concrete slab, no basement, and was a single-story home, meaning little likelihood of structural damage from the sheer weight of the accumulated hoard.

"There's a roof leak?" he asked.

Corrine nodded and headed down what looked like it might have been a hallway. He followed her, and she squeezed into a doorway of a room and finally found the light switch. What was probably a full-size bed was only half-usable, the other side piled high with clothes.

"Over there," she said, pointing.

On the ceiling were water stains, but the lack of mold and their relatively light color told him they were fresh.

"The roof is over thirty years old," she said. "If you can recommend someone to fix it, I'd be grateful. I don't know who to call."

Ross had followed them down the path. "I'll call Seth," he said, meeting Mark's gaze. "He'll know who to recommend."

Seth was another of their "mutual friends." He'd been a contractor in a former life.

Now, he was married to Leah, who was also his slave.

"Your husband slept in here?" Mark asked.

"Yes. I slept on the couch. Trying to clean the bed off was a nightly war I got tired of fighting. I figured if I was more important to him than the stuff, he'd do it." She blew her nose. "Obviously, I wasn't."

"How many bathrooms do you have?"

"Two and a half. The master bathroom isn't accessible because of all his stuff, but it used to work." She turned off the light and eased her way past them, her agility making her way around the mountains of stuff a sad result of her being forced to live like this.

She led the way back down the hall, through the kitchen where Essie and Loren stood waiting. He noted that Loren now had her arm draped around Essie's shoulder. Essie looked like she'd been crying.

He wanted to stop, pull her into his arms, and hold her, but knew he had work to do to get this process started.

He and Ross followed Corrine down another path that led through what likely had been the dining room. Rabbit trails branched off in a couple of places, and then they were at a bathroom.

She turned on a light. Again, relief. While lots of things cluttered the space, the tub itself was clean, as was the toilet, and the sink. "My other victory," she quietly said. "I told him if I was going to be forced to live with this stuff, then he would help me keep at least one bathroom usable."

"But one of the other bathrooms doesn't actually work?"

"The powder room," she said. "The toilet stopped working and he never fixed it."

She then led them to the living room. She had what they called in their line of work a "cockpit" area, containing the TV, the couch, and a small coffee table doubling as a desk with a laptop on it. The TV sat on top of a two-drawer filing cabinet.

"That cabinet," she said, "is where I have our papers. That has to be saved."

"Of course," he said. "We'll come in and get that out first thing so there's no worries."

"I need to take stuff out of it now, I suppose," she said, sounding close to tears again. "I need to find out about the life insurance policy. How to collect it. And the truck title is in there."

He looked at Ross. "If you want to help me, we can probably move it."

Ross nodded. "Might be easier to grab it now."

"Can we get some of my clothes, too?" She pointed at four large, clear plastic storage tubs. Inside appeared to be neatly folded clothing.

"Of course we can," Mark told her. "Did you want your computer?"

"Yes, I guess I need that." She unplugged it from an extension cord and closed the lid, picking it up and hugging it and the charger cord to her. "This feels so…strange," she whispered. "I'm sorry if I look like I'm being heartless, but you have no idea how many times I woke up wishing this mess was a nightmare, and that I had the house I wanted to have."

"I understand."

He'd started to ask Ross if he wanted them to stash her file cabinet in his garage when he realized something.

The garage was where Ross usually kept their play equipment stored. When they had parties, they folded up the Murphy beds in their two spare bedrooms and moved in the play equipment to there, and to their living room area.

"Um, where do you want to put the file cabinet?" Mark asked.

"We can move it into the guest room she's in," he said without missing a beat, his gaze squarely on Mark's. "And her clothes."

"All right."

Corrine rejoined the women in the kitchen while the men worked to excavate the file cabinet and the tubs of clothing. It took them the better part of half an hour, and they moved it all out to the driveway, close to the house, as a temporary staging area.

"How are you keeping them out of your garage?" Mark mumbled to Ross while outside.

"A damn good lock," he said with a smile. I've got tarps over the stuff, so I'll be able to get the mower out while Loren keeps them distracted, but I don't want them in there."

"I don't blame you."

They returned to the kitchen. "Okay," Mark said. "My brother, Ted, will be here at two to talk with you. I need to make a couple of phone calls, and then I can draw up a contract giving us permission to get started."

"But can I sign it today?" Corrine asked, desperation threaded through her tone.

He smiled. "Yes, it'll be on my iPad. We'll print you out a copy for your records."

"Oh, no. Just e-mail it to me."

Essie let out a laugh before she clapped her hand over her mouth. "Sorry," she mumbled.

"What?" Corrine asked her.

She finally lowered her hand. "I have all my stuff done paperless whenever I can," she admitted. "I have an app on my iPad. I can scan stuff and then get rid of the paper copies. I hate paperwork."

Her mom hugged her. "I'm so sorry you have to go through this," she said. "But can you show me how to do that? I want one of those iPads. I don't want to bring anything else into this house once it's cleaned out except groceries. I want a fresh start without any junk."

Mark was ready to head back to Ross and Loren's house. He'd assessed what they needed to do, which would be first clearing a path through the living room to the back sliders so they could then make enough of a dent to work their way to the front door. Corrine had given him a good idea of what was keepable—fortunately not much—and what could be gotten rid of—most of it.

The garage would be tricky. One of his guys was good at climbing, and could probably scale the mountain of stuff in there to get to the front door. If they could pry it open, they could easily start cleaning it out. Corrine had assured him there was nothing in the garage she wanted to keep unless they located documents, family photos, and lawn and garden implements.

Ross would help Corrine arrange for a roofing contractor to come give an estimate, with Seth's input.

Now Mark had to draw up their contract.

"Can I talk with you for a minute?" Essie quietly asked him outside his mom's earshot.

"Sure."

They let Ross and Loren take her mom back outside to wait. When they were alone in the house, Essie seemed to take a moment to gather her thoughts. She clasped her hands in front of her and stared at the messy floor.

"I wanted to say I'm sorry," she softly said.

"Sorry?"

"For…before. In high school." Her gaze darted up just long enough to meet his before dropping to the floor again. "I really liked you," she whispered. "I'm so sorry I cut you off like that." She drew in a shuddering breath. "Dad insisted that if I wanted to go out with you again, I had to bring you here to meet them."

Elation that his instinct was correct warred with his common sense to try to stay objective. He didn't interrupt her.

"I panicked. I couldn't let anyone know about my dad. It wasn't nearly this bad when I was in high school, but it was still pretty bad. I was terrified that if anyone knew they might put me in foster care, or if they didn't do that, life would be hell for me with people picking on me."

"I wouldn't have told anyone." He realized how wrong that sounded before the words even hit the air. "I mean—"

"No, it's okay. I really meant it when I said it wasn't about you back then. I'm so sorry I had to do it. I just didn't know of any other way to handle it."

Fuck this, fuck objectivity, and fuck Josh's and Ted's opinions.

He stepped close and pulled her into his arms, holding her through her initial resistance, until he felt her sobbing and melting against him.

"It's okay," he whispered. "I'm here for you now. You won't be doing this alone, I promise."

He felt her fingers tighten against his shoulders as another wave of sobs hit her. "I loved my dad, but I hated him so much for all of this, what he did to Mom for all these years. I hate him!"

"Shh, it's okay." He didn't know what kind of shampoo she used, but he wanted to so he could start using it, too. He wanted to stand there in the middle of that disaster and hold her until she felt better again.

Even if that meant forever.

* * * *

Essie hated herself for breaking down, but she'd deal with any fallout from that later. For now, she needed to cry, wanted to scream and rage, and if Mark was willing to let her slobber and snot all over his shoulder, she'd take it.

"I feel like a horrible daughter for running away."

"You're *not* horrible," he insisted, his tone gently firm, much the way Ross had sounded. "You did what you had to do."

"You must think I'm a coward."

"I don't. I think you were in survival mode. You aren't the first child of a hoarder to leave home. You can't fix someone else if they don't want to be fixed. They have to want it. It's even harder to deal with when it's a parent."

After a few minutes she realized she was growing uncomfortably comfortable in his arms. Like if she stayed there too dang long, she'd never want to leave. With great reluctance, she finally stepped back, wiping at her face with her hands.

"Sorry," she quietly said. "I guess your wife probably wouldn't like this. Me hanging off you."

He smiled. "Well, considering we've been divorced for a few years now, it's none of her damn business."

She stared into his brown eyes. They'd only shared one kiss, right after the movie, a sweet, tender kiss she'd often thought about since that night until the normal stresses of being a responsible adult shoved the memory into a lockbox where it would quit pulling at her heart and conscience every time she wanted to recall it.

Before she realized what she was doing, she leaned in and kissed him, hard. At first he seemed too shocked to respond, but just as it finally hit her what she was doing, and that she probably should not have done it, he started kissing her back.

Not only kissing her back, but grabbing her and pulling her tightly against him, one hand firmly clamped around the nape of her neck, the other arm around her waist, so that she had no other option but to drape her arms around his neck and hold on tight.

Which she did.

When he finally broke their kiss, he pressed his forehead against hers. "Okay, sorry, what were you saying again?" he breathlessly asked.

"I…" She couldn't remember. There'd been an apology and snot-sobbing tears and…

That was when he kissed her again, his hand deliciously curling around the nape of her neck once more, holding her there. He took his time with his lips, gently exploring, completely in control.

After shoving back her initial ingrained reflex of wanting to pull away, she let go to him, let him take control.

This time when he ended their kiss her brain was blissfully silent and free of all the recriminations and wildly swirling thoughts that normally plagued her.

Feeling secure for the first time that she could remember in her adult life.

She stared into his eyes, not sure what to say. Hell, she was afraid to say the wrong thing.

"How about dinner tonight?" he asked. "My place. Josh will be there, too. We live together. I can even have Ted come over. He eats with us a lot. You know, we can talk, catch up. Discuss all…this."

"The house?"

"Anything you want to discuss. Just…I'm single. You're single. If nothing else, let's catch up, even if only as friends. No pressure. Please? We can tell your mom we need to plan the decluttering."

She remembered meeting his two older brothers. Back then, they were just as cute as Mark. And if the other two brothers were there, maybe it would help keep her from doing something stupid, like throwing herself at Mark again.

I live in Spokane. This is a really, really *bad idea.*

But she wasn't a teenager anymore. She wasn't beholden to her father's rules.

"Okay. Dinner. Sure."

She would have killed for the grin he gave her. "We'll cook," he said. "You just come, relax, talk."

Reality set in. "What about my mom?"

"I'll talk to Ross and Loren and I'm sure they'll be fine keeping her busy."

"Okay," she said, nodding. "Thank you."

Chapter Seven

Ted wasn't sure what was going through his youngest brother's head…

Scratch that, I know exactly what's going through his head.

He knew Mark wanted to help Essline Barrone and her mom, but he also remembered far too well how his brother had reacted to getting dumped by the woman in high school.

He and Josh had tried for months to shake their little brother out of his funk.

He also thought it was no surprise that Mark's ex-wife, Carolyn, had strongly resembled Essie in appearance.

He didn't know what the woman looked like now, but he remembered the cute, albeit quiet, brown-haired, brown-eyed girl. He even remembered the thread of envy running through him at the time. She was smart, got fantastic grades, and was cute without being a stuck-up snobby bitch.

Hell, he'd even been jealous of his little brother at the time.

And then she'd dumped Mark without much of an explanation.

Now Ted understood that, when he talked with her, it would likely prove to have been a case of not wanting anyone to get too close and expose her father's hoarding. But back then he'd had to deal with the fallout as Mark's big brother.

And he damn sure didn't want to have to deal with it again when she left Florida to return home to Spokane.

Not to mention, the last thing they needed during a televised case was anyone getting too close to any of them emotionally. They'd lucked out so far that their close group of friends were trustworthy and helped them take great care to keep their extracurricular activities quiet, but one could only risk that for so long.

Then again, all three of them were pretty much in a dry spell in terms of relationships.

Josh knocked on Ted's doorway. "Got a minute?" He had his iPad in his hand.

"Yeah." Ted got an actual office since he had to see clients in private. They could afford a larger facility, but none of them wanted to put the money into doing that when their current arrangement was only a minor annoyance on occasion.

"Got two of the large containers scheduled for delivery at the Barrone house tomorrow morning, early. By seven, they said. What'd Purson say?"

"He'll be down in a couple of hours. He's going to meet us there at the house at two."

"I'm going?"

"Damn right you're going, in case I need you to help me beat some sense into Mark."

Screw the sensitive approach. He didn't want his brother getting hurt.

Again.

"Fast-tracking this might not be a bad thing," Josh said.

"I know. I suspect I'll be helping the family more through grief than working on letting go of things."

"They already signed the contract, and our waivers and releases for filming."

"I saw those come through," Ted said. "I wish he'd let me talk to them before doing that."

"Well, it's not a bad thing."

"I don't want this backfiring in the middle of a job, much less a shoot."

And he didn't want it backfiring on his little brother, either.

"Do you think we should talk to Ross and Loren?" Josh asked. "They might be able to help us with him. Tony, too. Voices of reason?"

"I already thought about that."

"And?"

"No arguments there." Ted sat back in his chair. "Ross texted me that he's already rounding up help for this weekend."

"See? That's good. Maybe we can get the house cleared out in a few days and then put it past us."

"Do you really think it's going to be that easy if he falls for her again?" Ted asked. "She'll head back to Spokane, but you and I will be left dealing with the aftermath."

"Then again, maybe we're underestimating him."

Ted gave him one of "those" looks.

After a moment, Josh let out a sigh. "Yeah, you're right."

"Of course I'm right." He scowled. "Which sucks, because this is the first time it's looked like he's had any light in his eyes since his divorce."

"Too bad we don't have a nice subbie girl to fool around with," Josh said. "Keep his mind off Essie."

They'd each had play partners off and on, but other than their brief dabbling with a poly arrangement, no one they felt a strong enough connection with to take it outside of the dungeon. Definitely not enough to take it to a sexual relationship level, especially considering how emotionally gun-shy they all were as a result of their divorces.

Brothers first, their business second. Any woman in their lives would have to understand that.

Any woman who was right for them *would* understand that. And yes, he realized how outside the norm it was to think in terms of having a closed poly group with his brothers, but they'd already tried the other, vanilla route, and each of them had failed miserably. They had several friends successfully living in poly situations, so why couldn't they? They'd already had a successful poly relationship, until the woman wanted heavier kinds of play than they could give her.

It's way too soon to think about that. Right now, they needed to get the Barrone case done, handled, and get Essline back to Spokane.

Then the three of them could get together and Ted could tell his brothers what he'd like to do. That he'd like to see if they could find a kinky woman who would want not one, but three guys in her life on a permanent basis. If it was something Mark and Josh would even be interested in. They'd all joked about it at some point, but they'd never had a serious sit-down discussion about it since amicably dissolving their other poly quad.

I think it's time we do.

* * * *

Essie still couldn't believe what she'd done. It was totally out of character for her to act like that. To just grab someone and kiss him like that—well, okay, he wasn't a total stranger, but close enough to one.

And he'd kissed her back.

Twice.

The fact that she'd had such a visceral reaction to him didn't help her sort things out, either.

What the hell *am I thinking?*

She followed him outside and they locked up behind them before she headed to Ross and Loren's. The men started moving her mom's things into her room for her while Loren got lunch preparations underway.

"Are you all right?" Loren quietly asked Essie while they were alone in the kitchen.

"Yeah, I'm just…still in shock, I guess." *As good an excuse as any.* Not like she was going to admit to the woman, *Hey, I was sucking face with your friend in the middle of that freaking disaster area.*

She already felt like enough of a failure as a daughter. Her dormant libido getting the better of her for a few weak moments certainly didn't need to get added to her rapidly growing list of personality flaws.

Essie didn't know if Mark staying around was because of his normal job or because of their little interlude, but she certainly didn't mind it. After they finished eating, her mom called and made arrangements to have her father's body picked up from the hospital morgue he'd been transported to for the autopsy. She also set up an appointment for the next afternoon, to go to the funeral home and finalize the arrangements.

Before Essie could bring up the topic of going to Mark's house for dinner, he handled it for her.

"Mrs. Barrone, I hope you don't mind if my brothers and I borrow your daughter tonight. We'd like to have her over for dinner to talk. Fast-track the arrangements for the decluttering as well as pick her brain. Professionally," he added, glancing at Essie.

"Oh?" her mom asked.

He flashed her mom a smile that nearly made Essie wet right there. "We get some animal hoarding cases, and—"

Her mom waved her hand at him. "Say no more, please. I always wished we could have pets, but you can see why I put my foot down." She turned to Essie. "I'm so sorry, sweetheart. I know you always wanted pets."

"It's okay, Mom. I get it now."

Mark winked at her, leaving her both horny and feeling slightly guilty. A few minutes later, he said, "I'd like to go back over there one more time before my brothers and the producer arrive, if that's okay?"

Her mom handed him the key. "Be my guest. You don't need my permission."

Essie opted to walk over with Mark. "Nice fib," she muttered as they headed up the driveway.

He shrugged. "Not totally a fib. Usually when we get an animal hoarding case, county animal services has already been called in. I wouldn't mind picking your brain about it." He smiled at her. "Among other things."

She didn't understand why he had this effect on her, if it was just the stressful circumstances, or unrequited teen love, or what.

She also didn't understand the uncertainty she felt, the disturbance in her normally perfect and well-controlled equilibrium. Never in her life did she ever feel uncertain, except in the past couple of hours about this particular man.

"How are you holding up?" he asked as he unlocked the door. "With your dad's death?"

She thought maybe he'd want to talk about what happened between them earlier, or, quite possibly, do it again.

"I don't know," she admitted. "I'm a little surprised she's not having a service, but I certainly don't want to have one. It'll be bad enough I'm cursing his name over the next couple of weeks while we excavate this place."

"Hopefully it won't take that long to complete the initial decluttering."

He followed her inside to the kitchen. Then, she headed off in the direction where the bedroom she used to call home lay. She had to turn sideways to make it through the rabbit trail leading down the hallway.

It came as no surprise that the room was filled, as best she could tell pretty much to the ceiling, with crap.

Mark had silently followed behind her.

She blew out an aggravated breath. If it wasn't for Mark's expertise and a shitload of helping hands, there would be no way she could get this place cleaned out in a month, much less a week.

"Son of a bitch," she muttered, kicking at a box blocking the doorway.

It was too much for her. She kicked it again. "You son of a bitch!" she screamed.

"I take it you're not talking to me," Mark said from behind her.

"No. *Him*. My asshole of a father." She kicked the box again, getting a little satisfaction when she heard something rattle inside it. "Was all this shit worth more to you than we were? Huh?" Another kick, and the side of the box caved in.

Unfortunately, it was the lynchpin in a pile, and the entire pile tipped over.

Toward her.

"Watch out!" Mark grabbed her by the arm and yanked her out of the way as Mount Trashmore toppled, filling the space where she'd been standing with more junk.

"Are you okay?" he asked when they got back to the kitchen.

"No, I'm not fucking okay," she sobbed, happy to let him hold her close. "I'm not. Fucking. Okay."

He seemed as happy to console her as she was to be consoled by him.

"You're *not* alone," he said, his arms feeling way too comfortable around her again. "I swear you're not alone here. You can lean on me."

"This sucks so bad," she mumbled against his chest. "And I'm sorry I'm acting like an idiot right now."

* * * *

I'm not sorry.

But he knew that would sound really, really wrong. "I don't think you're acting like an idiot." And he didn't. He'd seen, almost verbatim, this kind of reaction before. Or close enough for government work.

This was the first time, however, that he'd been pulled so personally into the situation. Even with their aunt, while they felt badly for their cousins and they loved their aunt, it was apart from them.

It was different.

This was personal, because it was affecting Essie.

"How soon are we going to be able to start this?" she asked.

"Josh sent me a text. We'll have trash containers here tomorrow morning. You and your mom are free to do whatever you want, but I know the producer will want to start filming as soon as possible."

"And he'll be here today?"

"At two, yes. Look, I'll talk to him for you, see if he can minimize your screen time."

"Thank you. I'd really appreciate that." She seemed to realize he still had his arms around her. She carefully pulled away. "Sorry," she mumbled.

"Hey, seriously. I want us to be friends. Tonight at dinner, just hang out with us, relax, decompress. I already talked to Ross about it, he said no problem in keeping your mom busy."

"Thank you. I appreciate you being so nice about all this. I know it's your job and everything, but still, thank you."

He made her look at him. "This isn't just about my job, okay? I know a lot of years have passed, but I get it." He didn't want to tell her the full extent of his pining for her. Not yet, at least. It might scare her off. "I feel badly that I didn't make you feel secure enough back then to confide in me."

"It's not your fault. I didn't confide in anyone. I was roommates in college with Amy for over six months before I told her even a little about it. I felt too ashamed."

"The shame isn't yours to bear."

"I know that now," she said, staring around them again. "But..." She met his gaze head-on. "Growing up like this, it took me a while to realize most people don't live like this. I couldn't bring friends home to play, or have sleepovers, or even enjoy holiday dinners. I couldn't enjoy having a Christmas tree proudly displayed in our front window. None of that. Birthday parties."

She looked around again. "I never felt good enough. Because of all this…crap. It sucks knowing your father would rather have this shit than a happy kid, you know? And Mom couldn't stand up to him. I get it. I do. But I felt angry for a lot of years. Still am, at him. I know he was sick, but it doesn't change what he took from me, and from Mom, for all of those years in exchange for the crap."

Mark left Essie in the kitchen while he explored the rest of the house, taking pictures with his cell phone. Excavating the front door and hallway would be one of their first challenges. At least in the living room they could use the cockpit area to move stuff into while they got the path clear to the sliding glass doors in back.

He'd seen worse in terms of hazardous conditions. But in terms of sheer volume, this house was right up there with the worst of the worst. In another bedroom that Essie told him was a guest room, he couldn't see to the other wall over the ceiling-high press of stuff.

When he returned to the kitchen, she was sitting in one of the two chairs, staring at the floor.

"Just being in here depresses me," she softly said. "I didn't realize until I was back here how depressed I felt all the time growing up. Like all the joy was sucked out of my life when I walked into this house. That's why I loved school so much. I could escape this disaster for a few hours every day."

When she looked up at him, her brown eyes were full of tears again. "I can't imagine how badly Mom must be depressed about this, but I'm finding it really hard to feel sympathetic about Dad dying, and I feel horrible about that, too. I feel horrible that I feel glad he's gone. Because Mom's still young enough she can enjoy life. So his love of all this crap stole that from me, too, a relationship with him."

"Just keep remembering it was the illness."

"Yeah, but people get help for stuff all the time. Addicts get into recovery. He thought there was nothing wrong with him living like this, making Mom live like this. Making me grow up like this."

"The sickest people sometimes don't realize just how sick they are." He glanced at the time on his phone. "We should go back to Ross and Loren's. My brothers and the producer will be here soon."

He offered her a hand to help her up but she stared at it without taking it. "I'm going to look like a horrible person," she softly said. "I'm going to look like I didn't give a shit about him or my mom."

"No," he insisted. "You won't. You'll be a voice of hope. Who knows how many kids out there will see you, see your story, and think okay, someone else survived this, so will I?"

That's when she met his gaze again. "You think so?"

He firmly nodded. "I know so."

With a sad breath even he felt to the depths of his soul, she took his hand and let him help her up. "Thank you, Mark. I really appreciate this. I know I've said it before, and probably will again, but you've made this just a little bit easier to deal with."

He squeezed her hand and leaned in to kiss her, glad when she didn't pull away. "You don't have to be afraid anymore. I've seen your worst secret, and it doesn't scare me. I can handle this. I can deal with this. I can *fix* this for you, and I will. If you'll let me."

She threw her arms around him, hugging him. "Thank you."

As he held her, content to stand there as long as she'd let him, he inhaled the scent of her hair. "You're very welcome."

Chapter Eight

Around one thirty, Ted gathered Josh and headed for the Barrone house. Since he knew exactly where Ross and Loren lived, he didn't even need to consult his GPS to find the place.

Not to mention, Mark's truck sat parked outside.

"Well?" Josh muttered. "Do we pull him aside now and give him an attitude adjustment, or what?"

"Or what," Ted said as he reached for the door handle. "I don't want to jump all over him about this and drive him away. We need to work together as a team, the way we always do. We can't let him forget that."

"Good plan. Lacking specifics, but still greeeat."

Ted turned on him. "You want to offer up something more helpful than sarcasm, be my guest. Until then, shut your pie hole."

Josh snapped him a two-fingered salute from his brow, but kept his mouth shut.

Ted had parked on the street behind Mark's truck. Getting out, they headed across the street to Ross and Loren's house. Josh rang the doorbell.

Ross answered the door. "Hey, guys," he greeted them, shaking hands with them. "Come on in."

They'd been to the Connellys' house several times, but under far different circumstances. Like there were normally people in various states of nakedness being beaten, or scening in some other way.

In the living room, Mark was talking with Loren, and a woman who Ted guessed was Corrine Barrone.

And Essie.

He would have known her anywhere. A little older, as they all were, she still looked like she used to.

Only better. Prettier. More mature.

Hell.

If he was already feeling like that and hadn't even spoken with her yet, he suspected what Mark must be going through.

They were about to sit down and get started when the doorbell rang.

"That must be Purson," Josh said.

Ross went to answer the door and returned a moment later with Purson Gibraltar. Ted considered himself firmly in the straight department, but if he'd been inclined to swing the other way, the producer's piercing blue eyes would have been enough to coax him in that direction. He liked Purson as a, well, person. The man was personable, easy to work with, and always had a knack for gently coaxing difficult clients into doing what needed to be done.

For some reason, their relations with the hoarders always went more smoothly when the film crews were present. Ted didn't know if it was because the people were aware of being filmed, or because of Purson's special flavor of persuasion, or a combination of the two.

Whatever it was, despite the extra logistical aggravations it sometimes caused them, and the inconvenience it caused in their personal lives in terms of needing to be especially discreet, Ted never minded working with Purson.

Mark introduced them. "Corrine and Essie Barrone, this is Purson Gibraltar. He's the producer we told you about."

"Nice to meet you both," Purson said as he shook hands with them. He carried a large laptop bag Ted suspected had more than just a laptop in it. "Have they explained to you what we do?"

"Sort of," Corrine said. "He said the network will underwrite some of the expenses if you film it."

"Yes. The network pays for at least half of the expenses in exchange for filming the process."

"Essie has some concerns," Mark said. "Can I talk with you for a moment before we begin?"

Shit. Ted closely watched his younger brother. Whatever had happened between Mark and Essie in the hours before he and Josh arrived, it had hit Mark squarely in the heart. He could recognize that look anywhere.

When Mark started to lead Purson down the hall, Ted grabbed Josh by the arm and set out after them.

He didn't give Mark a chance to protest. "Whatever you're going to say, it needs to be said to us, too," Ted softly said when they were out of earshot of the others.

They stepped into a bedroom and pulled the door shut. Mark looked uncomfortable. "Essie doesn't want a lot of screen time. She left home when she graduated high school and was estranged from her father since then because of his hoarding. I agree with her, that she doesn't want to be made to look like she abandoned her mother and is acting callous about her father's death. I know you all are pretty good about that, but I wanted to make sure."

Purson nodded. "I see. So what is the situation with her father?"

"She's not happy he's dead, but she's very angry. Understandably so. She felt abandoned by him."

"And her mom?"

"She's here for her mom, isn't she? Essie hasn't seen or spoken to her mom in over five years, yet she immediately flew home without her mom even asking her to."

Purson fingered the bloodstone amulet he wore around his neck as he seemed to ponder what Mark had said. "Okay, I get it. We need to be sensitive to her, minimize her air time, and make sure in edits she doesn't look like she just turned her back on what happened."

Mark looked relieved. "Exactly. She was a kid when she left. She didn't have any power against her father. I'd really like that to be the message, that kids feel powerless."

"Okay. No problem." He shook with Mark. "Let's go make this deal."

They returned to the living room. Ted couldn't help but feel a little bad at how nervous Essie looked.

Cut it out.

The unrequited protective side of Ted wanted to drape an arm around Essie's shoulders, cuddle her close, and tell her everything would be all right. He was smart enough to recognize "damsel in distress" syndrome when he saw it, even in himself.

Didn't mean he was immune to it.

And if he wasn't immune to it, he knew Mark wouldn't be, either.

Before any of them could explain things, Purson jumped right in, sitting next to the women at the table and flashing them a brilliant smile.

"I really appreciate you allowing us to do this in what I know is a very trying time. Our goal isn't to sensationalize what happened. Our goal is to give others hope that there is help, a better life out there."

Ted watched as the producer turned his focus on Essie. "While we would like to film you, to get your statements about what you went through growing up, I want to make sure we honor your experience in as respectful and truthful a way as possible. I assure you, we don't capitalize on situations just to raise our ad revenue. We produce a show that has helped others with hoarding disorders seek help. That has given the families of hoarders the strength to know they're not alone, and to help them get through this. That's our goal."

Essie nodded. "Thank you." She glanced at her mom. "Look, I loved my dad. But I can't lie about how angry I am at him for what he did to me growing up, what he did to Mom all these years."

She reached out and wrapped her fingers around her mom's hand. "Nothing I said or did was going to make him change. He had to want to. He didn't want to, and I couldn't keep living like that. Now I've got my mom back, and I want her to have a good life."

Her mom covered Essie's hand with her other hand. "This will be okay, sweetheart. We'll get through it together."

Purson flashed them another of his smiles, the kind that Ted knew would make him wet if he was a hetero woman. "Good. We're on the same page."

They spent an hour going through the network's contracts, release forms, and setting up a shooting schedule. They'd have a skeleton film crew there early the next morning, in time to catch the delivery of the storage containers. Today, Purson wanted to do a walk-through of the house and property with a portable camera he'd brought with him, stashed in his laptop bag, as Ted had suspected.

Ted also knew he'd have a struggle to maintain his professional distance. Essie wasn't just a beautiful woman, she was emotionally fragile, no matter how strong she was trying to be for her mom.

She had deep emotional wounds from her childhood that she was just now beginning to debride.

It was also clear to him now why she'd jilted their brother. And Ted felt more than a little shame at the thoughts he'd had about her back then, the anger toward her over dumping Mark. Had he known what she was going through then, he'd like to think he would have helped Mark support her emotionally, as a friend at least, to get through it.

Then again, teenaged boys were sometimes lacking in that department. They could be total jackasses. He remembered his jealousy that she'd been interested in Mark back then, and how he'd felt more than a little smug satisfaction when she'd dumped Mark, before realizing how deeply his brother had cared for her.

That's in the past. It was time for a clean sweep, time to get to work and help her and her mom get through this. And to help Mark however he'd need them.

Because if the look on Mark's face was any indication, his brother was once again an enamored teenager, entranced by the quiet girl who'd managed to fly under everyone's radar.

* * * *

Josh kept his mouth shut while Mark, Ted, and Purson handled getting the paperwork and schedule arranged. He couldn't help but watch Essie as they went through everything.

She was still as beautiful as he remembered her.

Yes, he'd felt jealous of his little brother, and then angry at the girl who'd broken Mark's heart.

He could bust Mark's balls all he wanted, but he wasn't exactly in a position to throw stones at the walls of his glass house. He'd been lucky that his divorce had been quick and tidy, in terms of paperwork and execution.

That it had happened at all still left his heart raw and chafing. No, he and Suzanne hadn't been the most compatible of people in the beginning, but he'd thought they'd worked well together.

It wasn't until one day she announced that he wasn't submissive enough for her and that she'd found someone else that he realized just how much in trouble their relationship had been. Sure they'd argued from time to time, and sure, they liked to play around in the bedroom, but he'd never realized how deeply their hidden discord ran. How much they butted heads about things in their relationship, both of them vying for control.

Until he went to a munch with another friend of his and was introduced to a whole new world. He didn't realize how mainstream people like him really were, that there was a world out there he'd been clueless about.

How there were women who wanted a man to step in and take charge, and that he wasn't a domineering asshole for wanting to find one of those women.

Maybe a woman who enjoyed being tied up while he fucked her brains out.

A lot of missing pieces had fallen into place for him the more he learned. And then once he'd gotten Ted, and then Mark, involved with his "mutual friends," his brothers had also realized what was lacking in their own lives.

The Dominant in Josh wanted to drape an arm around Essie's shoulders, hold her close, and tell her to stand back and watch this while he fixed everything for her.

The man used to dealing with hoarders for a living knew he couldn't quite do that.

Especially since Mark was making moonie eyes over her. Sharing a woman and a play partner was one thing. Sharing his brother's first true love, a love Mark had never gotten over, was another thing entirely.

Then again, the point was moot. Essie didn't live here and had a life to get back to. Entertaining any kind of thoughts along those lines was a guaranteed path toward disappointment.

No, better to sit back and wait. If we're ever meant to find a woman to have a permanent relationship with, we will.

For now, he'd simply do what he did best—be a big brother and try to help restore order where chaos reigned.

Chapter Nine

Essie tried and failed to regain her equilibrium following her little interludes with Mark. It didn't help that his older brothers were still as hunky as she remembered. The producer, Purson Gibraltar, was equally hunky, although she didn't feel the same urges toward him that she felt toward Mark, Josh, and Ted.

Especially Mark.

This could be trouble.

Here she was, dealing with all this crap, and her libido had picked now of all times to rise up like a *Hallelujah* chorus.

It's not fair.

Then again, one thing she'd had hammered home into her brain from when she was a kid was life was anything but fair.

Tonight she'd be torturing herself again by willingly going to their place for dinner.

I'm an idiot.

The next step in the process was for Purson to set both her and her mother up with wearable microphones before taking them across the street.

"I'm going to ask you a series of questions," he said, "and then in edits there will be a narrator who leads in with the comment or question that puts your statement into context. Okay?"

She wasn't stupid enough to think "reality" shows didn't have some level of scripting, but to now be in the middle of one herself felt surreal and added to her discomfort and unsettled mental state.

Essie hated feeling like that with a passion.

"Okay," she agreed.

He got her mom's microphone set up first, then checked the sound levels. Then it was Essie's turn.

"Do you guys have to wear these during the taping?" she asked Mark.

He gave her what she interpreted as a kind smile. "Sometimes. Depends on what they're shooting." He hooked a thumb at Ted. "He spends more time in front of the cameras than Josh and I do. And they have sound techs with boom mics that record, too."

Once they were ready, and Purson was happy with how the mics were recording, they headed over to the house. Essie's mom got to be the one to unlock the garage door. Purson had her go first, as he followed her with the video camera.

"How long were you married, Mrs. Barrone?" he asked as she led the way through the garage.

"Thirty-six years," she said.

"And Essie is your only child?"

"Yes."

"Why did you stay with your husband so long when he was a hoarder?"

"Because he wasn't this bad at first. And I took a vow to stick by him until death do us part." She stopped and turned to face him. "Now, he's dead. And as horrible as it sounds, now I can have a life again."

"Did you love your husband?"

"Of course I loved him. I loved him very much. That doesn't mean I didn't get very angry with him or what he did. If I didn't love him, I wouldn't have stayed all these years. I always hoped I could change him. That he *could* change."

"That was good, Mrs. Barrone," Purson said. "Let's go on into the kitchen."

They made their way there. Essie hung back, uncomfortably aware of how close Mark stood to her, his two brothers behind him. Ross and Loren hung back to stay out of the shots for now.

"Where did you find your husband?" Purson asked.

Her mom pointed at the floor. "Right here. When I came out yesterday morning."

"Where did you sleep?"

She led the way into the living room, where her cockpit area had been set up. "They were nice enough to move my clothes for me already." She spread her arms, indicating the sofa. "This is all the room I had for myself. I couldn't even sleep in my own bed anymore because of all the stuff he put in there."

"Okay, I'm going to ask you a question, and I understand it might upset you, but it's something people are going to want to know. And you're not the only one who's felt like this, but it will help others to hear your explanation, all right?"

Essie's gut tightened, but she didn't interrupt.

"All right," her mom said.

"Why didn't you clean out the house?"

"Oh, believe me, I tried to clean up behind him. He'd yell and scream and argue and fight with me and bring more stuff in when I wasn't home. It got to the point where, after years of it, I didn't have the energy to fight him any longer. I picked and fought the battles I knew I could win and stuck with those. I know it looks bad, but I can't do anything about what people think about me. They didn't live through what I lived through. Or what my daughter had to endure. Now that he's gone, I can get rid of all this...*junk* for good and finally have a relationship with my daughter again."

Essie swallowed as Purson turned around and focused the camera on her. "When did you leave home?"

"When I graduated high school." He asked her several more questions about how and why she left, how she felt about coming back.

It was with great relief that he shut the camera off at that point and gave her a kindly smile. "Okay, that was really good. I'm sure we'll get some shots of you while you're talking with Ted in a family session. Right now, I'm going to walk around the house and film it. You don't have to stay in here with me if you don't want to, but I might have some questions once I'm finished."

"You film whatever you need," her mom told him.

Essie pushed past the brothers and Ross and Loren and bolted for the side door. She didn't stop running until she hit the yard, where she stood, hands on her knees and gulping in fresh air.

"Are you all right?" Mark asked from behind her.

She was aware Josh, and likely Ted, too, had all followed her.

"No," she whispered. "I won't be all right until this is over. Even then I don't know if I will. It can't bring Dad back and fix him before this happened, can it?"

She was aware of Loren slipping her arm around her. "It's okay to be upset," she softly said. "No one expects you to hold it in."

"That's a good thing, because I don't think I can."

Ross spoke up. "While we're all over here, I'm going to get my mower out and do that once Purson shoots the backyard."

"Good idea," Mark said.

Once Purson finished with the shots he needed, he called Essie in to the kitchen, alone, to film her again.

"What do you hope will happen with this process?" he asked.

She had to think about it. "I want my mom to be happy and not lose her home. I want the house cleaned out and the repairs made so she can live like a normal person and not be held hostage by this stuff or by my dad any longer."

"Do you think you and your mom will be able to resume your relationship now?"

"I hope so. I want to. I didn't want to lose touch with her. I didn't want to lose touch with my dad, either. He was the one who used his hoarding to build a wall between us. He didn't have to act the way he did."

"How does that make you feel, what he did?"

"Angry. Pissed off. Oh, sorry, can I say that?"

Purson laughed. "Yes, it's cable."

"I wanted a relationship with him. We were close when I was little. Then when the hoarding started, it was like that was more important. And that makes me sad as well as angry."

The light went off on the camera and he lowered it. "Do you have a picture of where you live now? Interior shots?"

"No, but I can have my roommate send me some."

"Great. That'd be fine. You can e-mail them to me."

"Why?"

"To show the compare and contrast. As sad as it sounds, to show that you are not your father's daughter." The man really did have gorgeous blue eyes. Despite his good looks, he still didn't do to her insides what Mark, and even Josh and Ted, did to them.

"Oh. Okay. I'll ask her to do that."

He started to lead the way to the garage and stopped, turning. With his voice lowered, he said, "Just for the record? Mark, Josh, and Ted are nice guys. I've seen them do a lot of good for people who let them. You can trust them."

She felt her face burning. It was as if he'd sensed her thoughts.

He smiled. "I can tell they really like you in a different way than I'm used to seeing. Follow your heart and your gut. They won't steer you wrong." With that, he turned and headed back toward the garage.

What the hell?

She didn't have time to ponder his statements, because it felt like the world was closing in on her. She had to escape the house again.

When she emerged into the sunlight once more, Ross was busy mowing the backyard while Mark, Josh, and Ted had moved the pile of branches closer to the gate. Her mom and Loren were standing in the shade next to the driveway.

"Are you all right, sweetheart?"

She didn't want to lie to her mom, but she didn't want her mom to feel any worse than she knew she already did. "I'm...dealing."

Her mom hugged her. "Go have a good meal tonight," she said. "Don't worry about me. I'm going to sleep well knowing that tomorrow is the beginning of my freedom."

"What about your job?"

"I told them what happened and what I'm going through right now with the house. They said I could have at least two weeks off, and if I need more to tell them."

She hoped two weeks would be enough. "Paid?"

"Oh, no. Not paid. But I don't mind." She walked over to her husband's truck and kicked one of the front tires. "Seriously, boys. I don't want this. I found the title in my files. I want it out of here. I'll give it away. It still runs."

"Let me call Tracy at the office," Josh said. "Maybe she knows if any of our crew needs a vehicle."

Purson got their microphones disconnected and put away. Essie needed a break from it all. Other than work, this was the most "together" time she'd spent with a group of people, other than Amy's family, since college. "I'm going to…" She pointed at Loren and Ross' house.

"I'll stay here with your mom," Loren said. "Go ahead. It's okay."

It took Essie every ounce of will she possessed not to break into a run as she crossed the street. Once she had herself locked in the guest bedroom, she sat on the bed and texted Amy.

SOS

It startled her when her phone rang in her hand less than a minute later.

"What happened?" Amy demanded, her protective tone sending Essie's control over the edge.

Essie flopped back on the bed and tearfully spilled her guts to her friend, leaving out the part about her kissing Mark.

When she finished, Amy sounded dubious. "What aren't you telling me, honey? I'm your friend. I won't judge."

Heat filled her face again. She briefly explained about Mark and their all-too-short history in high school. And what happened with him that morning.

Amy let out what sounded like a snort. "Okay. So you kissed him. He obviously didn't have a problem with it."

"You don't think this is a problem?"

"No, I don't. Girl, I've seen your Kindle. Don't go all uber-prude on me now."

"This isn't a joke. It's not funny."

"Do you hear me laughing? No. If your question is should you still go to their place for dinner? The answer is yes. Unless there's some sort of underground cannibal torture ring they're all a member of, I doubt you'll be in any danger."

"I wasn't worried about that," Essie mumbled.

"Okay, then. What's the problem?"

"I…" She had to think about it. "My life's upended."

Amy kindly laughed. "Aaaand there she is. There's my control-freak girl."

"Am I really that predictable?"

"Yes, and it's one of the reasons we get along so well. Go have dinner with hunky guy and his brothers tonight. Nurse's orders."

After using the bathroom and washing her face, Essie returned to her mom's driveway where everyone had assembled. It was after five, and Essie's stomach let out a grumble.

"These guys grill killer steaks," Ross said in response. "I hope you worked up an appetite today."

"I'm going to text you our address," Mark said. "They have to run back to the office to pick up Josh's truck. So meet us at our place at six thirty, if that's all right?" He started thumbing a message into his phone.

"Okay." Her phone vibrated in her pocket. Yep, there was the address. Then guilt hit her again. "Mom, are you sure you don't want me to—"

Her mom waved away her objections. "Honey, I've got papers to go through. Ross said he'll help me figure out the life insurance policy and your father's pension, all that stuff. We'll be busy with that tonight. Please, go and have fun." She looked at the house, where lengthening shadows were cast by the sun dropping in the western sky. "I think we won't have much fun of any kind until this mess is cleaned up."

* * * *

After grabbing a shower, Essie looked up the men's address on her phone and timed her trip to arrive right at six thirty. Three trucks sat in the driveway, all bearing Collins Cleaning Management signs on the sides.

Another case of nerves hit her. Not just because of the brothers.

They're bachelors.

Yeah, but they run a cleaning service.

But they're bachelors.

The last guy she'd gone out with, despite having a tidy car, his apartment had been…Well, okay, nowhere on the scale of her parents' house, but it had sufficiently grossed her out enough that she didn't have a second date with him.

She knew all guys weren't like that, but it had soured her on dating, she'd have to admit. Amy's boyfriend, Pete, was wonderful at cleaning up after himself.

I can do this. Just dinner.

She grabbed her purse and headed for the front door. Josh answered, looking freshly showered and wearing shorts and a T-shirt. "Hey, glad you found it okay. Come on in."

She immediately began to relax. The house felt lived-in and homey, but was also neat and tidy. Especially the kitchen, she was pleased to see, which was as clean, if not cleaner, than her own.

What a relief.

Mark, who was standing at the stove and stirring something in a pot, flashed her a smile. "Hey, we were just getting ready to put the steaks on. Ted's got the grill ready."

By the time they were sitting down to eat, she hadn't been left alone with Mark, and had relaxed as the men talked about what they did for a living and not about her case in particular.

"How do you three live and work together and not kill each other?"

"Oh, I don't live here," Ted said. "I have my own place."

"He might as well live here," Josh said. "He's here enough. We keep asking him to move in. We try long enough, hopefully he'll accept our invitation and move back in with us."

"I think Mom worries about him," Mark offered.

"Where do your parents live?"

"They retired to Naples," Ted said.

"Oh, Italy?"

The men laughed. "A few hours from here. South of Fort Myers," Josh said.

"Oh." She felt heat fill her face. "That's right. Sorry. Been away too long. I don't remember the geography like I used to."

"No worries," Josh assured her.

She thought she might feel nervous around the three brothers, but the exact opposite happened. By the time they'd finished with their meal, she'd laughed more than she had in the past several months, and she wished the night would stretch on for another day.

She also felt more of an attraction for Mark's older brothers than she realized she would.

That both unnerved and excited her.

Maybe I can finally find someone. She'd seriously begun to wonder if maybe she wasn't one of those people who just didn't have a sex drive. Despite being lonely for intimate companionship, even of a nonsexual kind, her motor only seemed to rev a little when reading some of the kinkier books on her Kindle.

And it wasn't like anything out of *those* books was ever going to happen to her in real life.

But the fact that she felt an attraction to more than one man, maybe it was triggered by her father's death and her mom's newfound freedom. She didn't know.

All she felt certain about was that the new undercurrent of excitement in her own life, despite the circumstances surrounding it, was welcomed. Something she hadn't felt since leaving home for college, and then again moving from Gainesville with Amy to their apartment in Spokane.

Like a fresh start was within her grasp if she'd only stretch herself out on that flimsy branch just a little farther.

The men wouldn't let her help clean up. Josh and Mark took care of the dishes while Ted led Essie back to the living room and turned on the TV.

She started to sit on the couch when she spied the floor-to-ceiling bookshelves, filled with what looked like thousands of books and DVDs, all neatly arranged and dusted. The movies were arranged alphabetically by title, while the books were arranged alphabetically by author.

The tidy order to the full shelves soothed her.

"Holy wow," she said. "That's a lot of books." She looked up at another shelf. "And movies."

"Yeah, the books are Mark's, mostly. The movies are Josh's, mostly."

She turned to him. "What about you?"

He grinned. "You should see my Amazon and Netflix accounts."

"Ah. I have a Kindle." She turned back to the shelves. "Sometimes I feel bad that I don't buy paper books. But I've got thousands of e-books. Unless it's something I needed for school, or for work, or for a continuing credits course I'm taking, I try to buy digital. Or I check it out from the library." She smiled. "Netflix is my friend, too."

He shrugged. "I lost a lot in my divorce. All those streaming services were just really getting started then. I opted to go that route. I can access them pretty much anywhere, and when I finally move again, I don't have to pack them up and haul them around."

"Or dust them," she said, smiling.

He grinned. "Or sort them, or get rid of any of them. I always hated downsizing my books."

"Me, too. That's why I love e-books. I can always keep them." She ran her fingers over the spines, everything from classic fiction, to horror, to sci-fi, and even some nonfiction titles.

The movies were also widely varied, including a copy of *Sleepless in Seattle*.

She laughed as she pulled it from the shelf and held it up. "Whose DVD is this?"

In the kitchen, Mark and Josh looked up, saw what was in her hand, and pointed guilty fingers at each other, making her laugh again.

"No one's going to admit it, huh?" she asked.

"Hell, no," they echoed.

Ted sat at one end of the couch, a smile on his face. "I'm not ashamed to admit I enjoyed the movie."

"Good for you. I loved it." She slid it back into its position on the shelf and took the other end of the couch.

* * * *

Ted knew there was something about her. The more time he spent with her, the more he grew to realize he was attracted to her.

That, he knew, could be a very dangerous thing. Especially when he knew Mark was crazy for her.

Then again...

He shoved those thoughts out of his mind as he channel surfed, trying to find something he could put on that wouldn't distract them all too much while they talked.

Yes, he and his brothers had been poly and it had worked reasonably well for them. But that had been kinky, a BDSM dynamic. Okay, technically they all had dated her, too, and all had sex with her, but it was…different.

They'd known what they were getting into from the start, as had the woman.

This is not the unicorn we seek.

He nearly snickered at that thought as he paused on one of the older Star Wars movies.

"Oh, I love these movies," she said.

Choice made, he set the remote on the coffee table. "Then there it will stay." He knew he couldn't segue into a discussion of their own personal lives with her. "So without cameras or microphones or your mom around, how are you *really* doing?"

He gave her credit for putting on a brave face. Her sweet lips pressed into a tight, thin line as she struggled for control.

Finally, "Better than I thought I would, in some ways. And horrible in others."

"This is what I get paid to do," he tried to joke. "You can talk to me." He hooked a thumb over his shoulder. "Or, I can kick them out and we can be alone."

"Hey," Mark and Josh countered from the kitchen.

"It's *our* house," Mark reminded him.

But it worked. She smiled for him.

Yes.

"Please don't kick them out," she said. "It's all right." She settled back into the cushions. "I just…I think I should be more upset over his death than I am, but it feels like I'm more upset over the house. And that doesn't seem normal."

"Normal is a setting on a clothes dryer," Mark called from the kitchen.

"Quiet, you," Ted called back. "No counseling from the peanut gallery."

Another smile crossed her lips.

His heart twisted in a familiar way he knew could lead to absolutely no good if he let it get out of hand.

"Normal," he said slowly, hoping he wasn't grinning too widely, "is actually a setting on a washing machine."

"Asshole," Josh called out, his tone light and playful.

Yet another smile from her, this one almost reaching her eyes.

I could sit here and do this all night.

And that scared the crap out of him, how easily he could do that.

How much he wanted to do just that.

Chapter Ten

Essie got to bed a little before midnight Thursday, and felt like she'd just closed her eyes to sleep when the alarm on her phone scrambled her awake at five o'clock the next morning.

Heart racing from the alarm's loud screech, she stumbled her way out of bed and over to the dresser, where she'd left the phone on its charger, to silence it.

Oh, yeah. Today. It starts today.

She sat on the bed, rubbing at her face and trying to shove sleep out of her system. She wanted to crawl back under the covers and knew she couldn't.

She might be incapable of mourning her father right now, but she wouldn't allow her mom to go through this alone.

I need to wake up. By the time she stepped out of the shower, she smelled coffee brewing.

Oh, I love Loren.

She threw on jeans, a T-shirt, and sneakers and made her way out to the kitchen. Loren was also dressed in dejunking chic fashion, jeans and sneakers and a tank top under a denim shirt with the sleeves rolled up. She'd also pulled her hair up into a messy bun on the back of her head.

Good idea. Essie had stopped at a ponytail. She pulled the band out of her hair and quickly twisted it up and off her neck. *Less chance of catching it on something in that fricking maze.*

"Thank you sooo much," Essie moaned as Loren poured her a mug of coffee.

"Like I said, coffee is mandatory in this house." Loren prepared her own mug. "So how was dinner last night?"

"They were very nice." She sipped at her own coffee. Truth be told, she hadn't wanted to leave their house, wanted to curl up on their couch, preferably in their laps.

And that scared her.

It wasn't like her to just feel that way about someone.

I hope this isn't a bad thing.

Her mom appeared, dressed and looking far too chipper for that early hour and also allowing Essie to shove her thoughts about the men out of her mind.

"Good morning, sweetheart."

"Are you all right?" Essie asked her.

"I'm great." Her mom's bright and cheery mask slipped only a fraction before she firmly fixed it in place again. "I'm ready to get started as soon as possible."

Once Ross was up, he took the keys to the truck and to her mom's car, as well as Essie's rental, and moved them across the street to their driveway and yard. Essie helped Loren cook them breakfast, and then Mark showed up a little after six.

Essie felt somewhat guilty that she was attracted to his brothers, even though she knew they likely didn't feel anything like that toward her. She never should have kissed Mark. It was wrong to dump him twice when he was such a nice guy.

I won't be here long-term, so it doesn't matter. I'll just be more careful.

Moments later, Mark's brothers showed up with a work crew, as did Purson and his film crew. And by the time Purson had Essie, her mom, and Ted set up with mics, two large trucks had arrived and were looking for guidance on where to drop the large trash containers they hauled.

Mark and his brothers helped guide the trucks, one at a time, into the driveway, and from there it felt like Essie was swept up into a tornado.

Ross coordinated the arrival and assistance of their friends, who also seemed to know the three brothers. Essie was introduced to so many people in such a short amount of time she knew she wouldn't remember most of their names.

By eight o'clock, Loren had guided Essie back across the street under the guise of getting more coffee. Apparently Purson had instructed his film crew not to follow her.

"How are you doing?" Loren asked.

"Apparently not as good as Mom is," she said as she stared through the front windows at the anthill of activity. Already, the first things were being hauled out of the garage and tossed into the trash containers. Someone had set up two portable picnic tents in the front yard, with tarps spread out under them, to use as a holding area for items they wanted her mom to look at to decide their fate. In the backyard, another set of tents and tarps were set up for the same purpose.

A portable storage unit had also been delivered, and several boxes of photographs and papers had been deposited there for temporary storage.

Her mom had shocked Essie by declaring she wanted the house stripped down to the bare floors where possible, all the carpeting ripped out, the beds, sofa, and any other "soft" furniture thrown away. She only wanted to keep things like the table and chairs, bookcases, and other items of furniture that could be cleaned.

Then a small cheer went up. Essie watched as a group of about fifteen men forced the large garage door up while her mom clapped in glee. They helped another man, who'd been inside, extricate himself from the mound of stuff that seemed to flow from the opening, like a mudslide of junk.

Her mom, standing nearby, made an unmistakable gesture, waving both her arms at the garage and then at the trash containers.

Throw it all away.

The men set upon the pile, using large shovels and their bare hands as they began digging out the space.

"I should be out there with her," Essie said, feeling guilty.

"No one blames you for feeling overwhelmed," Loren said, making her take the mug of coffee.

"Oh, dammit. I forgot to ask Amy to send me those pictures Purson wanted." She quickly texted her friend, who responded a few minutes later that she would do it as soon as she got home from her shift.

Apparently all efforts had been shifted to the garage. By the time Essie finished her coffee and rejoined her mom twenty minutes later, they'd only made a few feet of progress despite every available worker getting involved.

"Isn't it wonderful?" her mom asked with a smile on her face. "I'll have a garage again. I'll be able to park my car in there."

Essie draped an arm around her mom's shoulders, holding her close and feeling horribly sad that her mother's existence had been rendered to such a sad benchmark of progress. "Yeah, it'll be nice for you."

Ted took a moment to join them. "How are you holding up?" he asked them.

"This is so wonderful," her mom gushed.

"I feel guilty I'm not doing more," Essie said.

He gave her a kindly smile. "We decided to focus on the garage because if it rains, we can also use it as a staging area."

"That makes sense."

He looked to where everyone was pitching in. "I think we have enough people in there right now." He returned to her. "But if you want to go into the kitchen and start on the floor in there, that's a one-person job."

"Okay."

He led her to a trailer, where they had all their supplies stored, and handed her two boxes of contractor's bags. A cameraman and sound tech broke off and followed them.

"Just fill them and put them near the doorway," Ted told her. "I'll have someone come take them out for you."

"Thanks."

Aware of her shadows, Essie rounded the garage and headed into the kitchen. Like Purson had the day before, she knew the cameraman would periodically ask her questions. Essie set the boxes of plastic bags in the kitchen sink and looked around, trying to decide where to start, the crew scrambling to stay out of her way as much as possible.

I shouldn't have to do this.

But she knew she had to do it, to help her mom.

Essie ripped the box open and pulled a bag out, deciding to work from the corner where the fridge was located and make her way across the kitchen. It took her less than a minute to fill the first bag with newspapers and magazines and tie the top flaps off. She dragged it over to the doorway and started filling a second bag.

She tried to remember the good times with her father and had to dig deep, back to her childhood, before middle school, to find one. Standing next to him at the stove while he cooked, frying up a batch of fish he'd caught that afternoon from a local fishing pier.

Before she'd realized how flawed her father was. When he was still her daddy and could do no wrong in her eyes.

By the time she'd finished filling the first box of bags, she was crying and didn't realize it. It wasn't until the cameraman spoke to her that she remembered they were there, wedged into the hallway to stay out of her way while unobtrusively documenting her progress.

"What are you thinking about right now?"

She sniffled back tears. "How my father wasn't always like this. How I wish I could have *that* man back, the one who spent time with me and Mom."

Josh appeared in the doorway and, without a word, grabbed two of the bags and hauled them out. In a few minutes, a steady line of people coming to take out the filled bags had whittled the pile down to nothing.

For Essie's part, she felt like she wasn't making any progress. Although there was now a larger clear space on the kitchen floor, it only served to accentuate the clutter in the rest of the kitchen, and the house.

Ted returned to check on her, bringing her three more boxes of contractor's bags.

"Is someone bringing more stuff in while I'm not looking?" she tried to joke. "I feel like Dad's ghost is here adding crap as fast as I get it out of here."

"That's a normal feeling," he assured her. "We haven't really begun the process inside yet. You should come take a break and check out the garage."

She did, following him out through the side door. It was weird being able to see daylight over the top of the canyon wall of the path from the doorway. She couldn't remember the last time she'd seen the large garage door standing open. When she walked around to the front of the garage, her mom's beaming smile greeted her.

"Look!" she happily exclaimed, walking inside the garage. They'd excavated about ten feet inside. "And I haven't saved anything so far except a rake and a shovel," she proudly announced.

"That's great, Mom," Essie said, hoping her smile looked real.

Inside, she was crying, her soul curled up in a tight little ball. Again, how sad was it that her mom had been forced to find joy in excavating her husband's legacy from her home?

Ted rested his hand on Essie's shoulder. "Let's take you and your mom into the backyard for a few minutes, okay?"

She nodded, letting him guide them back there, a film crew following.

No one had started using this staging area yet. "Corrine," he started, "how are you holding up?"

Her mom eagerly nodded. "You have no idea how happy I feel right now. I know I should be upset, but I'm not. I'm free!"

"However you feel is valid," Ted assured her. "Purson asked how you'd feel about a crew going with you to the funeral home this afternoon."

"I'm fine with that if Essie is." Her mom looked at her.

Essie shrugged. "Whatever Mom wants."

"Okay," her mom said. "That's fine then." A look of horror crossed her face. "Will things stop while we're gone? Because I don't want to hold up the cleaning."

Ted kindly smiled. "No, nothing will stop. You've made it clear what items we're looking for, what you want to personally check before it gets tossed, and we'll make sure anything we're doubtful about will be saved in a staging area."

"Oh, okay." She smiled. "I really feel happy for the first time in…I can't remember since when." She hugged Essie. "Thank you for coming home, sweetheart. I love you so much."

Essie choked back her emotions as she hugged her mom. "Love you, too. I just wish it'd been under better circumstances."

* * * *

Essie threw herself into the process, making what she considered visible progress in the kitchen after several hours and refusing to stop for a lunch break when everyone else did.

She didn't want to stop. She wanted every last scrap of useless crap gone from the house. The film crew left her alone so they could go eat as she continued filling bags. New, old, she didn't care what the stuff was, if it wasn't something she knew belonged to her mom, she trashed it.

Mark walked into the kitchen, alone. She wondered what he was doing when he made her turn around and lifted the hem of her shirt.

Then she realized he was turning off her mic pack.

He put his arms around her, hugging her from behind. "How are you *really*?" he softly asked.

She shook her head. "If I start crying now, I might not stop for a long, long time."

He turned her around to face him and held her. "Are you going to be okay at the funeral home today? I can ask Purson to call off the crew."

"I'll be okay." She let out a ragged laugh. "At least if I cry there I'll appear to be a reasonably sympathetic human being and not a coldhearted bitch."

"Stop. No one thinks that about you."

She was about to respond when her phone buzzed in her pocket. Untangling herself from Mark, she pulled it out and found a text from Amy.

Went home @ lunch. Check UR mail. Luv U!

She thumbed through to her e-mail and downloaded ten pictures. The first five were of their apartment, including Amy's room, showing how neat and tidy they were compared to…this.

She let Mark look over her shoulder. "Wow, you weren't kidding when you said you're not messy."

"No." The next picture made Essie burst out laughing. Amy had taken a close-up selfie, eyes crossed, cheeks puckered, and her tongue stuck out.

Mark smiled. "She seems like a good friend."

"She is. I love her like a sister." She thumbed through the rest of the pictures showing their apartment before texting her friend back.

Thank U. I needed that. Love U 2.

Amy texted her back immediately.

:)

Mark turned her microphone back on before leading her outside to where everyone was eating. He prepared Essie a plate of food while she e-mailed Purson the pictures of the apartment.

As the producer previewed them on his phone, he walked over to Essie, also switching off her microphone as well as his own before speaking with her. "I don't mean this to sound the wrong way, but believe me, you won't look bad when this episode airs. This here shows the contrast. A child of a hoarder reclaiming her life and controlling it. This is hope for others. This is a good thing."

"I hope you're right."

"I'm rarely wrong. This will be a powerful episode in a good way."

He switched their mics back on and the rest of the crew started clearing the garage again while Essie sat and watched as she ate. When she finished, she was going to return to the kitchen when her mom stopped her.

"One of the men on the cleaning crew said his brother-in-law needs a work truck. Can you help me clean out your dad's truck?"

Essie cast a longing look at the house. At least in there, even when she was being filmed, she hadn't felt like she was on display.

"Okay. Let me get some bags." Now knowing where they kept the supplies in the trailer, Essie grabbed a box of contractor's bags and headed over to the truck with her mom. With them working on each side of the truck, it only took them a few minutes to get the worst of the stuff emptied out of the cab.

It wasn't until Essie pried open the glove box, which likely hadn't been opened in years, that she felt like she'd been punched in the gut.

Inside, nestled among outdated registration paperwork, long-dead ink pens, scraps of paper, and other assorted detritus, she found one of her school pictures, maybe from fourth or fifth grade. She also found a faded Polaroid of her and her father, taken in front of the garage. He stood behind her, a smile on his face, while Essie held up a stringer of four fish they'd caught that day.

Written on the bottom of the picture in her dad's handwriting—*My little fisherman.*

She slid to the ground, landing on her ass with the pictures clamped in her fingers as she rocked back and forth, crying. Her mom hurried around the truck to the passenger side and sat next to her.

"What is it—oh, sweetie."

She let her mom hold her close as she cried. She remembered that day, one of the few good memories she had of her father.

Like the picture, the memory had become buried under a mountain of other crap.

Mark and Ted both rushed over, soon followed by Josh, when they realized there was a problem.

Essie held the picture against her chest, her eyes clamped tightly closed. "Why, Mom?" she whispered. "*Why* weren't we good enough for him?"

She was aware of Ted kneeling behind them, his hands on Essie's shoulders. "You didn't do anything wrong. Neither of you. He was sick, and unless he wanted to get help for it, nothing either of you could have done would have changed what or who he was. He had to want it. It wasn't a reflection on either of you."

"But he had a choice," Essie said. "He had a choice, and he chose wrong. For years."

"And nothing you say or do will change that now," Ted gently said. "All you can do is try to understand that it wasn't about you or your mom. It wasn't that he didn't love the two of you. It was about a silent battle he waged and lost inside himself."

Someone pressed a wad of tissues into Essie's hand. Loren, if Essie had to guess, but she wasn't ready to open her eyes yet.

She wanted to cling to the precious, bittersweet memory.

Wanted to hold on to the illusion that this was all a nightmare.

Eventually she opened her eyes and, laying the pictures in her lap, blew her nose. After a moment, she threw the tissues away in one of the bags and picked up the pictures. Getting to her feet, she tucked the photos in her back pocket.

"I want this done," she said, wiping at her eyes with the backs of her hands. "Let's get the truck emptied, and then it's one more thing checked off the list."

"Do you want to go talk in private?" Ted asked.

She shook her head, not daring to look him in the eyes. She knew if she did, if she saw the concern that would certainly be mirrored there considering his tone of voice, she knew she'd break down crying again.

Instead, she forced a smile. "Nope. I want this truck cleaned out and off their lawn."

Thirty minutes later, the truck was emptied, her mother had given the title and a bill of sale to the new owner, who'd come to get it, and the new owner was driving it down the street with a promise to bring back the old license plate later that day, once he'd gotten the new one for it.

Essie felt a mix of joy and sadness at war within her as she watched it go. One less piece of crap weighing her mother down.

And a piece of her childhood—gone. For good or bad.

I have memories. I need to try to weed the good ones out and toss the rest.

Chapter Eleven

Ross volunteered to drive Essie and her mom to the funeral home.

And by volunteer, he used *that* tone on Essie again, gently telling her he was driving them and brooking no resistance to his offer.

Ted asked to go with them. Essie was glad to have him there, although she would have liked it even more if it was Mark.

Essie was going to grab a shower and change clothes, at least, but her mom nixed that idea. "No, we need to get moving."

Aware that the cameras were filming, Essie gently tried to change her mom's mind. "Don't you think we should be properly attired?"

"You don't stink. I don't stink. I'll be damned if I'm going to let Edgar dictate my life anymore when he's dead. Now let's get going, or we'll be late."

Essie looked to Ted for advice, but he only gave her a little shrug.

"All right. Let me at least get my purse and go to the bathroom."

"Um, might want to turn off your mic," the sound guy suggested.

"Thanks."

She retreated to Ross and Loren's house and locked herself in the bathroom. After using the toilet, she washed her hands and her face and stood in front of the mirror, trying to take deep breaths and control herself.

The woman staring back at her was a stranger in some ways. She looked haggard, drawn. Sleep deprived.

More than a little pissed off.

And very, very sad.

I can do this. I can do this.

She changed from the T-shirt to a clean blouse, grabbed her purse, and went to wait in the living room with Ross and Ted. The crew would follow them to the funeral home in one of their vehicles.

When her mom emerged from her bedroom, carrying her own purse, she smiled. "Let's go."

Essie and Ted volunteered to sit in the backseat so her mom could ride shotgun. She realized as Ross drove that while the street names were familiar, many of the buildings were totally unknown to her, new shopping centers having been built, and even already creeping into decay since she'd last been to Sarasota.

Ted reached across the seat and took her hand. Essie was in no mood to refuse the contact. When he gently squeezed, she met his gaze.

"You okay?" he mouthed.

She didn't want to lie to him. She shrugged and turned back to the window to watch the scenery go by.

* * * *

Between dinner the night before and how she was handling herself now, Ted knew he was already heading down the dangerous slope toward love, headfirst and gaining speed at a ridiculous rate.

I barely know her.

Despite this damsel's current distress, he knew his feelings ran deeper than that. He now understood why Mark had swooned over her.

And if she was okay with him holding her hand, he damn sure wasn't going to let go. Not until she made him.

Except he finally had to let go when they reached the mortuary. They waited a moment for the film crew to catch up and get their microphones turned on again before going inside. Purson had ridden with his crew, and explained to the staff who they were and what they wanted. A few signed film releases later, they had the funeral director micced and ready to record.

Ross held back, staying out of the shot. Ted didn't blame him. Ross was fairly well known within their BDSM community and didn't need the additional exposure being featured on the show would bring. At least he owned his own business and didn't have to worry about his job.

Which had been another factor Ted took into consideration when he went into practice for himself, working with his brothers.

Ted stood by, out of the shot but ready to intercede if necessary to stop the filming if he thought it was getting to be too much for either woman. But to Essie's credit she held it together, her eyes growing red, but no tears breaking through.

Even her mom, while teary and emotional, held it together. Essie didn't challenge any of her mom's decisions, including what urn to pick out, and held her mom's hand through most of the process.

He fought the urge to stand on Essie's other side and hold her free hand.

I'm in trouble.

He would need to talk to his brothers, or at least Mark. Not that there would be anything to come from it, since she'd be returning to Spokane. But if they were ever to have a successful poly relationship, they needed to start working on their communications skills.

Including he needed to admit to Mark and Josh what he felt for Essie.

* * * *

Essie knew her mom was either handling this far better than she herself was, or was hiding it much better. She offered Essie a smile when they emerged into the bright Sarasota afternoon sunlight.

"That wasn't so bad," her mom said. "It's done, and we can move on. All we need to do is pick him up when they call us."

Ross led the way to the car. "Are you sure you feel like working on the house when we get back? No one would blame you if you want to take the rest of the afternoon off."

Her mother looked horrified. "No! I want to get right back to work. Do you have any idea how much of a weight is off me right now? I'm finally in control of my life again, the way I want to be. I will keep working until I get too tired to stand tonight. Even if everyone else goes home, I'm going to keep working."

She turned to Essie. "I know you have to be exhausted, sweetheart. I want you to get a good night's sleep tonight. But…I feel like I have energy for the first time in years. You have no idea what it's like."

"Yeah, kind of do, Mom. Why do you think I escaped to college?" It wasn't until the words were out of her mouth that Essie realized maybe her internal filter had a sleep-deprived glitch.

Her mom's eyes widened.

"Mom," she quickly said, "I'm sorry, I didn't mean it like that."

Her mom hugged her. "No, I understand. I'm sorry, sweetheart. I'm sorry I couldn't stand up to him before. I've spent too many years in my own survival mode."

Essie was aware of the film crew discreetly filming their exchange.

After a moment, her mom stepped back and smiled again. "Let's get back to the house. I'm dying to see my garage."

There were a thousand questions running through Essie's mind that she couldn't pose to Ted with her mom sitting right there in the car. She knew she'd have to pull him aside at some point, without a film crew or microphone within range, and talk to him.

When they got into the car, his blue gaze caught hers, stirring something deep inside her. She didn't know what it was about the brothers that did that to her, although she didn't have to be a genius to suspect it had something to do with her old feelings for Mark.

He reached out and took her hand in his again, gently squeezing as he stared into her eyes.

She squeezed back and settled into the seat for the return ride.

* * * *

Essie's mom was delighted to see the crew had made drastic progress since they'd left. Over half the garage was now cleared out.

Corrine threw her arms around Mark and hugged him. "You boys are a blessing, do you know that? This is amazing."

Essie loved that he hugged her mom back. "Hey, it's what we do. Helping people is what we enjoy doing."

More people had arrived to help during their absence, including some more friends of Ross and Loren and the brothers. More introductions Essie was sure she'd never remember.

"I need to go put my purse up," Essie said. "And change out of this shirt."

Essie's mom handed her purse to her. "Please take mine, too, dear."

"Sure thing."

Essie returned to the house, put her mom's purse on her bed, and walked through the bathroom to her own bedroom where she changed. She was about to leave when her phone buzzed from Amy.

U ok?

Essie sat on the bed. *Hanging in there.*

Then her phone rang. "You sure you're all right?" Amy asked.

Essie flopped back onto the bed. "Yeah. Mom's doing a happy dance that the garage is almost empty."

"Yeah, well, sometimes it's the little things in life."

"This wasn't little. I'll send you some pics." She'd snapped a few to e-mail to Amy later. Essie wanted them so if she ever started to slip in her own habits, she'd have an immediate reminder why she couldn't let go of the strict control she exerted over her life. Why she couldn't afford to slide in the slightest in terms of her routines and habits.

A reminder that, as Purson said, she wasn't her father's daughter.

Chatting with Amy helped Essie feel a little better. After ending the call with her, Essie opened her bedroom door but stopped in the doorway when she heard Loren talking with someone in the kitchen.

"Are you guys going to the next munch?" Loren asked.

Essie listened even though she knew it was wrong. She'd seen that term before—munch. It was something she'd read about in some of the books on her Kindle.

The erotic BDSM books.

A woman replied. "I think so. Are you coming to the club tomorrow night?"

"I doubt it," Loren said. "While Corrine and Essie are here, we're trying to keep a low profile. Sir doesn't want to scare the 'nillas."

The women chuckled.

"I don't blame you," the other woman said. "Cris and I are trying to keep Landry from doing too much. He'll work himself to death helping if we don't rein him in."

"Damn Doms, anyway," Loren teased, drawing another laugh from the woman Essie now assumed was Tilly, based on the context. "How is Landry doing, anyway?"

"Knock on wood, his last blood work showed he's still in remission. It'll be another couple of years before they declare it safe for us to relax, but it's looking good. He caught that last round early, and we pursued aggressive treatment."

"I'm glad." Loren seemed to hesitate. "I'm glad it's working out okay with you and Cris, too. I know I was really hard on him when he came back, but you have to see why."

"It's okay," Tilly assured her. "I get it, believe me." Another laugh. "But it worked out for the best. I never thought I could be happy again when he left. Then when Landry brought him back, I never thought I'd trust Cris again. But here we are, a couple of years later, and I'm really happy with both of them."

Essie knew her eyes had to be bugged out.

Both *of them?*

"Poly isn't for everyone," Loren said. "But I'm glad it's working for you three. Sir and I love you, you know that. We were just afraid for you when Cris returned, that he'd hurt you." Loren laughed. "I promise I don't want to charbroil him anymore."

Poly? Three? Essie's mind raced.

Realizing she'd crossed a line in a horrible way, Essie closed the bedroom door just loudly enough she knew the women could hear it. Carefully schooling her expression, she walked into the kitchen, where both women were staring at her and looking more than a little guilty.

Essie's intention had been to pretend she hadn't heard anything and move along to get back to work on her mom's kitchen.

Instead, she found herself staring at the woman and opening her mouth. "Are you guys into that BDSM stuff?"

Both women's faces turned red as they looked at each other for a moment.

"A simple nod will do," Essie said when neither responded. "I won't freak out. I promise."

Both women slowly nodded.

"I'm sorry. I overheard some of what you were talking about. Look, it's okay. I'm not a prude. I read plenty of dirty books. I just didn't realize it was…real."

Loren seemed to cede the conversation to Tilly. The woman cleared her throat before finally speaking. "A lot of our friends are into the lifestyle, yes."

"So you and your husband and that guy…" Essie didn't know how to continue and hoped Tilly would fill in the blank.

Tilly nodded. "Yes. We're poly together. Our situation, it's…complicated."

Loren snorted. "You got *that* right," she muttered.

Essie stepped closer. "It's okay. I'm not offended or anything like that. I'm sorry my mom and I are uprooting your lives."

"No," Loren quickly said. "It's not like that, honey, I promise." She walked over and took Essie's hands, squeezing them. "We really care about your mom. She's a sweetheart. This isn't a burden on us, believe me. We're glad we're able to help out. I don't want you thinking you're imposing on us."

"But we are, if you can't really be yourselves around us."

"It's not like that," Tilly repeated. "Yes, we do a lot of vanilla things with our kinky friends and can be a little more open around them in terms of not having to watch everything we say. But that's a choice we make in exchange for living the life we want to live. And we're happy to do it."

"So who else here is into that?"

The women glanced at each other again. "Look, we really don't want you to think any less of anyone," Loren said.

"I won't. I promise. And I won't say anything to my mom. But I'd like to know." A thought hit her. "Mark, Josh, and Ted, right? That's why so many of your 'mutual friends' offered to help, isn't it?"

The women nodded.

Essie had always envied the submissives in the books she read. How they could be strong women in charge of their lives, and then have a man—or men—they could trust and let go to and know that everything would be okay on the other end of whatever life threw at them. That was one of the reasons Essie allowed herself the indulgence of reading. It took her to places she knew she could never go in her real life and allowed her a few hours here and there to escape reality.

What she hadn't counted on was it being something possible outside of those erotic romances she read.

"Why?" Essie asked.

Loren's brow furrowed. "Why what?"

"Why do you do it?"

"It's not really something I can condense into a few sentences," Loren said. "I love Sir. I trust him. I enjoy knowing that I can be myself and be strong and yet I can still have him to fall back on when I need a mental vacation for a little while."

"Mental vacation how?"

"Subspace. I like when we play and he puts me in that mindset where my world revolves around him and what he's doing to me, until he says otherwise. It's a feeling unlike any other."

"What about you?" she asked Tilly.

Tilly laughed as she held up her hands. "No, don't ask me. I'm a switch, and it really is complicated. Even our good friends are still sometimes confused by our dynamic. But yeah, I love subspace when I go there. I won't deny that."

"What's a switch?"

"Someone who plays on both ends of the flogger," Loren said with a smile.

"You you let your guys beat you?" she asked Tilly, but it was Loren who responded.

"It's about way more than that. Think of it this way. Do you know anything about scuba diving?"

Essie nodded.

"Okay then. You know how there are all sorts of different types of diving, from photographers to cave divers, even underwater welders?"

Essie nodded again.

"Okay. That's an apt analogy for what it is we're doing. Some people only snorkel on the weekends. Some people are professional deep cave divers. And everything in between. There's no one right or wrong way to do BDSM as long as everyone's an adult, they're consenting, no one is harmed, and everyone is getting what they need from the dynamic. That's it."

"That sounds too simple," Essie said.

Tilly giggled. "Everyone thinks that at first. But it really *is* that simple. It's like a Mongolian barbecue. You stack what you want on your plate and then have it grilled together. You choose."

The front door opened and Essie's mom walked in, silencing further conversation. "Oh, there you are. Come see the garage now, sweetheart. It's great!"

Essie glanced at the two women one last time. "Thanks for the info."

"Any time," Loren assured her.

As Essie followed her mom across the street, she now understood what it was about Ross that had struck her just right. His quiet commands.

He was a Dom.

Would I have noticed it under any other circumstances? More importantly, would I have welcomed it the way I did?

Normally she wasn't this emotionally vulnerable and stripped bare. Under usual circumstances, if anyone tried to assert themselves over her, she pushed back, hard, refusing to be bullied.

And Mark and his brothers are Doms, too?

She glanced across the yard to where Josh and Mark were conferring with one of their work crew. She didn't see Ted right away, until she spotted him talking with the film crew on the other side of the yard.

In a fit of horror, she checked her microphone and felt relief to see it was turned off.

I need to be more careful. I don't want to get anyone in trouble.

But now that she had a deeper insight into the brothers, and several of their friends, a niggling part of her mind didn't want to let go of it.

And she definitely wanted to talk more with Loren, Tilly, and the brothers.

Especially the brothers.

* * * *

Essie was exhausted when the men and her mom forced her to call it a day at nine that night. She hadn't had much time to think about the things she'd learned from Loren and Tilly. There was just too much to do.

Too much she wanted to do to keep other, noisier thoughts from crowding into her mind.

Not just about the BDSM stuff, but about her dad, too.

The crew was exhausted, most of the volunteers had left or were leaving, and the garage had not only been emptied and swept out, but the very few things her mom had selected to stay were neatly stacked on or next to a built-in workbench that even her mom had forgotten was there.

"Look at this!" her mom said, slowly spinning around, a grin on her face and her arms outstretched in the two-car garage. "Isn't this great?" Someone had found replacement bulbs for the fluorescent light fixtures that hadn't worked since before Essie had left home simply because her father couldn't reach them to replace them.

The space was filled with light and her mom's glowing smile. As filled as it had been with garbage just a few hours before.

"I almost don't want to park my car in here," her mom said as she stopped and stared at the side window, which had been blocked by cardboard boxes. "It's beautiful."

Essie leaned against the workbench. "It's a garage, Mom."

"It's a beautiful garage."

Ted stood to the side, an amused smile on his face. "Corrine, you don't have to be afraid to park your car in here. It's your space. You reclaim it however you want, as long as it's in a healthy way."

"Oh, I was just joking. Of course I'll park my car in here. I'd park it in here tonight if those trash containers weren't in the way." She stared up at the ceiling. "Do you think they can put one of those electric openers in here for the door?"

"I'm sure we can find a trustworthy contractor to take care of that for you," Ted said.

"I'd like that," she said, finally pulling her gaze from the cobweb-free ceiling. "I'd really like that." She walked to the opening and stopped, turning to face them. Then she held out her hands in front of her, waist-high, and slowly walked in. "I'll be able to bring my car inside, even if it's raining, without having to get out. I can stay dry while I unload my groceries. I won't have to juggle an umbrella and the bags."

She stopped by the workbench and stared at it. "I could even put the bags here while I unload, before I bring them inside." Her tone held more than a touch of wonder. "Do you know how long it's been since I've been able to do that?"

Her mom turned to where Mark and Josh now stood in the doorway. One last cameraman was still filming, and Essie, her mom, and Ted still had live mics.

Essie had been told that the network was trying to get their usual "star" crew in to film shots with her and her mom, but because of the short notice they hadn't arrived yet.

Frankly, Essie didn't want them there. She was happy with Ted, who seemed to understand her.

Mom. He understands Mom.

Then again, maybe Ted, and Mark, did understand Essie more than she wished they did. As Ted's gaze met and locked with hers, his blue eyes seeming to delve deep into her soul to shed light on her secrets, she felt a stirring within her, one she wished she could explore.

One she knew, based on the circumstances, she likely never could.

She was shocked to realize *that* thought made her sadder than even the death of her father.

What the hell *is wrong with me? What kind of* damn *freak am I?*

Once they were free of the mics and the cameraman had quit filming, her mom stretched, a smile on her face. "I will sleep so good tonight, you have no idea. Are you ready to go back?"

"Yeah, in a minute. I'll lock up. You go ahead and get your shower first."

"All right. Thank you, boys, so much." She hugged the brothers before walking across the street toward Ross and Loren's house.

That left Essie alone with the men.

Mark stepped forward, concern on his face. It made her feel vaguely guilty that it was his eldest brother she wanted to talk to right now. "Are you all right?" he asked. "I know that's a stupid question under the circumstances."

"No, it's not a stupid question. I guess I'm as okay as I can be. Under the circumstances," she added. "Can I talk to Ted alone for a few?"

"Sure," Mark said. Josh nodded. She didn't miss the slightly puzzled look on Mark's face before he turned with Josh and headed over to their supply trailer.

She pulled the large garage door down and locked it, finding the solid, clanking sound more satisfying than she'd ever imagined it would be.

"Wow. Mom's right. That's pretty neat."

"I think your mom would stand out here and open and close that door all night if we let her," Ted lightly observed.

She ran her hand over the handle. Someone had used a broom or something on the inside of the door, sweeping it clean, free of dust and cobwebs. They'd also oiled the rollers, hinges, latch, and other mechanical parts of it.

"You might be right," Essie agreed.

"So what's going through your mind?"

She couldn't turn and face him yet. "I accidentally overheard Loren and Tilly talking earlier today," she said to the door handle. "About BDSM. I asked, and they answered." She finally forced herself to turn, her eyes focused on his knees. "Tell me about it."

He let out a long breath before sticking his hands in the pockets of his jeans and shifting his stance, feet a little wider apart. His voice dropped, softer. "What do you want me to say, Essie?"

Even his tone sounded different, and not just the volume.

Now she knew she couldn't look up and meet his gaze, afraid she'd want to drop to her knees in front of him.

Make it go away for me. Please, make it all better. I don't want to do this alone anymore.

"You and your brothers are into it?" she asked.

"Into BDSM, yes. Does that bother you?"

"No."

When she didn't continue, he pressed. "Then what did you want to ask me?"

"You're a professional. How do you reconcile that?"

"Back up a step. A professional what?"

"Counselor."

"Yes, I am. The mental health community is finally recognizing that consensual BDSM isn't an indication of a psychiatric disorder." He smiled. "Something a lot of us have known for years."

She didn't know how to respond to that. "Tilly was talking about being poly. What does that mean?" She risked a glance at his face again before her gaze dropped to his knees.

He took a slow, deliberate step forward. She didn't flinch away. He stopped a few feet from her, hands still in his pockets. "It means a non-monogamous relationship where people are involved with more than just their primary partner. It can take many forms, and it usually means all the people involved in the arrangement have consented and agreed to the rules the group sets."

"So they can have sex with whoever they want?"

"Not necessarily. You might be thinking about swingers, and even then, there's a hugely malformed public image about what they do. They frequently have their own rules about what can and can't happen, but I suspect that's straying from your topic."

She nodded. "How many poly people do you know?"

"Besides myself and my brothers? Quite a few."

"You don't, you know, *with* your brothers, do you?"

"Eh, no. We were in a poly relationship with a woman, a submissive, for a while. She wanted and enjoyed having more than one partner at a time. We enjoyed playing with her. When she needed more from us than we could give her, we parted friends and went our separate ways."

"Needed more how?"

"Every sadist has their limits, just as every sub has theirs. She pegged us out at the top end of our scales and needed more." He shrugged. "Communication is key in poly relationships. Well, it's key in BDSM, too. It's about trust and communication. If you can't manage either of those, it won't work."

"And Mark and Josh?"

"Yes, they're Dominants, too."

"Are you seeing anyone now?"

"No. I'm single. Can I ask why you're so interested in this?"

She felt heat fill her face. "I just wanted to know."

"And now that the secret's out, can we depend on you to be discreet about it? We have a lot of friends who came out today to help, and more who will be here tomorrow."

"I won't say anything, I promise." It took every ounce of strength she had, but she looked him in the eyes. "I'm okay with it."

"Good. I'm glad it's not an issue. Our private lives are nobody's business. You will find the same mix of people in BDSM as you will in the general population. All occupations, economic situations, genders and sexualities, and with countless interests." He looked around, smiling. "Hell, there are probably people out there paying top-dollar for clean-garage porn."

That made her laugh, as well as relax a little. "Think Purson will set us up with that to make more money?"

"You never know. Look, it's late, and you have to be exhausted. I promise, if you need to talk to me about this at any time, feel free. But I'd prefer we make sure we don't have a film crew tagging along, and we make sure our mics are off. Deal?" He withdrew his right hand from his pocket and extended it.

She shook with him. No magic zap of energy raced through her, although she did wonder what his strong hands would feel like roaming over her body.

"Deal," she said.

He helped her get the garage locked up and they rejoined Mark and Josh by the supply trailer.

"Everything all right?" Mark asked.

She smiled. "I'm good. Really. Thank you." She hugged—just hugged—him, Josh, and then Ted, before bidding them good night and heading back to Ross and Loren's.

Her mom was just finishing up her shower. Essie opted for a quick shower, followed by a soak in the tub. Closing her eyes, she envisioned first Mark, then Ted.

Don't forget Josh.

No, don't forget him, with his black hair and brown eyes. They all strongly resembled each other. You could see they were brothers.

Is it any coincidence they all turned out to be Doms? Were there any case studies on that?

Probably not.

Closing her eyes, she tried to relax without falling asleep. When she caught herself nodding off, she let the tub drain and rinsed off, cleaning the shower as she did, before getting out and toweling dry.

Pulling on a T-shirt and sleeping shorts, she crawled into bed and had a thought about calling or texting Amy before sleep took over and dragged her down into its depths for the rest of the night.

Chapter Twelve

Ted called Mark and Josh into his office early Saturday morning before they headed over to the Barrone house. They'd met at the office first to take care of some administrivia for other parts of their business that Tracy needed them to handle.

He closed the door for privacy since their weekend receptionist was in the office. *No reason to soft-pedal it.* "I can't consult with Essie anymore," he announced without fanfare.

Mark found his voice first. "But they need you."

"I'll still work with her mom, don't worry. But I can't counsel Essie."

"Why not?" Mark asked, frowning. "What the hell?"

"Is this about why she wanted to talk to you alone last night?" Josh asked.

Ted stared at the floor, hating he had to say this. "Because I'm attracted to her," he said. "And I can't be objective with her." He finally looked up at Mark. "And because I know how you feel about her. And, heads-up, she knows about our involvement in BDSM. Loren and Tilly spilled the beans."

"You like her?" Mark asked.

Ted looked at him. "That's *all* you can think to ask? *Really?*"

"Just answer the question," Josh said.

Ted stared at them. "Yes, I like Essie. Happy?"

A slow grin spread across Mark's face as he turned to Josh. "What about you?"

"Wait," Ted said. "What?"

"Shh." Mark waved his objection down. "Josh, what do you think?"

His brother's face turned red as he jammed his hands into his pockets and suddenly found the carpet very interesting. "She's nice."

"Be honest."

Josh took a deep breath and let it out again before finally meeting Mark's steady gaze. "I like her, okay? I like her a lot. There, are you happy?"

Mark's grin widened. "I am now."

Ted stared at his youngest brother. "What are you saying? She lives in Spokane."

"Who's to say we can't maybe talk her into moving here?"

"We barely know her."

"I don't mean tomorrow. But let's be honest, with her now having a relationship with her mom again, she's going to have a pull toward moving here, right?" Mark looked to Josh. "Tell me I'm wrong."

Josh rubbed the back of his neck. "In theory, it sounds good. But you know as well as we do that theory and reality are two different things when it comes to being poly." He dropped his hand. "So I'm not going to count on this as a sure thing when we don't even know if she'd be interested in that in the first place."

Ted silently gave Josh credit for being sensitive. "Mark," Josh continued, "we don't even know if she's kinky. Just because she's okay with *us* being kinky doesn't mean she wants that, too. We all did that once. Marrying the wrong woman. As much as I'd love poly with you guys, I'm not going to give up all other hopes for love because of some flimsy what-if that might possibly be out there…or not. And, likewise, I don't expect either of you to give up a chance for love if you meet a woman who decides she wants no part of being poly. It takes a special kind of woman to want to be in a BDSM dynamic as a submissive, much less be poly. That's a tiny subgenre of an already minuscule slice of the general population."

"Just stay open to it," Mark said. "Please?"

"We are," Ted and Josh parroted. Ted glanced at his younger brother before continuing. "Just don't get your hopes up unrealistically, all right?"

"I won't. I just want to know you two have my back."

"We *do* have your back," Ted assured him. "We always *will* have it. That's why we're asking you to please keep your feet planted firmly on the ground."

Well, this conversation went better than I thought it would.

It also had taken a far left turn from the direction he'd thought it would go.

"So have you told Essie yet?" Mark asked.

"No. I'll talk to her as a friend, but I think for the purpose of filming the show, she needs to work with Kennedy." Kennedy Porter was the network's handpicked mental health specialist for the series. She looked good on camera and definitely had great rapport with their clients.

But off-camera, none of the men could stand her. She was arrogant, pushy, and frequently rude to them and the work crews, except for Ted. She sucked up to Ted.

For that reason alone, Ted despised her. *Love me, love my bros.*

Ted secretly suspected she was a Domme in her private life and, somehow, had reacted badly to Mark and Josh. They were always polite and professional with her, but even Purson had noticed how she acted around the men and apologized to them for it.

"Boss likes her ratings appeal," Purson had once said. "You guys ever have a better choice to replace her, I'll take it to him."

"Kennedy might not be in until Monday," Josh said. "If then. Hell, at the rate we're going, we might have most of the house emptied by Sunday."

"No," Mark said. "We need to make Sunday a half day. Give the crew a rest. And give Essie and her mom a rest, whether they want it or not."

"Good luck with *that*," Josh muttered. "Corrine is an absolute machine."

"We'll need a trash dump by then anyway," Ted said. "Hell, both containers are over three quarters full and that was just mostly the garage. Imagine what will happen when we dig into the house."

"They'll come swap them out Monday morning," Mark said. "I already arranged it."

"And we're supposed to have rain tomorrow," Ted said. "We can use that as an excuse to shut down filming."

Mark nodded. "Seth already said he'll get a tarp up on the roof this morning. He found the leak. That'll prevent more damage."

"Okay, fine," Josh said. "So what do we do meanwhile?"

"Our job," Mark and Ted said. Mark gave the floor to Ted. "The thought of chasing someone who's emotionally vulnerable doesn't sit well with me anyway."

* * * *

Mark didn't want to admit to his brothers that he'd already done more than just talk with Essie. Unfortunately, with all the volunteers and crew around, he hadn't had any other opportunities alone with her to repeat their kiss.

He knew, deep in his heart, that she was more than a little interested in him, at least, and possibly even Ted. He could tell from the way she'd watched Ted yesterday. Now that he knew Essie was aware of their private proclivities, he wouldn't hide that from her.

"I kissed her," Mark admitted.

Josh and Ted stared at him. "What?" they both finally asked.

"Kissed her. Well, she kissed me first." He told them what happened.

Ted scrubbed at his face with his hands. "Jesus, Mark—"

"Open mind, right?"

He let out one of *those* sighs, the big-brother kind. "Don't screw with her mind or her heart."

"I'm not. I'm keeping an open mind."

If she was interested, she would respond. If not…

Well, then she'd push him away.

He damn sure hoped that didn't happen. He didn't want his heart broken twice by the same woman.

And while he knew Essie was going through a lot, he suspected she was a lot stronger than Ted thought she was. He sensed an inner strength and determination in her that went deeper than he could remember seeing in other clients.

Then again, he recognized it could be more wishful thinking on his part.

Neither brother seemed to have anything else to say.

"If that's all you wanted to talk to us about, can we get moving?" Mark asked. "I want to get over there and get started."

"Yeah, that's it," Ted said. "I just wanted to make sure we are on the same page, and make sure I handled this sooner rather than later."

"When are you going to tell her?" Josh asked.

"I don't know. I'll figure that out when we get to that point."

* * * *

Saturday morning, Essie was able to sleep until six thirty. After grabbing a toasted bagel and cup of coffee, she headed over to her mom's house and got it unlocked. The film crew, workers, and volunteers wouldn't arrive until after seven.

The peace she felt when she stepped through the side garage door and flipped on the lights shocked her. It was a far cry from the tensing in her gut the first time Ross led her in there.

Mom's right. It is a beautiful garage.

She walked to the center of the space. Like her mom the night before, she extended her arms and slowly spun in circles, relishing the ability to freely move without having to turn or dip or wiggle or worry about dislodging a mountain of crap.

Her mom's gentle laughter from the side door froze her. "I'm glad you understand me."

Essie stopped and turned to face her mom. "I'm sorry I left you alone with him."

Her mom walked in and over to her, stopping in front of her. "Honey, I chose to stay. I was so proud of you for getting that scholarship and getting out of here. I wish I'd said it better before." She hugged Essie, long and hard. "Believe it or not, your father was proud of you, too."

"He never said it." They had driven up to Gainesville for her graduation, which had shocked the hell out of her.

"I know. He said some stuff at the time, when we were driving up for your graduation. Sideways comments." She finally released Essie and stared around the garage. "I think he kept his emotions as bottled up inside him as he did junk in this house. They were a shield." She focused her gaze on Essie again. "But he did love you. And me. The only way he knew how to."

"Forget the wedding vows. Why did you stay?"

Corrine shrugged. "It was my vows. And…as stupid as it sounded, I always thought I could change him. I never gave up hope even though I rationally understood how hopeless it was. When you truly love someone, you don't always think with your mind. You think with your heart and with your feelings. I didn't want to leave him. I knew if I did that he would bury himself. I had no doubts about that. I gave him the best life I could, and now it's time for me. And you."

Her mom walked over to the large garage door and opened it. Her smile broadened. "I can't wait to get a garage door opener," she said. "And I want to paint the house. I want colors. And I want to put down some of that laminate flooring that looks like wood. I want to be able to run a dust mop around the floors in a few minutes and have them clean."

"Sounds like you want to redecorate the whole house."

"I do. And I will. I know I can't do it all at once. I want to go to IKEA and get a new couch, and a chair for the living room. And a bed." She smiled. "And a new guest bed. So when you're here, you have a place to stay."

That actually sounded really nice. "Thanks, Mom. It'll be good to be able to come back here and visit."

"Maybe I can talk you into moving back here one day." She shrugged. "A woman can hope. No guilt, though. I understand you have your life and friends and stuff."

No guilt intended, and Essie knew that, but she felt guilty nonetheless. "We'll see. Let's get your house cleaned up first. There's plenty of time to talk about that later."

* * * *

The men still hadn't arrived by eight o'clock, but that didn't slow down the work crew foreman or film crew. The foreman got the volunteers organized and working on clearing a path through the living room to the back door while Essie returned to the kitchen.

The clutter didn't emotionally crush Essie as much as it had before. All she had to do was look through the open utility room door and see the now-emptied garage.

Her mom started work on the utility room. She separated her clothes into a laundry basket and threw away everything that was her husband's.

"Do you want my help in there?" Essie asked.

"No, I'm okay. You're doing a great job in there."

By the time the men arrived a little after eight thirty, Essie had most of the kitchen floor space cleared, the top of the fridge emptied, and had started making a dent in the pile on the table. They were able to bring wheelbarrows into the garage now, and dollies to move fifty-five gallon garbage drums, so Essie was able to make faster progress once her mom had completely cleared a wide path through the utility room.

Essie felt a little thump in her chest as all three brothers joined her in the kitchen.

"You're making great progress," Mark assured her, holding her gaze with his longer than she knew was normal.

Her stomach fluttered in response. If she looked at Ted, his blue eyes bored into hers. That left Josh the only safe one, and even then not so much. While she hadn't had the one-on-one contact with him that she'd had with the other two, she was still viscerally attracted to him, too.

Stop it. Focus.

By the time the work foreman called a lunch break, the mop sink in the utility room was actually useable for the first time in over a decade. Her mom hadn't cleaned out the cabinets in there yet, but the other stuff on the floor and stacked on top of the counter was gone.

Her mom beamed. "I can't wait to get a mop in here and get it cleaned up!" She turned to Essie. "I'm going to paint it yellow. That's a cheery color."

Essie smiled. "One step at a time, Mom. Let's get the house emptied, first. And you have a job to get back to."

"Oh, I know." Her mom turned again, taking in her progress. "It's just…I feel like I'm over the moon. I know that's wrong and weird, and maybe I'm using this as a way to delay grieving for your father. I don't care. Grieving for him will be easier to do when I'm not despising my existence or losing my home."

Essie hugged her from behind, resting her chin on her mom's shoulder. "True. I won't be nearly as worried about you when I have to return home, either."

"I'm glad he died first," her mom softly said.

Essie was aware of the two camera crews filming them, one from the garage door and one from the kitchen.

"Why's that?"

"Because I would have hated to die first and left you saddled with him. Worse, he wouldn't have reached out to you. He wouldn't have tried to bridge the gap, I think. He certainly wouldn't have done the work needed to save this place."

"True." That thought made Essie sad because she knew it would have been exactly what happened. She might have been lucky if her father had even been able to find her landline phone number in Spokane, much less called her to let her know.

"Time for lunch," her mom announced, patting Essie's hands before gently breaking away. "I feel like I can relax now. I didn't understand before how fast this would go. How easy it would be to empty this place."

"We're not done yet."

"But we will be. And it's going to be beautiful again. It'll finally feel like a home instead of a prison."

Chapter Thirteen

Essie found herself alone in the backyard Saturday evening with Josh as the crew wound down for the day. They were both free of their microphones or a crew shadowing them. She stood there, unsure what to say to him and filled with a lot of emotions now that she knew more about him and his brothers.

"Thank you," she finally settled on, even though it felt lame.

"You're very welcome," he said. "I'm glad we're able to help you with this."

Without thinking what she was doing, she grabbed him and hugged him, relieved when his arms encircled her. As she relaxed in his embrace, it hit her how comfortable she felt standing there with him.

And wondered if dreams could become reality if she wished hard enough.

Before she could stop herself, she rose up on her toes and kissed him on the lips. "Still, thank you."

Shaking, she hurried from the yard and back to Ross and Loren's.

* * * *

Josh was still standing there, in shock, when Mark and Ted found him a minute later. "You ready to head home?"

He nodded. "Yeah."

"What's wrong?" Ted asked.

Besides thinking I might be falling in love with her, too?

"Um, she just kissed me."

"Who?" they asked together.

"Who the hell do you think?"

A slow smile filled Mark's face.

"Stop it," Ted warned.

"You can't stop me from being hopeful." He looked positively giddy as he smacked them both on the shoulders and left them standing there.

Josh looked at Ted. "I sense a disturbance in the Force."

Ted rolled his eyes. "I sense a disturbance in your jeans," he said. "Remember, she's still a client."

* * * *

Ted drove back to his apartment complex that night, full of conflicted emotions. He couldn't deny his feelings for Essie.

Then again, feelings were just that. Feelings lied—all the time. He damn well knew that.

It was his fricking *job* to know that.

When he made the final turn, he was aggravated to see his usual way into the complex blocked by construction barricades and heavy equipment. Several bright klieg lights illuminated the parking area, where it looked like a dozen workers were gathered and working around a gigantic hole in the middle of the asphalt. Large mounds of dirt and chunks of asphalt lay to the side.

This can't be good.

Ted rolled down his window as the complex manager walked over to his truck. "What's going on?" Ted asked him.

"Utilities break. Water and gas lines."

"We don't have gas in here."

"I know. It's a through-line that apparently no one knew about before they started working on the irrigation system. The water will likely be off until tomorrow morning, at the earliest. Maybe longer. We're putting everyone up at hotels for the night if they need it."

"Dammit." He needed it. He'd wanted a long, hot shower. "Hold on." He grabbed his cell phone and called Mark. "Hey, long story short, my complex has no water until tomorrow, at least. Can I bunk there tonight?"

"Sure. You know you can. We're already home."

"Thanks. I'll see you soon." He ended the call. "I'm good. Will they let me in?"

"Yeah, you have to go around to the back entrance. We have it unlocked for tonight."

"Thanks."

Ted got turned around, found the back entrance that he usually didn't use because it was only open during daylight hours, and parked as close to his unit as he could. Thirty minutes later, he'd packed a few days' worth of clothes just in case and was on his way to his brothers' house.

He had a key, but they'd left the front door unlocked for him. Mark stood in the kitchen, hair damp from a shower, and was unloading their dishwasher.

"So what happened?" Mark asked.

"I don't know. Apparently they were working on the irrigation system and took out a water line and a gas line at the same time."

Mark laughed. "That takes serious skills."

"Tell me about it." He headed back to what was now a guest room and home office, but had been his room growing up. He set his bag on the dresser and stared around. It felt so different.

Josh stepped into the doorway. "Guest bath's all yours, dude. I'm done."

"Thanks."

"You know, I understand you like your privacy, but you could move back here and pay a fraction of what it costs you every month there."

Immediately following his divorce, Ted had needed privacy and time to lick his emotional wounds. Yes, he'd stayed with his brothers for a couple of weeks while he got an apartment lined up, but other than that, he'd been on his own.

Part of it was he'd wanted to prove he was more evolved than his little brothers, especially since his degree was in mental health counseling. He'd wanted to prove to himself that he could live alone and be successful at it. He'd moved from home to college with roommates, then married, then…

Six years after his divorce, he was still alone.

And lonely.

He turned to Josh. "You guys mean it?"

Mark appeared next to him. "Duh. We've been bugging you about it for a while now. I know Mom and Dad would feel better if we were all together. They keep asking me how you're doing every time I talk to them."

"Why wouldn't they ask me?"

"Mom says she does, and you say you're fine and change the subject."

"Shrink, heal thyself," Josh teased.

Ted heavily sat on the edge of the bed. "You don't think we'd get on each other's nerves?"

"Not any more than we already do," Mark joked. "Come on, bro. We miss having you around all the time. We're three bachelors. Maybe we can find someone to play with again like we did before."

"That was pretty fun," Josh agreed.

"I thought you had eyes for Essie?" Ted asked Mark.

"I do." Mark glanced at Josh, then back to Ted. "Maybe we could…you know…talk to her."

"She's not from here," Ted reminded him.

"You like her. You said so."

"I do, but me liking her, and Josh liking her, and you liking her, that doesn't means she's going to like any of us, or want all of us together."

"Tell us to our faces you wouldn't want to be poly," Mark challenged.

Ted reined in his irritation. "That'd be a lie and you know it. But wanting it and finding someone compatible with all three of us who wants us, too, are different things."

"Just keep an open mind," Mark asked. "Please?"

"Yes, fine. Can I get a shower now?"

"When are you moving in?" Mark pressed.

"If it'll get me into the shower faster, consider me moved now. My lease is due for renewal next month anyway."

Mark and Josh high-fived each other. "For the win!" Josh said.

* * * *

After his shower, Ted rummaged through the kitchen for a snack. After settling on a handful of almonds from a jar on the counter, he turned to find Josh standing there.

He held out his hand. "Almond?"

"No thanks." Josh leaned against the counter. "Did you mean it? That you'd want to try being poly?"

His instincts of being a big brother instantly waged war with his training as a counselor. "Yes," he finally said. "If the right unicorn comes our way. One who won't up and leave and go back to Washington state, yes." He popped an almond into his mouth to buy him some time.

Josh slowly nodded. "Okay. I just wanted to make sure you really meant it and weren't just saying it to get Mark off your case."

"I really meant it. I think Essie is great. But she's not local. And we don't even know if she's kinky. I don't think a long-distance relationship would work well for any of us. Not that long a distance, at least. It's Spokane, not St. Pete."

"Mark and I have both kissed her."

Jesus. "I know." *Don't rub it in.*

Apparently Josh realized what he said. "I didn't mean it like that. I meant she was interested in us. Why wouldn't she be interested in you, too?"

"Again, the whole thing about her life being in Spokane. Look, let's give it a rest for tonight, okay? Table the topic for now. Get through the Barrone job and go from there. Hey, I've moved back in. Consider it a battle won and move the frak on."

Josh smiled. "It's good to have you home, bro."

"Thanks. Just remember that next time I make my special chili for dinner."

Josh grinned. "We can totally gas Mark out."

"Yep."

Josh left him alone in the kitchen. Ted hoped this wasn't a mistake. That moving back in with his brothers wouldn't turn out to be a really bad move.

Then again, being alone hadn't helped him move forward. He was stuck in stasis with no change in sight.

Maybe I need to be the change.

On that thought, he headed for his bedroom.

* * * *

Essie hoped she hadn't made a horrible mistake kissing Josh, but at the time it felt right and she went with it.

It's what they do in books, right?

And Josh hadn't seemed to object to it.

She went to bed early Saturday evening and got a good night's sleep, albeit spent the night having sexy dreams about the three brothers. She awoke invigorated Sunday morning, her mood only boosted by her mother's positive attitude.

They made more slow progress. They had plenty of volunteers, but they had to shoot a few scenes for the show with one of the organizational experts who'd managed to arrive a day earlier than expected.

Essie kept it to herself that she thought it was little more than a circle jerk as the prissy, snooty guy talked with her mom, suggesting ways to prevent a return to such a cluttered state.

She finally let out a giggle when her mom had apparently had enough of his condescension as well. "You were told it was my husband who was the hoarder, right? Did they show you the difference between my car and his truck? I managed to keep the kitchen semi-functional all these years. Frankly I don't like a lot of your ideas because it means bringing stuff, even organizational stuff, *into* the house. I want to get rid of as much stuff as I can, *out* of the house, and not bring it back. Believe me, young man, you come back a year from now, this house will be spotless without an ounce of clutter."

Even Purson turned away, his shoulders shaking and betraying that he was laughing.

The expert quickly recovered, however. "Well, I'm certainly glad to hear that. It's good you have a positive attitude."

"I'm positive once my house is cleaned out that it's going to stay like that for the rest of my life."

Essie caught Ted's attention and walked out the side door, switching off her mic as she did.

He followed and switched off his as well.

She rose up on tiptoe to whisper in his ear. "That guy is an ass."

Ted shrugged. "He's a well-paid ass, apparently. He's on a couple of the network's home improvement shows. I think he either didn't read the background package on your mom, or he decided to disregard it. Usually he's not this much of a jerk."

"Okay, so it's not just me?"

"Not just you."

They switched their mics back on and returned to the house.

By lunch, clouds had started building to the west. Someone checked the weather and found a line of severe thunderstorms was moving their way from off the Gulf.

"As much as I hate to do this," Mark told Corrine, "I'm going to call it a day now. We need time to button up the site, get the tents down, all of that."

"Can I keep working?" her mom asked. "I can use the trash bags, right?"

He kindly smiled. "You sure you don't want to take time off?"

"No. Absolutely not. I want to keep working."

"It's your house. Now that we've got some of the clutter out, it's not quite as bad a fire hazard as it was. But please don't wear yourself out."

"Oh, I won't do that," she assured him.

The film crew had shut down, and most of the volunteers had left for the day, when Ted motioned to Essie. He led her through the house to the living room, where light now slanted through the sliding glass doors into the living room.

"Wow," she said. "That's great."

The film crew had already taken their mics back. Ted gently held her hands. "I wanted to talk with you. Alone."

Her heart trip-hammered in her chest. "Yes?"

"I'm going to keep working with your mom and with the show. But I needed to let you know that I can't counsel you any longer. I'll be here for you as a friend, but not professionally."

Now her heart sank. "Why?" she breathed.

She didn't think he was going to answer at first. But then he squeezed her hands, harder this time, and turned the full force of his blue eyes on her. "Because I really like you. I'm attracted to you. And it wouldn't be ethical for me to date someone I'm technically treating. If I have a choice of possibly having more than just a friendship with you, or treating you as nothing more than a patient, I'll take the risk."

Outside, someone called for Ted.

He leaned in and kissed Essie on the forehead before releasing her hands and hurrying out of the living room.

Unable to think, much less move, she stood there, his words still sinking into her brain.

He...likes me.

So there it was, two guys who definitely liked her, two brothers.

Should I try for a hat trick?

Okay, that was a horrible way to think. But it wouldn't leave her brain, either.

Then again, Josh hadn't pulled away from her when she'd kissed him the evening before.

Worse, she knew she really couldn't ask Amy her opinion. She didn't want to admit she was seriously contemplating this potentially kinky relationship.

Relationship*s*.

It was a few minutes later, just a little after two, when the first of the rain bands hit. The temperature dropped, wind picking up, the smell of rain on the breeze.

"Why don't you go relax," her mom told her. "Go call Amy. I'm going to stay over here and putter around."

She kissed her mom on the cheek and dashed through the rain to Ross and Loren's. Her mom certainly looked happier by the day. It was as if the hoard had been a weight holding her smile into a frown.

As the house emptied, her mom's smile grew, even her posture looked a little straighter.

Essie took a quick shower and texted Amy to see if she was even available to talk.

Her phone rang, a FaceTime call.

It was so good to see her friend's smiling face she almost burst into tears. "Hey."

"Hiya, stranger," Amy said, grinning.

Essie laid back on the bed. "You're a sight for sore eyes."

"I saw the pics you sent me. Holy crap. I'm really sorry. Now I'm wishing I had taken time off and come with you."

"No, it's okay. We have plenty of help."

"So these are the guys from that show?"

Essie proceeded to tell her about the brothers, answer her questions, and they ended up talking for over an hour.

After dinner, Essie retreated to her bedroom. She turned the TV on low and channel surfed, finally finding *Clue* playing on a station.

Always a guaranteed laugh for her. She knew the movie by heart but laughed every time. She set the sleep timer and settled in to watch.

Tonight, though, her mind drifted. She thought about her kiss with Mark, her tamer one with Josh, what Ted had confessed—and her feelings for all three brothers.

And she thought about BDSM.

How maybe it wouldn't be the worst thing in the world if she experimented a little.

Maybe, just maybe, she could try moving back to Florida. She could live with her mom, for a while, at least. Maybe try dating the men.

Do something different for a change. Obviously, what she was doing now wasn't working for her. She was alone and lonely.

Mom's not getting any younger. How many years do I have left with her?

Essie had honestly thought somewhere in the back of her mind that maybe one day her father would change his ways and come around.

The two pictures from the truck's glove box were sitting propped up on the dresser next to her cell phone. They'd found a long-missing photo album that morning and set it aside to look at later.

Essie knew she felt too raw, too emotional to go through it now. Besides, she didn't want to stall the cleanup just to look through it, even though Purson said he did want to get a shot of her and her mom going through pictures at some point in the process.

If I was here, I could pay rent to her. Give her more money to fix up the house.

That's not your responsibility.

She's my mom.

You love Spokane.

I miss Florida.

There it was. She never had fully adjusted to the Washington winters. She still froze her keister off while others were wearing light jackets, or even running around in shirt sleeves. The first year she'd had to drive in snow she'd nearly wrecked when she hit ice on the road.

Florida was flat and snow free.

She even missed the hot Sarasota summers, where getting into the shade meant the temperature dropped at least ten degrees because the ever-present sea breeze off the Gulf of Mexico kept temperatures comfortable.

Muggy, sure. But she'd take eighty-five and humid over a hundred-degree day with lower humidity.

In a heartbeat.

Am I really thinking about doing this?

She could rent a truck and a car hauler. She and Amy had moved themselves from Florida to Spokane after graduation. Essie, who'd learned how to drive in her dad's truck, had done most of the driving, Amy only driving on long, flat stretches of interstate.

Those thoughts, and others, scrambled through her mind as sleep and exhaustion finally took hold of her system.

Chapter Fourteen

Essie awoke Monday morning with misgivings. Despite what she'd thought the night before, she knew that was a mistake. A grief-fueled, emotionally charged mistake.

I have a life, a job in Spokane. I can't just uproot myself and move back to Florida because my libido suddenly woke up and said huzzah.

It wouldn't be fair to Amy, or to her boss, who'd been so gracious to work with her on the time off.

Even for three hunks like Mark, Josh, and Ted. Besides, how would she ever choose between them anyway? Well, she didn't even know how Josh might feel. For all she knew, he might not be attracted to her the way she was to all of them despite their kiss. A kiss wasn't a sure thing to build a future on.

I need to talk to Mark.

And she'd had every intention of doing just that. First thing, her plan was to find Mark and pull him aside, without a camera crew there, to talk.

She'd located him behind the house a little after seven that morning, just getting started with the crew and talking with Josh when Josh's phone rang. He offered them an apologetic smile and stepped away to take the call.

Nervous, she watched him as his body language changed as he talked. He held up a staying finger at Mark before she could lead him away for their talk. She hadn't been micced yet and knew Purson wouldn't sic a film crew on her until she was ready.

Then Josh said, "Hold on." When he turned, searching and pausing as his gaze fell on her, he said, "You're a vet tech, right?"

"Yeah?"

He spoke into the phone. "Tell them we'll be there in twenty minutes. Text me the address." He hung up. "That was Tracy," he said to Mark. "Just had an emergency called in." Before Essie could react, Josh grabbed her by the hand, practically sprinting for the front yard where his truck was parked along the street.

He let go of her hand as they reached his truck, and she automatically reached for the passenger door as he headed for the driver's side.

"I don't have my purse."

"You won't need it. Get in."

"What's going on?" she asked.

He barely checked his mirrors before pulling out into the street. "East Bradenton. Tracy just had a hysterical woman call the office. Her elderly mother was taken to the hospital yesterday. She fell and broke her hip while taking out the garbage. The daughter didn't even know she had dogs until her mom finally admitted it this morning when the mom realized she wasn't going to be released. When the daughter entered the house to take care of them, she…" He didn't finish.

Essie didn't think she wanted him to.

He hit I-75 and headed north. Two exits later, he was making a turnoff into a rural neighborhood with multi-acre properties. Older homes mixed with newer ones. He consulted his phone and then finally pulled into a dirt driveway outside an older, wood-framed house. Typical older Florida home, the two-story house was set up on short concrete pylons with a wraparound porch.

It had seen better days. The once-yellow paint was peeling, bare wood visible around some of the window frames on the second floor.

There was an older Ford sedan parked in the weed-pocked yard, a newer Toyota parked behind it.

An obviously distraught middle-aged woman in jeans and a T-shirt sat on the front steps. She stood when they got out of the truck and approached her.

"Thank you for coming so quickly."

Josh introduced himself and Essie to the woman, whose name turned out to be Lisa Parker.

"What's the situation?" he asked her.

Inside the house, Essie heard at least two dogs barking, smaller dogs from the sound of it.

"I...I..." Lisa burst into tears. "Now I know why she never let me inside," she said. "I don't want to call Animal Control to catch them for me, but they won't come to me, and I'm afraid to even try to chase them down. I'm sure they need to go to the vet. I don't want my mom going to jail, but I...I can't do this. Yesterday, they told her she'd have to be in a rehab facility for at least a month. When Dad died eight years ago, I got her to give me a power of attorney in case anything happened, you know? I just...I can't leave it like this. I have to clean this out. I just..." She stared at him, more tears in her eyes. "Please, I need your help."

Essie exchanged a knowing glance with Josh. "How many dogs?" she asked.

"Three," the woman said. She led them around the side of the house to another door that opened into the kitchen. "At least, that's what she told me. Who knows if there's that many in there?"

The smell hit Essie first, even before the woman opened the door.

When she opened it...

Oh, thank god.

Essie never thought she'd ever be thankful that her father "only" hoarded stuff, not garbage, not food, not animals. The cloud of stench that hit them was almost like a wave rolling in from the Gulf and crashing onto the beach. Essie felt like the smell would totally coat her body.

A disgusting layer of garbage and animal waste mixed together and pressed into the linoleum covered the kitchen floor. The counters were completely covered in old food, garbage, and dirty dishes.

Josh stopped Essie and Lisa at the door with an outstretched arm. "We need to go get protective equipment. We can't go in there like this."

Essie spotted a small dog peeking around the corner at them before it bolted back into the narrow canyon of garbage it had emerged from.

Josh turned both women around and made them step back onto the porch, closing the door behind him.

"We can't leave them in there," Essie protested.

"They've been in there for years. Another hour won't hurt." He turned to Lisa. "You said you have a power of attorney?"

She nodded. "My mom is eighty-four years old. I thought maybe she was having some issues, but she seemed like she was still okay mentally. She's always been stubborn and independent. But this..." She shuddered. "I'll sign whatever I need to hire you."

"You understand that by doing that, she's probably going to be very upset with you."

"I don't care. My husband's a lawyer. I've already called him, and he's going to file an emergency motion for guardianship as soon as he can get the papers drawn up and over to a family judge. I texted him pictures of the kitchen. She obviously cannot live by herself any longer. She was always a little disorganized, but this is totally out of character for her. I'm not even sure there's just three dogs in there at this point. That's what she told me, but how do I even know?" The woman sounded close to hysterics.

"I'll stay here with her," Essie told Josh. "You go get what we need."

"I need to get a signature first," he said. He returned to his truck and retrieved his iPad, thumbing through it as he returned to the porch. "This is an emergency contract," he explained to Lisa. "It gives us permission to be on the property, to enter the house, recover the animals, and is a liability waiver. Let's get the dogs safe first, then we can sit down and go through the details of what we need to do and arrange a full contract. Unfortunately, our main crew is tied up on another job right now, so the earliest we can start is next week."

She nodded. "Okay, that's fine. As long as the dogs are safe. Where do I sign?"

Josh got her information from her to fill out the form, then showed her where to sign with her finger. Once that was done, he sent copies to the office and to Lisa's e-mail address. "I'll be back shortly."

Essie was peeking through the window in the door and spotted the dog again, which barked at her before running away. "Bring some crates," she called out to him. "Pick up at least three crates, medium sized or larger. Wire crates, not the plastic kind. And some kennel leads."

"Some what?"

"Just go to a pet store. They'll know what they are. And some dog treats. Something meaty that will smell good."

He nodded before getting in his truck and quickly driving off.

Essie sat on the porch steps with the woman, listening as Lisa cried through her story. Her father had died of cancer eight years before. She hadn't been super close to her mother before that, but after her father's death, and with her own three children busy with high school sports and other activities, she accepted her mom's word that everything was fine. Her mom came over to eat dinner with them at their home a couple of times a month and seemed all right.

It wasn't until the neighbor across the street found her on the ground in the driveway the morning before and called her that Lisa had been aware there was a problem. Her mother had spent the entire day before insisting she would go home from the hospital, and everyone thinking her stubbornness was a combination of just normal confusion, pain medication, and the result of the anesthesia.

Until that morning.

That was when her mother admitted to having the three dogs.

Lisa sat with her head in her hands. "I feel like a horrible person," she said. "I feel awful. Like I'm the world's crappiest daughter."

Essie somehow held back her inward giggle that, no, she felt the title rightfully belonged to *her*, but that she'd gladly hand it over to Lisa.

Then again, her father hadn't hoarded animals.

"You're not awful," Essie assured her. "It's hard to tell a parent it's time to get help. Believe me, I know."

And as they sat there, Essie confessed her troubles.

About her dad and his hoarding, and how the case that the crew was currently tied up with was her own.

When Essie finished her story, Lisa hugged her. "Thank you," she softly said. "That did help. Thank you for telling me I'm not alone."

"I just don't want you to think that you're the only one to ever go through this. And we're the 'lucky' ones, believe it or not. There are no telling how many other hoarders out there whose families still don't know. They'll get the shock of their life when something happens, their loved one dies and leaves this all on their shoulders. Some of them might know or suspect there's a problem, but they don't know the full extent."

When Josh finally returned an hour later, Essie had circled the house and looked in the windows on the lower floor. All of them had the curtains drawn. Only the window in the kitchen door wasn't covered. Twice more she'd spotted a dog, different than the first one she'd glimpsed.

Although she had heard a bark that sounded different from the first two, lending credence to the theory of three dogs. She didn't think there was more than that in there, but she knew she could be mistaken.

Josh dropped the tailgate on his truck and unloaded a large plastic storage tote. Inside he had disposable protective suits, nitrile gloves, face masks like hospitals handed out for visitors, and protective goggles.

"Put these on," he said, handing them both suits. "We don't know how bad the rest of the house is."

The suits even had elasticized hoods that covered their hair, and he'd brought protective outer booties as well. They used several turns of duct tape around the cuffs of their pants and sleeves to close any gaps.

Then he unboxed the three new wire crates he'd bought, Essie quickly unfolding and assembling them.

He handed her the leads and treats. "This what you wanted?"

She smiled. "Exactly. Thank you."

Thus armed, they returned to the kitchen. "Let me go first," she said.

Trying not to gag on the stench, she stooped down as she slowly made her way through the kitchen to the doorway leading into the rest of the house. She hoped being crouched would appear less threatening to the dogs.

The rest of the house looked just as bad. The narrow path through the stuff was also coated in animal waste ground into the carpet. When she looked down at her feet, she realized fleas were coating her legs.

"Go wait outside," she told them. "No reason for all of us to be in here."

"I'm not leaving you alone in here," Josh said.

While she was grateful for and more than a little bit horny over the protective tone in his voice, on this point she wouldn't cave.

"Seriously, Josh. This is a literal health hazard. I don't need to tell you that. Go wait out on the porch. I'll bring them out as I find them. If you both are in here spooking them, it'll only make my job harder." She spotted empty food and water bowls on the floor. "See if you can find usable bowls and a bag of food in here, and get them some water. They're probably starving and thirsty."

She caught sight of one fur-covered rump disappearing into a darkened room. She fumbled for and found the light switch, wishing she hadn't when one dim bulb illuminated the room. It turned out to be a bathroom, and if she'd thought she had to go, the sight of the nasty space would have dried her bladder right up. It looked like something out of a horror movie.

A small dog cowered in the corner, next to the bathtub. Essie wanted to push the door closed to at least keep the poor animal from escaping, but the inches-deep layers of filth and garbage on the floor prevented her from budging it.

"Hey, sweetheart," she cooed, not moving from where she stood. "It's okay, sweetie. I bet you're hungry, aren't you?" She slowly ripped open the bag of treats Josh had brought and took one out.

It looked like it might have been a black and white shih tzu mix, but right now it was one matted fur ball of brownish gunk. She swallowed back her anger and her bile. The poor thing needed help, and the owner obviously wasn't in her right mind. It didn't make the situation any easier to stomach, but it helped Essie calm herself.

It lifted its nose to the air and sniffed the treat she slowly held out. Essie finally gave the treat a gentle flick, letting it land in front of the dog.

The dog kept its eyes on her as it lowered its head to sniff at the treat, then scarfed it up.

"Good, baby. That's real good." She pulled out another one and tossed it in front of the dog.

It took her fifteen minutes and five more treats to finally get the dog to stop growling at her. Once it did that, she slowly looped one of the kennel leads, tightening it only so far that she had a large enough loop to slip over the terrified dog's head. Ideally, she'd have a catchpole she could use to snag the dog and not risk getting bit, but they didn't have time for that. She had to make do. Cautiously, she stepped forward and reached out.

"It's okay, baby. Going to get you out of here and get you cleaned up, I swear. Get you some food and water." The dog sniffed at the loop of braided nylon, trying to keep an eye on her and the kennel lead at the same time.

Behind her she heard a noise but didn't take her attention off the dog in front of her. The dog glanced at whatever made the noise and then immediately focused back on her, so she suspected it was probably one of the other dogs behind her.

She knew she'd likely only get one good attempt per dog, and knew she needed to make each attempt count.

Apparently the air-conditioning in the house either didn't work or wasn't turned on. It felt at least fifteen degrees hotter inside than out, the disgusting stench stifling like a rancid cocoon. Sweat trickled down her neck and her back as she kept her tone light and soothing.

"Heeey, baby. It's okay." Finally, she was able to swoop the lead around the dog's neck and give a quick tug to tighten it. The dog tried to pull back and away, growling at her again, but it was trapped in the corner between the wall and the tub.

She stepped forward, scooping one arm under its midsection, the other keeping the kennel lead pulled taut so the struggling dog couldn't turn and snap at her. She didn't think it was really aggressive, just poorly socialized and terrified out of its mind.

And probably more than a little batshit crazy from being cooped up in that disaster area.

"I've got one!" she called out as she backed out of the bathroom. "Get a crate ready!"

She squirmed her way through the passage and back into the kitchen, where Josh held the kitchen door open for her. Lisa had one of the crates open. Essie slid the dog, lead and all, into the crate and quickly closed the door.

The terrified dog cowered in the far corner of the crate. It had felt like it was probably close to twenty pounds, but how much of that was matted fur was hard to tell.

"Holy crap," Lisa muttered.

"I hope you've told your vet we'll be bringing them in," she said, now able to get a better look at the poor dog. "I don't know how the other two are, but this one needs to be shaved down. It's going to have flea and skin problems, probably worms, dental, ears…" She shook her head. "I can't tell how old it is, but it doesn't look like an elderly dog. Please get it some water, at least."

Josh and Lisa had already rescued a couple of plastic bowls from the kitchen and rinsed and filled them with an outside hose. Josh handed one to Essie, who dropped a couple of treats into the crate in front of the dog before easing the door open just enough to get the water in.

Once she closed the door, the dog immediately lapped at the water for almost a minute before scarfing up the treats.

"I called my vet," Lisa said. "I already warned them. They told me to call when we were pulling in, and to meet them at the back door so they could evaluate them outside before they bring them in."

"They might want to shave them down outside," Essie said. "They're absolutely covered with fleas. They're going to have to be completely shaved from head to toe." She'd seen cases of animal neglect before, and abuse. But she'd never seen dogs matted this badly before.

"We can load the crates in the back of my truck," Josh said. "I've got a cargo net we can put over them so they stay secure. Lisa, I don't think you want them in your car like this."

"I can't believe my mom let this happen," the woman said, her eyes welling up again. "She was never like this before. A few piles of papers here and there, sure, but always clean."

Essie stared down at her arms and legs, where fleas were still jumping off her. "The place is crawling with fleas," she said. "Once we get the dogs out, someone needs to set off a couple of bug bombs in there."

"I'm halfway tempted to let the county fire department come burn it down as a practice run," Lisa said, frowning. "If it wasn't for the fact that there's some family pictures and things like that in there I need to find first."

"We've got a couple of exterminators we work with on a regular basis," Josh told her. "I can get you all their numbers. They handle emergency cases, too."

"Thanks."

Essie picked up another kennel lead. "Let me get back in there."

Josh reached out and grabbed her arm, his gaze piercing her through to her core. "Be careful," he warned.

Dominant, concerned.

She nodded, shoving her growing feelings for him out of her mind. "Oh, believe me, I will."

Essie worked her way back into the house through the kitchen. Somewhere deep in the house, she heard a noise, like something moving around.

It even feels like a damn horror movie.

The house had the high ceilings typical in many old Florida wooden framed houses, to help draw the heat up and away from residents.

Unfortunately, those same high ceilings had allowed the owner to hoard more stuff. Essie couldn't see over the tops of most of it. Whereas her father's hoard had grown from neat stacks of boxes and items that had morphed out of control, it looked like this woman had created a landfill inside her home. New clothes with tags still attached were piled under empty egg cartons and soup cans, many of the latter which looked like they'd never been rinsed out. The blocked windows only made it appear darker inside.

She's lucky she fell and broke her hip outside and not inside. She would have died in here.

Suppressing a shudder at that thought, Essie turned back to the kitchen and opened the door enough to speak to Josh. "Do you have a flashlight?"

"Yeah, hold on." He retrieved a small LED light from his truck and passed it through to her.

"Thanks." Inside, with the light to better illuminate her progress, she followed the sounds through the downstairs until she reached what was likely the foyer area.

It was hard to tell from the junk stacked around.

But the stairs were there, a very narrow path leading through piles of garbage on either side of the risers to the second floor.

She was almost afraid to play the beam of the light around the dim space. The last thing she wanted to see were tiny eyes of rats or other vermin reflected back at her.

There was old and dried dog feces everywhere, some of it ground into what once was a carpet, some of it petrified.

She must not have a sense of smell left. The house reeked of ammonia from urine, and she already felt a headache coming on.

She had to get the dogs out of there and get herself out of there before she became sick. So far, she hadn't seen any indication of cats or their feces, and while eye-watering, to her experienced nose the urine stench smelled like dog pee, not cat.

"Here, puppy," she called out. More noises came from upstairs, including a faint growling.

Dammit. Cautiously eyeing the stairs, she made her way up them, unable to grab onto the banister because of the piles of garbage in the way.

Chapter Fifteen

Josh nervously hovered by the kitchen door, cracking it open every minute or so to listen for Essie. He had a bad feeling about the entire situation, and didn't like the fact that Essie was alone inside. Old wooden houses like this, especially when filled with the weight of hoarded stuff, were especially susceptible to structural damage.

He'd never forgive himself if she got hurt.

I should have told her not to go upstairs. Thirty minutes later, he'd almost made up his mind to do just that when he heard her call out.

"I have number two. Get ready." He was waiting at the door, with Lisa ready at the crate and a bowl of water already inside it, when Essie made her way through the kitchen. Fortunately, this dog was short-haired, maybe a dachshund mix from the look of it. She eased it into the crate where instead of growling at her it immediately drank from the water bowl.

"I hope that doesn't make them sick," Lisa said after she closed the crate door. "Drinking that much."

"That's the least of their worries," Essie told her. She turned to Josh. "I know there's at least one more, but after I finally catch it, I want to take one more turn through the house to make sure."

He read the determination in her brown gaze. Despite his overwhelming urge to pull her into his arms and kiss her right there, their shared stench made that not only impractical but more than a little gross.

"I'd rather you didn't if you don't think there's more than three."

"I don't know if there is or not. That place is a damn maze. I think the last one ran back downstairs while I cornered this one. It's hard to tell."

"Is the upstairs as bad as downstairs?"

She nodded.

"You need to look up at the ceilings on the first floor. Make sure none of them are buckling. If they are, you don't go back upstairs, understand me? And don't spend any more time than necessary downstairs, either. I don't want the upstairs collapsing on you."

"I'm *not* leaving that dog in there."

You will if I tell you to. But he didn't say that. "If it's dangerous, come get me and I'll go in after it. I don't want you getting hurt." *Because it'd kill me if you did.*

The thought shocked him, but it hit him hard and fast.

And he knew it was the truth.

"I'll be okay." Before he could argue with Essie, she slipped into the kitchen again and disappeared around the corner.

With tension building to a nerve-snapping level in his gut, he waited by the kitchen door, keeping it cracked open to listen.

* * * *

Essie searched downstairs but didn't find the dog. "Hey, baby. Hey, puppy."

Upstairs, she heard a noise.

Of course. She did look up, as Josh had told her. She didn't see anything unusual, no buckled floors, but knew that didn't mean anything to her untrained eye.

Carefully making her way up the treacherous stairs again, she started searching room by room, closing doors as she went. Sometimes that meant kicking piles of junk out of the way and pulling her entire weight against the doorknob to make it move, but she did it.

When she heard a noise coming from what might have been the master bathroom, she started climbing over more piles to reach it.

There, revealed in the beam of her flashlight and cowering on a layer of garbage inside the bathtub, she found the final dog and the other one she'd seen from the kitchen door.

"Hey, baby," she said, relieved to have trapped it. Unfortunately, the room's light didn't work in this bathroom when she tried the switch. There was a little light filtering in through a half-covered window in the bedroom, so she let the half-opened door stay that way, hoping the terrified animal wouldn't dash around her. She propped the flashlight on what had been the counter but was otherwise covered with junk.

She dumped a handful of treats into her hand. "Here, sweetie. Look at this. Smell this." She carefully tossed a few so they'd land in front of the dog. One immediately rolled off a piece of cardboard and under the other layers of junk, but others landed in front of the dog. It only gave the treats one sniff before inhaling them.

"Gooood. Good baby." This dog was also matted like the first, but not as severely. She suspected it was either a shorter-haired breed than the first, or hadn't been there as long to become as matted. Its coat was a uniform shade of nasty brownish grey that she suspected was more from being filthy than anything resembling its true color. Her instinct was that it might be a yellow or peach cocker spaniel mix, based on the shape of its head and its long ears. It was hard to guess its weight, but it looked like it might be around thirty pounds or so.

It trembled as she talked to it and slowly approached. Footing in the bathroom was tricky due to walking on layers of stuff instead of the actual floor, but she kept her gaze focused on the dog.

"Hey, baby. Goood baby." Her heart broke for these animals at the same time she once again gave thanks her mom had kept her foot firmly down about not having any pets.

I don't have it nearly as bad as Lisa.

Essie finally got close enough to the dog she could slowly move the noosed kennel lead toward its head with her left hand. She held a treat in her right hand, moving it around so the dog kept its focus on the yummy treat and not the kennel lead approaching it.

Finally, knowing she was risking getting bit, she extended her right hand through the noose and closer to the dog. It sniffed at her fingers, its tongue flicking out to lick at the treat.

"Good, baby. Goood puppy." In one swift movement, she let the dog take the treat as she swooped the noose around the dog's neck and tightened it.

The dog exploded in a flurry of movement, catching Essie off-guard. She managed to get hold of its scruff with her left hand, digging into the matted fur tightly as she picked it up and hugged it under her right arm.

She backed up, unable to see where she was going as the struggling dog tried to break free from her grip. That was when she felt herself losing her balance. Unwilling to let go of the dog, Essie rolled onto her back as she fell, hitting the door and slamming it closed as a pile of clutter fell over on her and the dog in the darkness.

"Josh!" she screamed. "Help!" The flashlight, dislodged by her fall, was now pointed down, giving her barely any light. "Josh!"

* * * *

Josh was listening at the kitchen door and trying to hear over the sounds from the road and from Lisa trying to soothe the two scared dogs in the crates. He was about to shush her when he heard what sounded like a heavy thump, followed by screaming, from somewhere inside the house.

Heart pounding and self-recriminations flying in his brain, he flung the kitchen door open and ran inside. "Essie! Where are you?"

He followed the sound wrong the first time, ending up under her on the first floor. Getting himself turned around, he finally located the stairs and tripped up them as fast as he could until he made his way down the choked hallway to the last bedroom.

"Essie!"

"In here!"

Scrambling over the piles of crap, he made it to the closed door and tried it. The knob was unlocked, but when he shouldered the door, it barely budged.

"Are you okay?"

"Stuff fell and blocked the door."

He tried to slow his pounding heart. She wasn't hurt. If anything had happened to her…

"Stand back."

"Hold on." He heard sounds inside, including the dog growling and barking, sounds of things shifting around. "Okay."

He took a step back and slammed his body against the door, only managing to budge it an inch. Several more times, and his shoulder was killing him and he'd only managed to pry it open another six inches. "You'll have to dig out from in there."

"I'm not letting go of the dog!"

He swore under his breath and took another step back, kicking at the door. Fortunately it had a hollow core, and after the third kick he heard it splinter and crack. Then he used his shoulder again and was finally able to bust enough of the door that he could start ripping it apart.

"Okay," she said. "That should do." He reached in to steady her as she squirmed through the door, the struggling dog firmly hugged against her. "We need to get it to a crate before it stresses itself out any worse."

He refused to let go of her, keeping a hand on her arm, shoulder, or resting on her waist, until they reached the kitchen. Lisa was waiting at the third crate, and closed it after Essie got the dog safely inside.

The other two dogs, who'd both calmed down, seemed happy to see their compatriot.

Josh ripped his face mask off. "What the *hell* was *that*? You could have been hurt!"

She ripped her mask off. "It took me too damn long to get hold of it. I wasn't about to let go once I did because it wouldn't have given me another chance!"

He stepped close, into her face. "You could have been hurt!" he yelled again, worry now flooding to relief that she was safe.

"And I wasn't leaving it there!"

Their eyes locked. Before he realized what he was doing, despite how grungy both their overalls now were, he grabbed her by the back of the neck and kissed her, hard, possessively. He wrapped his other arm around her waist, refusing to let her go.

There was only the briefest resistance on her part before she melted against him, kissing him back.

Oooohhh fuck. But he didn't stop kissing her, not until he'd satisfied himself that she was all right.

From the way she kissed him back, apparently she was all right.

Very all right.

Then she tucked her face against him and burst into tears. At first he thought maybe it was because of him kissing her, when logic took over.

She was clinging to him, sobbing.

He held her as best he could, softly soothing her. "It's okay," he said. "You did good. You did a good thing. I was just scared for you. I'm sorry I yelled at you."

"I know. It's just…that could have been my parents' house. Those poor dogs…"

It was relief hitting her, the adrenaline crash. He'd seen subs post-scene have a cathartic cry and recognized this was along those lines.

He'd stand there holding her as long as she needed him to. Be a rock for her.

"They're safe now, because of you," he soothed. "You did good. They're going to be all right. This is a good thing."

It was the sound of Lisa clearing her throat that finally brought him back to reality a few minutes later. "Um, how did you want to load the crates in your truck?"

Josh gave Essie one final, silent kiss, hoping she understood the message he wanted to send her.

Mine.

Only then did he release her and step away, taking a deep breath. "I think there's a box of tissues in my truck," he said. "Go take a minute for yourself. Then let's get these guys loaded and the cargo net secured over them before we take off these." He tugged at his coveralls. "I have more so we can put fresh ones on at the vet's office."

He pulled her close and dropped his voice. "You *ever* do anything like that again and risk getting yourself hurt, I'll spank your ass. Understand me?"

Wide-eyed, she nodded. "Okay," she softly said.

He wanted to correct her, to draw a "Yes, Sir" out of her, but didn't push it.

If she knew what he and his brothers were, and she wasn't fighting him off, maybe there was a chance for them with her.

If they could prove to her how good it could be with them.

* * * *

Several hours later, Essie stood under a scalding hot shower in the guest bath at Ross and Loren's house and vigorously scrubbed herself from head to toe. It was late afternoon and heavy thunderstorms had shut down the operation at her mom's for the rest of the day.

Her mom, however, was still busy sorting things and cleaning the kitchen.

The vet's office had been crazy busy since it was a Monday, so Essie had offered to shave the two matted dogs in the parking lot. With Josh and Lisa helping her hold them, she shaved the mats off the two longer-haired dogs while the staff bathed the short-haired one and got it ensconced in a cage in their kennel. After disposing of their second set of protective coveralls and accepting teary hugs of gratitude from Lisa, Essie and Josh had returned to Essie's mom's house.

They didn't talk. She didn't want to, too overwhelmed processing everything that had happened to speak yet. She suspected he felt that way, too, his silence not feeling chilly in the slightest.

She couldn't believe she'd broken down in tears. She could cry over a scare and over neglected dogs, but still found it hard to cry over her father?

What's wrong with me?

In fact, she kept replaying Josh's threat in her mind, the protective, territorial tone in his voice when he'd threatened to spank her.

She had no doubts he meant it.

What shocked her was that she hadn't recoiled. In fact, even thinking about it again had made her wet.

Well, it answered my question about whether or not Josh likes me.

Josh had left after dropping her off when Purson, who'd been helping his crew pack their gear, told him work was shut down for the day due to the storms.

I need to talk with Josh. She wouldn't force it today, though. She suspected he needed as much time to process things as she did.

Ross had gone to work that afternoon, leaving Loren alone at home. When Essie finally emerged from the shower after using up most of the hot water, she towel-dried her hair and got dressed. Then she took her filthy clothes to the utility room and set the washer to hot, running them through without any other laundry to contaminate.

"Can I make you something to eat?" Loren asked when Essie returned to the kitchen.

At first she wanted to refuse, but at the thought of food her stomach grumbled. "I was going to say no, that I wanted to check on Mom, but maybe I should eat." She slid onto a barstool at the counter. "I feel luckier than ever now."

"Why's that?"

"It was..." She couldn't suppress her shudder. "Horrible. TV shows don't do that kind of stuff justice."

Loren's nose wrinkled. "That bad, huh?"

"Let's put it this way. Compare your house to what Mom's house was like. Well, now think about Mom's house being the equivalent of your house, and then compare *that* to the house we were at this morning. That drastic."

Loren's eyes widened. "Holy crap."

"Three dogs." She studied her hands. "I guess my motto through all of this needs to be, 'It could always be worse.'"

Loren heated her up a plate of leftover lasagna and poured her a glass of iced tea. "Feel like talking about it?"

She wasn't going to, at first, but then the story spilled out of her.

Before she realized what she was saying, she mentioned Josh's kiss.

Loren's playful smile startled her. "He likes you. Nothing wrong with that."

Heat filled Essie's face. "I guess. Can I tell you something else?"

"Of course."

She admitted kissing Mark. And her growing feelings for Ted, along with his admission that he liked her.

Loren didn't seem shocked in the slightest. Instead, she looked amused. "I don't see a problem here."

"You don't? Three guys? Brothers? Not like I could choose."

"Then don't. They've been poly before. Poly's not my thing. Then again, Sir's very territorial. You're a single adult. They're single adults. Have some fun. Who knows? You might enjoy it. Wouldn't hurt to talk to them about it."

Essie had expected pretty much any other advice except that.

"I don't live here."

"No, but it doesn't mean you can't experiment with them if they're willing. It doesn't even have to be sex. Ask them to play with you. I can vouch for their skills. I've seen them play many times before. They're good Tops and Doms."

Essie forked a bite of lasagna into her mouth to avoid answering.

She didn't fool Loren in the slightest. The other woman playfully smiled. "Nothing ventured, nothing gained."

"I'm supposed to be helping my mom," she finally answered.

"Yes, and you have been. But you need to decompress a little through this whole process or you'll have a meltdown. Consider it stress relief."

Stress relief, hmm?

Their conversation was cut short by her mom returning. "Well, I feel better now. Ready to start again tomorrow." Essie thought her mom looked ten years younger than the night she'd arrived at Ross and Loren's house.

Happier, for sure.

At peace.

Essie opted to leave the pondering for later and focus on her mom. It was what she should do, a good daughter's duty, to make up for lost time.

* * * *

Josh stood under the water and let it sluice the filth and stench off him. No matter how many times he'd handled a hoarding case involving animals, it never got easier.

I hope I didn't piss her off.

He couldn't believe he'd threatened to spank her, especially in front of someone else, but adrenaline had been flooding through him after getting Essie safely outside.

Considering how emotionally charged the whole situation was, it'd be better to talk to her, alone.

When he made it out to the kitchen, he found Mark and Ted waiting for him.

"What?"

"What happened today?" Ted asked. "Tell us."

Knowing he was about to get reamed out, he told them, not leaving out any details.

Mark scowled. "You're lucky she didn't get hurt. I would have beaten *your* ass."

Ted lightly backhanded Mark on the shoulder to silence him. "Tread lightly, guys. Okay?"

"You like her, too," Josh shot back. "Who are you to tell us that?"

"It's exactly why I'm telling you that," he said. "Need I remind you about sub frenzy? We don't need her regretting anything later on. If it's meant to be with her, it will happen. Take it slow." He pushed past them both and headed to his room, where they heard him shut the door. He'd brought some of his belongings over that afternoon from his apartment after rain shut down the Barrone job.

"Did I cross a line with her today?" Josh asked Mark.

He leaned against the counter. "Yeah, but I can't honestly say I wouldn't have done exactly the same thing in your shoes, so I don't hold it against you. I'm willing to bet big bro doesn't, either."

"Could've fooled me," Josh muttered.

"Let it go," Mark said. "Maybe we can talk to her tomorrow without film crews around." He headed down the hall to his room, leaving Josh alone in the kitchen.

He wanted to call Essie, talk to her, but wasn't sure that was the right thing, either.

Instead, after he ate dinner, he opted to go lie down and catch up on his sleep. Exhaustion had set in and he knew that wasn't the best mental state to conduct a heavy conversation. When he closed his eyes, he couldn't help but replay the scene in his mind, even with the gross circumstances, of having Essie in his arms and deliciously pressed against him.

I hope I didn't fuck things up.

Chapter Sixteen

Tuesday went smoothly. Essie was relieved when Josh told her he'd received a call from Lisa Parker. The three dogs were doing well. They'd been vetted, wormed, given their shots, and microchipped. They still needed dental work, and then they'd go home with her. Fortunately, they'd already been spayed or neutered, the short-haired dog a male and the two others female.

Essie was glad to hear the woman was going to keep them instead of uprooting them to yet another home. At least this way maybe Lisa's mom could visit with her dogs. Essie knew the elderly woman likely did love them, that the neglect wasn't deliberate.

Deliberate or not, the effect was the same. The woman would never live alone again.

After a full day of working, getting the kitchen nearly emptied except for stuff that belonged there, and an on-site visit from the investigator to check on their progress, Essie was exhausted by the time Mark called it a day a little before six that evening.

A shower, dinner, and a quick phone call with Amy didn't leave Essie feeling any more relaxed or centered. Not with her thoughts constantly turning to the three Collins brothers.

She felt like she was about to lose her mind. Between the disruption of her normal, calm, peaceful routine, the temporary displacement from home, the grief she didn't seem able to adequately express or expunge, and the stress of her mental confusion over what she was feeling for the three men, it felt like she'd been ripped out of her tidy, cherished reality and dumped into a surrealist painting.

And she *hated* that.

She didn't consider herself OCD, because she'd chosen her life, rigidly controlled it as much as possible, but could make changes as necessary. She wasn't a slave to her routines.

But her father's untimely demise, while an unexpected boon for her mother's life, had completely upended her own.

Even after a second hot shower she knew she didn't need she hadn't relaxed.

I have to get away and think and process.

She grabbed her purse and the keys to her rental car. "I need to go out for a few hours," she told Loren, who was on the sofa and watching TV. "I'm sorry, I hope that's not a bother? I don't want to disrupt you guys any more than I already have."

Loren kindly smiled. "Need some alone time after yesterday?"

Relieved that she understood, Essie nodded. "Yes. Exactly. It was…intense."

"Don't worry. If you're not back before we go to bed, we'll leave the front door unlocked. Just lock it when you come in."

"Thank you." She swooped in for a quick hug before practically sprinting out the front door.

She didn't know where she wanted to go. She pointed the car west, thinking about maybe just heading out to Siesta Key to sit and stare at the Gulf for a while. It'd be nice to stare at the ocean. Meditate under the stars.

It was one of the few things Essie missed about living in Florida. Yes, she could drive over to the Washington coast and see the Pacific Ocean, but it was different than the Gulf. It wasn't as serene on a calm, starry night like tonight.

Instead however, as her mind churned through what she'd learned about the men in the past couple of days, she found herself driving toward Mark and Josh's house. Even when she pulled into their driveway and shut the car off, she still wasn't sure why she was there.

It wasn't just about the animal hoarding case she'd helped with.

I guess there's only one way to find out.

Locking the car, she headed up their front walk.

* * * *

Ted closed his eyes and tried to relax. It was weird living in this room again. An alien familiarity. Things not quite the same, but not quite different, either. Except that now Mark had the master bedroom, while Josh had the bedroom he'd shared with Mark while growing up all to himself.

Then again, living alone wasn't everything he'd thought it'd be, either. It was okay for a few days here and there, but being alone all the time had proved...well, lonely. More lonely than he cared to admit to anyone, especially his two younger brothers.

Out in the living room, he heard Mark ask, "Who's that?"

"I don't know," Josh replied.

He was about to open his eyes when he heard the doorbell ring.

Okay, no meditation for the muddle-minded, I guess.

Sitting up, he swung his legs over the side of the bed and sat there for a moment. Being around Essie hadn't helped him maintain his center.

Damned if he wasn't attracted to her. He'd be lying if he said he wasn't. Especially when she'd outright asked him about the BDSM and hadn't flinched when he'd honestly answered her questions.

She was a strong, willful woman, used to rigidly controlling her life. And that she was as desperately alone as he was became painfully clear the more he talked to her.

Yet she likely would never admit it to herself, much less anyone else.

He heard the front door open and Mark's surprised sounding greeting. "Hey. What's up?"

It was the sound of Essie's voice that set his feet in motion before he even realized he was up and heading for his bedroom door.

"I'm sorry to drop by unannounced like this. May I come in?"

"Of course."

Ted yanked the bedroom door open. Belatedly, he realized he was only wearing a pair of running shorts, but screw it. She was just stepping inside the front door when he reached the foyer.

"Hey," he said, sliding to a stop, heart pounding.

Her eyes locked with his. "Hi."

Every logical reason he had for not getting involved with her flew right out the damn window when he stared into her eyes.

Fuck. I'm so screwed.

She looked from him, to Josh, to Mark. If he had to guess, the concern on her face was due to sheer nerves. "Can I talk with you guys about something?"

"About your mom?" Mark asked.

She shook her head a little, both hands holding on to her purse. "No," she softly said. "About the other…stuff."

It clicked home for Ted. "BDSM." He didn't phrase it as a question.

Now her gaze dropped to the tile floor. "Yeah," she quietly said. "That."

"Oh," Mark and Josh said together.

Idiots. Both of them.

"Sure," he said, reaching a hand out to her. "Anything you want."

After only a brief hesitation, she took his hand. That gave him hope, that maybe there was trust there.

Idiot. I'm the idiot, not them.

He realized he had it just as bad for her, if not worse, than Mark and Josh.

He led her to the living room and opted to stand while he got her settled on the sofa. "Can we get you anything to drink?"

She shook her head. "No, thank you."

Mark and Josh stared at him, apparently dumbfounded into silence.

Great. "So. What did you want to know?" he asked when it was apparent neither of his brothers were going to speak.

She drew in a deep breath. "Loren was telling me some stuff. About why she does it. About it giving her a mental vacation."

He nodded. "That's what it's like for some people, yes."

Her sweet brown gaze settled on his for just a moment before skipping away to his brothers, then back to the floor. She held her purse tucked in her lap, both hands around it, practically hugging it against her. "What's it like for you guys? Do you enjoy hurting women?"

"No!" the three of them responded in unison.

Mark and Josh looked at him before ceding the floor again. "The impact play is fun," Ted explained, "and bondage, but only if the person we're playing with wants that. We actually had a partner who was into far heavier play than we were comfortable with."

She met his gaze again. "You shared her?"

Now he felt uncomfortable. While poly and other forms of nonmonogamy were common among the people they socialized with in the BDSM lifestyle, it wasn't something they usually discussed outside that circle of friends. "Yes."

"Like those other friends of yours? Tilly and her guys?"

"Sort of," he said. "They're a little different, but same principle."

"So what do you like to do with a woman?" she asked.

Wow, the one time he wished he could melt out of the spotlight, and he couldn't pay his brothers to take over for him. He finally stepped a little closer. "You want me to be direct about it, or do you want me to sugar-coat it?"

"Direct."

His heart thumped a little in his chest. It'd been on the tip of his tongue to reply with, "Good girl," but he knew at this point it might be received the wrong way.

"We like to be in charge," he said. "Yes, we've shared women before. We've each been divorced. We separately realized that we needed more than a vanilla relationship. We didn't set out to be poly, but it just happened that way."

"In charge how?"

He sensed the minefield and treaded lightly. "In the bedroom. In the relationship part of it. Not overbearing," he quickly added when he sensed her tensing. "Not domineering, but with input and decision-making. But…" He tried to think of the best way to phrase it. "In charge, taking care of things, the safe lighthouse always there for you to come home to."

He knew that was taking a big risk, phrasing it like that, but decided if she was asking, maybe she had more on her mind than he'd guessed. "Just because others do things their way doesn't mean we do it the same way. A little over-the-knee spanking, some bondage, forced orgasm play, a little protocol."

He took another step closer, now standing in front of her, forcing her to look up to meet his gaze. He dropped his voice and prayed his cock didn't harden and tent his shorts right there.

"I enjoy knowing that at the end of the day, I can come home and let go of everything else and focus on one thing, and that I am, for a little while, the center of your world and your entire focus. That I can provide that safe, calm, dependable anchor when the rest of the world threatens to carry you away with its craziness."

Mark stepped forward, his voice sounding lower than usual, nearly choked with emotion. "That you can curl up with your head in my lap while I stroke your hair and tell you what a good girl you are."

Josh added his two cents. "That you can tell me what's wrong, and if you need me to fix it for you, I'll do my damnedest or die trying. That you never have to face anything alone ever again."

Ted glanced at his brothers, realizing they were, all three of them, idiots in love with this woman whom they barely knew. A woman who didn't even live here and who would likely break their hearts when she returned home.

"That we can take you to bed," he said, "and even if there's stuff going on in your life that is totally out of our control to fix for you, that at the very least we can take your mind off it and make you forget about it while you're with us."

Ted stepped around the coffee table and sat at an angle next to her on the couch, his arm draped across the back of the sofa, but not touching her...yet. "Someone we can take care of. Spoil rotten. But what we ask in return is willing submission. We can't and won't take it. You have to want to give it. We'll never force you to do something, but there might be plenty of times you find yourself faced with making the choice to submit or refuse."

He watched her throat work as she swallowed. "Like what?" she asked.

Taking another risk, he reached out with his other arm and tucked stray strands of her hair behind her ears. "My ideal is a relationship where I'm in control. I'll ask you to do what I say, when I say it. Not in terms of work or things like that." He waited until her gaze settled and focused on him. "I might make a rule that you don't wear panties at home without permission. And that if you break that rule, you get a spanking. Or I might make a rule that if you aren't at work, your cell phone is always on you. And if you don't answer a call, or at least text me back, you might get a spanking."

Mark chimed in. "Or a rule that if you ask me to make a decision for you, you will abide by that decision even if you decide you don't like it. Whether it's what to order at a restaurant, what movie to see, or how to handle a jerk hitting on you on Facebook."

"Like controlling who I can be friends with?" He heard the edgy tone in her voice, but Josh jumped in with a response before Ted could.

"No, not exactly. Not unless that person was dangerous for some reason. Or that person upset you on a regular basis and you let them walk all over you. We would never cut you off from your friends or you mom. But we would hope that you would have a level of trust in us that, if we saw a situation develop that was unhealthy, you would completely confide in us and allow us to make a decision on what to do about it."

"So…all three of you were in a relationship with the same woman?"

"The longest poly group we had was more play and sex than a real relationship," Ted said. "If you told us all you wanted for right now was to just be play partners, we'd be okay with that. Or if you'd like to see what might happen, we could agree to be exclusive for now."

He cupped her cheek with his hand and gently tipped her face up. "If you just wanted to let go for tonight and see what might happen without any thoughts about tomorrow, see if you'd even be okay with this, we can do that, too."

He wasn't expecting it when she nodded.

He glanced up at Mark and Josh, who both nodded.

Returning his attention to her, he decided to push more.

She wants this, she'll need to be ready for it.

He dropped into his "Dom" tone. "What do you want, Essline?" he asked. "You need to say it."

He caught the hitch in her breath and could barely hear her soft whisper. "I don't want to think tonight. I don't want to be in charge tonight."

Aaaaand there goes my cock.

He forced himself not to think about the painful erection straining against the front of his nylon shorts. "What are your hard limits?" When confusion furrowed her brow, he added, "Sex, yes or no?"

She nodded.

"You have to ask for it."

"I'd…like to see what it's like."

He desperately hoped this wasn't just a curiosity for her. A chance to sow wild oats and then return to Spokane and never speak to them again. "I would like to feel what it's like to put you over my lap, naked, and spank you with my bare hand while you're sucking one of their cocks," he said. "Maybe even use a paddle on that sweet ass of yours, until it's red and sore, before I slide my cock up your ass. Would you like that?"

That was pushing it, and he knew it, but if she wanted to play this game she needed to play by their rules. More importantly, she needed to know those rules and agree to them before they could play.

"Yes," she said.

"Yes, what?"

She swallowed again. "Yes, Sir."

He leaned in closer, so close he could feel her breath against his lips. "Then ask for it. Tell us what you want."

"I...I'm not into pain but I'd like to try to see if I can get to subspace like Loren talked about. Like...like in the books. I've read a lot of books. I didn't realize people did it in real life though."

Oh...shit.

He desperately hoped she wasn't one of *those*, who just wanted to play for a little while to scratch an itch because of a novel she'd read. Before he could ask more, she continued.

"I'm willing to try it but only as long as I know if I ask you to stop that you will. If it gets to be too much."

"This isn't a game to us," he said. "All you need to do is just say *red* and we'll stop, I promise. But up to and until you do, we won't stop. We won't give you more than you can take, though. We want it to be fun for you."

He watched her look at Mark, and then Josh, before she returned her focus to him. "You're all okay with sharing someone?"

"Sweetheart," Ted said, "it makes it that much hotter for us. Women have the advantage of multiple orgasms. We can tag team you and keep you coming all night and share the work. You sure *you* can handle all three of *us*?"

Chapter Seventeen

Ted's low tone sounded like a velvety purr. If that wasn't enough to turn her insides to melted butter, the playful smile that curled his lips would have finished her off.

"Just think," he continued. "Tied up, helpless, and forced to orgasm all night long. Three cocks filling you, three sets of hands, three mouths. Keeping you so busy that the only thing you can think about is how good it feels."

Hell, her clit was already throbbing, her pussy wet.

Mark spoke up. "A cock in your pussy, one in your ass, and one in your mouth." When she glanced his way, he wore the same sinfully seductive smile his eldest brother wore.

Josh added, "You know, I still have that Hitachi in my toy bag." His grin looked downright evil.

"Oooh," Ted and Mark said.

"Even better," Ted continued. "Three cocks filling you, while one of us holds a vibrator against your sweet little clit. You might never want to leave."

"No strings attached tonight," Josh said, "except that we're in charge unless or until you safeword."

"A chance to see us the way we really are," Mark added. "If you don't like us like that, we part as friends and no hard feelings. But if you do like it…" He shrugged.

Ted picked it up. "If you do like it," he said in that same delicious velvety tone, "then we can do it again. And again. Maybe get you to the point you think about moving back to Florida. Because I promise you, if you give us a chance to be in the driver's seat, we'll do everything in our power to show you how good it could be on a permanent basis."

Ooooh, that sounded tempting. Sooo fucking tempting, he had no idea.

Then again, maybe he did.

Dangling in front of her a chance to have not one, but *three* hunky guys filling, among other things, her heart and her bed? To be able to, for once, have someone she could lean on instead of shouldering the weight of the universe on her shoulders?

A chance to let someone else, someone she could trust, be in control for a change?

"We have a lot of friends," Ted said. "A lot of great people. It's like an extended family. Ross and Loren. Tilly, Landry, and Cris. Tony and Shayla. Bill and Gabe. And others. You've met a lot of them. Look at how Ross and Loren jumped into action to help your mom when they barely knew her and didn't know you at all. That's how they all are. Other than your friend Amy, and her family, who do you have keeping you in Spokane? Your mom is here. You could have a ready-made family of your own with us and our friends. Where if you have a problem, you could pick up a phone and call any of them and they'd be there for you in a heartbeat."

The sudden prickle of tears in her eyes surprised her. She blinked them away. "Can we just see how tonight goes?" she asked, his comments hitting far too close to home for her liking. She didn't want to think, and pondering the truth of his proposal would engage her brain in an emotionally painful way.

"Then tell us what you want," Ted quietly insisted.

"I want to be submissive to you three tonight."

Ted leaned in and kissed her, the hand cupping her chin gently but firmly holding her in place while his other hand slipped around the nape of her neck and gripped her there as well. He didn't have to force her lips apart. As soon as she felt the flick of his tongue against the seam of her lips, they parted for him.

He lifted his mouth from hers. "Such a good girl," he whispered before kissing her again, this time with more force, in charge and totally possessive.

With that simple sentence, it felt like he'd stuck a spatula in the middle of her melted-butter soul and gave it a quick stir.

She was aware of Josh and Mark closing in, one of them sitting on her other side on the couch and one of them now standing in front of her, but with her eyes closed she lost track of who was who. One of them took her purse from her lap and she heard him set it on the coffee table.

Then there were another set of lips caressing the side of her neck, and a hand slipping through and tangling in her hair.

"Just let go," Josh said. "We'll catch you. We promise."

Ted ended their kiss again and touched his forehead against hers. "Let us catch you. Just let us take care of you."

"I don't know how," she admitted, feeling the tears struggling to break through again. "I don't know how to let go."

Ted gently stroked her cheeks with the pads of his thumbs. "Then let us teach you how to let go. Just give us a chance to show you how good it could be, how freeing it can feel."

She wanted to. *Daaaammnn*, did she ever want to. Not just for the sexytime, either. Not just for the fun. She wanted to see what it was like, just once, to let go and know someone else could take control and make the world go away.

It was a luxury she'd never had, not since she was a child.

She nodded. "Okay."

He smiled, rubbing his nose against hers. "Okay?"

She thought about it. "Yes, Sir."

"Good girl."

She whimpered.

* * * *

Mark didn't know when he'd slipped from wanting to make her theirs, to desperately hoping she'd let them make her theirs, but it felt right. Better than right, it felt perfect. One woman who could understand and complete them. One woman they could spend their private time with, who could accept them fully as they were, the way they were, in the same way they wanted and accepted her.

It was a little selfish on his part, but he wanted to blow her mind in bed, to get her to the point that she didn't want to leave them, wouldn't leave them, wouldn't disappear to Spokane to drift away from them.

Yes, she had a shit-ton of emotional baggage. Who better to understand, love, and help her heal than them? They understood. They got it. They didn't have hoarders for parents, but they'd worked with enough of them to know the problems. To know how deeply the condition hurt their families.

They were lucky their own parents were alive, but the fact that she had unresolved issues with her own father was something they could and would help her with, if she'd let them in.

She turned her head to look at him. "Are you really okay with this?" she asked.

He smiled and kissed her. "Really. I'd kill any other guy who tried to lay a hand on you, but these are my brothers. I'd never worry about you if I wasn't with you if I know one of them is around."

"Yes," Ted and Josh echoed.

"See?" He kissed her again, savoring it. "I know this is new to you. But we also know this can work. We have friends who make this work. I'm not saying it's perfect or that there won't be hiccups, but with all of us there behind you, we'll be able to hold you up, help you find your way, and never abandon you. Sometimes, we'll each have alone time with you."

He chuckled. "And sometimes, we'll have you in bed between us, our hands all over you, our cocks inside you, and blow your mind so hard that you'll never want to be anywhere but here."

"You don't even know me," she said. "Not really. How can you be so sure?"

"Because I feel it. I know what didn't work, and what didn't feel right. This feels right, feels *good*. And I'm willing to do whatever it takes to prove to you how good it could be if you just let it happen and don't keep making excuses for why it couldn't work."

Big brother Ted suddenly applied the brakes. "Uh, guys, condoms?"

Mark silently swore, but Josh jumped up. "I think I still have some. Hold on." He ran down to his bedroom and returned a moment later, triumph on his face and Trojans in his hand. "Ta-da!"

Essie giggled, the sweet sound sending the good kind of shivers through Mark's soul.

Hers. Whether she knew it or not, whether she still wanted him or not tomorrow, he knew his heart irretrievably belonged to her.

* * * *

Essie realized she was really about to go through with this.

Really.

As every logical reason as to why this was a horribly irresponsible and dumbass move tried to scream its way through her mind, she shoved those thoughts away and did her best to ignore them.

Maybe this would be okay.

Maybe it would lead to something good.

Maybe she could find whatever it was that had been missing from her life all these years.

Maybe.

If she didn't try, she wouldn't know.

"I'm on the pill," she said.

"No offense, sweetheart," Mark said, "but at least for the first time, until we can have a better, more detailed conversation, for your peace of mind and ours we'd rather use them."

"Okay." She closed her eyes and let the men ease her back on the couch. Mark kissed her, nibbling his way down her jaw to her ear and back again. Hands lifted her blouse up and over her head. Then she felt her bra being removed.

Two warm mouths closed around her nipples, sucking, flicking, playing, teasing until they were hard, aching peaks and sending pulses of need to her clit with every pull.

"See?" Mark murmured. "How good is *that*?" He cupped her face with his hand and made her look him in the eyes. "Answer me, baby."

"Good."

"Good what?"

"Good...Sir."

He kissed her, hard, other hands now working on her jeans to get her belt loose and the button undone. All the while, Josh and Ted continued teasing her, sucking on her nipples, drawing soft whimpers from her.

Working together, they finally got her jeans and panties off her with her assistance. Then Ted relinquished her nipple and knelt in front of her, pushing her thighs apart. He hooked his arms under her legs, fingers digging into her flesh as he buried his face in her pussy.

Not only did her eyes drop closed, she was pretty sure they rolled back in her head in a complete three-sixty. His tongue found and flicked at her clit as Mark changed positions, his mouth now covering and sucking her abandoned nipple.

Holy...fuck. She'd never felt pleasure so intense before. Sure, she rubbed one out in bed or with the handheld showerhead on occasion, but that wasn't very often.

This...

Hell, if it felt *this* good every time she did it, she'd die of starvation because she'd *never* stop doing it.

Ted's tongue circled her clit, dipping into her pussy before returning. She felt the climb start, her head lolling back on the sofa as pleasure filled her, her orgasm washing over her. She tangled her hands in the men's hair, moaning, but then another jolt of pleasure shot through her when the men both took her wrists and pinned her arms over her head, against the couch.

"Please don't stop," she softly begged.

Ted burrowed even deeper, nibbling on her clit with his lips before sucking her sensitive nub into his mouth, where he flicked it with his tongue.

Searing pleasure that bordered on pain shot through her, rocketing from one end of her body to the other. That she couldn't move, between Mark and Josh pinning her arms down and Ted keeping her in place, impaled on his tongue, only added to the sensations.

Ted took her above and beyond, not stopping even when she didn't think she could take any more and tried squirming free.

Mark lifted his head. "Oh, no, sweetheart," he playfully said. "You don't get to safeword for pleasure. Only pain. You *will* stay right here and keep coming as long as we make you."

With that, he bent his head to her breast again, once again sucking on her nipple.

She tried to pull her hands free and that made the men only hold on tighter.

Which only fired her pleasure centers up again.

Essie found herself locked in a downward spiral into the deepest, most intense pleasure she'd ever experienced in her life. No other lover before had ever made her feel like this.

Damnnnn...

And then, impossibly, she felt her body responding, once again surging toward another orgasm.

Ménage with hot guys? Check.

Multiple orgasms in the space of a few minutes? Check.

When the release slammed into her, she sobbed at the sensation, pleasure so raw she didn't know if she'd remember what it felt like to have a plain old boring climax she gave herself, much less ever be satisfied by one again.

Josh lifted his head. "Look at me, baby." Her head lolled toward him and she opened her eyes.

He smiled. "Just think how good this could be every night. Oh, another of our rules might be you don't get to masturbate ever again. If you want to make yourself come, you have to ask permission."

Not that she did a lot of that, but that rule sounded so utterly H-A-dubya-T hot that she nearly came again from the thought.

"Would you like a rule like that, baby?"

She nodded. "Yes, Sir," she whispered, unable to put more strength into her voice.

Between her legs, Ted had eased up a little but was still circling her clit with his tongue, keeping the boiler primed, as it were.

And she thought she just might be able to come again.

Mark lifted his head. "Hey, go get the Hitachi." He grinned as Josh let go of her and went dashing down the hall again.

"Wait until you get a load of that," Mark promised with an evil grin.

Josh returned a moment later with a towel, a vibrator, and an extension cord. Ted finally sat up, smiling as he licked his lips before leaning in to kiss her. She loved tasting herself on him.

"Baby," he said, "I cannot wait to fuck that sweet pussy of yours."

"Change," Josh said. "My turn."

Ted climbed onto the sofa where Josh had been. Mark and Ted grabbed her wrists and held them over her head again, pinned against the couch. With their other arms, they each hooked one under her knees, holding her thighs spread wide open for Josh, who now sat on the floor.

"Eyes down here, baby," Josh ordered.

She could barely keep her head up, but complied.

He tucked the towel under her bum, then held up the vibrator. "Meet Señor Hitachi," he said. "He will be your new best friend." He held it up to her lips. "Kiss it."

She did, her heart racing in anticipation.

"Good girl," he said. With one hand, he spread her labia wide open, making her moan again.

Then he flicked the vibrator on and pressed it against her clit.

Had it felt good before? Holy crap, this made even that pale in comparison. She let out a cry as the intense sensation threatened to overwhelm her.

"Take it," he sternly ordered. "Come for me."

Mark and Ted tightened their grips on her as she struggled. "Take it, sweetheart," Ted ordered. "You can take this. This is nothing. This is just the warm-up."

"Eyes on me," Josh ordered.

She didn't try to keep her cry quiet as she tipped over the edge again. With the men firmly gripping her body, she sobbed her way through that orgasm, heaving in a relieved sigh when he pulled the vibrator away after a few moments.

"Oh, we're not done," he teased. "Not even close." He pressed it against her clit again.

This time, his goal was apparently to build her up to an even bigger release. He kept teasing her, tormenting her, driving her closer every time before pulling it away.

Finally, she found herself begging for release and didn't even realize it until Mark chuckled.

"You want to come, baby? A few minutes ago, you were trying to get away from Señor Hitachi. I think you need to make up your mind."

"Please make me come, Sir!" she begged.

It was only as Josh laughed and pressed the Hitachi against her clit once more that she realized her tactical error.

"Oh, I'll keep you coming, all right."

She thought she'd be close to hyperventilating when he finally relented several minutes later and switched it off.

"So much for foreplay," Josh teased.

Mark and Ted released their grips on her. She slumped against the couch, wrung out and sated and with a deep, pleasant, unfamiliar buzz floating through her brain.

Could this be subspace? She both wanted it to stop, and yet wanted to beg them to keep going. A nice, floaty feeling she'd never experienced before.

The men quickly stripped. All three men were in shape, not rock hard and leaving her feeling frumpy and fat, but nothing to be ashamed of, either. All three of them sported rigid, generous erections that were now pointed her direction.

Ted grabbed one of the condoms and rolled it onto his stiff shaft, then sat on the couch next to her. His brothers helped her straddle him, her back against his chest as Ted guided his cock into her ready pussy.

Her moans echoed his as he impaled her to the root, filling her.

"Arms over your head, baby. Behind you. Wrists together."

She did and he reached back, grabbing them with one hand. He flexed his hips, seating his cock even more deeply inside her drenched cunt.

"Oh, fuck yeah," he groaned. Then he reached out and snapped his fingers. "Señor Hitachi."

She started to protest, but then he had it in his hand, had flicked it on, and was pressing it against her exposed clit.

Mark and Josh leaned in, their hands on her thighs, keeping her from rising up and escaping, their mouths once again on her nipples.

"Come again," Ted roughly ordered in her ear, his voice sounding strained with the effort of holding back. "Come on my cock, baby."

With her body stretched out like that, she couldn't have refused even if she wanted to. His cock had found her G-spot and pressed against it perfectly at this angle. And with the men's bodies pinning her in place, all she could do was sit there and take it.

"That's it," he grunted as her orgasm started. "I feel you coming. You just keep doing that. So fucking perfect, baby."

She didn't know when she'd started crying again, but she found herself rocking in time with Ted's hips, as much as he'd let her, wishing he'd fuck her hard and fast and deep, and—

What would it feel like with one of them in my ass, too?

That thought pushed her over the edge again. Ted finally pulled the vibrator away and switched it off. He let go of her wrists, grabbing her hips and bouncing her on his lap as he started fucking her.

Mark and Josh draped her arms over their shoulders and she held on to them as Ted fucked her, hard and deep, while the last echoes of her orgasm still rolled through her.

Ted let out a loud groan, his fingers tightening on her hips before he finally fell still. After a moment he wrapped his arms around her and pulled her against him, kissing her.

"I hate to make you move, baby, but I need to get up and take care of something."

Mark and Josh helped her off him. As he disappeared down the hall, Mark rolled a condom onto his cock and climbed between her legs. "Hard and fast, baby," he said, "because if I don't do this hard and fast, my cock's going to beat me to death." He pushed her over sideways onto the couch and lifted her legs, pushing her knees up until they touched her chest.

He smiled down at her. "The next time I fuck you tonight, it'll be slow and I'll make sure you come at least twice." He lined up his cock with her cunt and speared her, drawing a moan out of her.

Yessss, this.

She wanted hard and fast, a thorough fucking to make her walk funny the next day.

Then again, they'd already accomplished that even before they'd started fucking her.

With her ankles over his shoulders, he grabbed her wrists and held them over her head, pinned down.

She'd never realized how sexy it felt being held down.

Must do it more often.

Mark's brown gaze held her, locked on hers as a smile curved his sweet lips. "See? Three guys to make you feel like a sexy princess all the time. All you have to do is follow our rules."

At this point she'd be willing to agree to anything if this just didn't stop. If they didn't stop.

Ted returned and sat at her head, sticking his thumb in her mouth. She sucked it like a cock, swirling her tongue around it, wishing it was a cock, one of their cocks, specifically.

"Ooh, baby," Ted moaned. "You are going to love being spit-roasted."

Josh stood next to them, slowly stroking his cock. "I want to feel her sucking my cock while she gets another session with Señor Hitachi. I bet she'll moan her brains out."

Ted and Mark both said, "Ooh."

"Good idea," Ted added. "We'll put that on the agenda."

Mark was right. He didn't last long, fucking her hard and fast and deep, even more deeply than his brother, until he took one final thrust and buried himself inside her with a satisfied grunt.

He fell still, breathing heavily before leaning in to kiss her and letting go of her wrists. "You're beautiful, sweetheart."

"I'm about to explode," Josh said as he grabbed a condom and rolled it onto his cock. "Move it."

There was a tumble of bodies, and then she found herself face-to-face and on top of Josh. "Grab my cock, baby. Put it in." He settled his hands on her hips.

She did, easing the head in and slowly impaling herself on him.

He sucked in a sharp breath. "Oh, fuck yeah. You're gorgeous, sweetheart."

Once his cock was all the way in her cunt to the hilt, he reached up and cupped her breasts in his hands. "Ted, do the honors."

"My pleasure." He knelt next to them and held up the vibrator.

"Hands behind your back," Ted ordered. "Keep them there."

She complied without hesitation, without question.

He turned the vibrator on and slid it between her legs.

Josh started pinching her nipples between his fingers, harder than before, enough to make her gasp through the pleasure of the vibrator.

"Yeah, you feel that, don't you, sweetheart," he teased. "A little bit of bite, a lot of pleasure. Give her a few swats on the ass."

Ted stroked her ass cheeks with his other hand before landing a stinging slap against her left ass cheek.

She started to howl in protest, which turned into a howl of pleasure as an unexpected orgasm slammed into her.

"That's it," Josh grunted. "Take it, baby. Take it for us."

Ted kept the vibrator pressed against her clit as he slapped her ass, back and forth, Josh still rolling and pinching her nipples.

The only thing she could equate it to was adding salt to a dessert recipe to make it taste that much sweeter and balance it out.

And the buzz in her brain turned into a full-blown blizzard.

Mark had returned at some point, because he stroked her hair, his fingers tangling and fisting her hair, making her look up at him.

He wore a pleased smile. "Oh, baby, just think if you had a cock in your mouth right now."

Another burst of pleasure spiraled through her nervous system, taking away her ability to speak, leaving her only with the ability to breathe and feel.

Ted dug his fingers into her ass. "See, sweetheart? Only as much as you can take." He gave her another stinging slap. "All the good stuff, none of the bad."

Josh released her breasts. "Okay, I have to fuck her." Ted pulled the vibrator away and Josh grabbed her hips, fucking his cock hard and deep inside her.

Mark held her in place, his hands buried in her hair, making her keep her eyes focused on him. "Such a beautiful girl for us," he cooed. "You're such a good girl, taking what we give you."

Hell, if he'd keep talking to her in that tone, she'd take any and everything they wanted to give her. Just to keep feeling *that*, that blissful release that wiped out every other thought from her mind.

Josh didn't last long. When he came, he pulled her down on top of him, his arms wrapped around her, and kissed her. "You're perfect, baby."

Predictably, he, too, had to get up. Ted sat on the couch and gathered her into his arms, curled against him.

That was when she burst into tears.

She didn't understand it, and she was afraid the men might freak out about it, but Mark and Ted only held her more tightly, Mark pulling her legs into his lap.

"It's all right, sweetheart," Ted soothed. "Let it all out."

Out it came. She turned her face against his stomach and sobbed, feeling everything draining out of her, all the bad, all the stress, all the worry.

All the grief.

Everything.

After a few minutes she pulled herself together and took a deep breath. "Sorry," she said. "I don't know why I did that."

Ted's smile looked loving, kind, nothing like the sexy, stern Dom of a few minutes earlier. "It's normal. Some people have cathartic cries after a scene." He tucked her hair behind her ear. "Just surf the zen."

Mark laced his fingers through hers. "Did you hit subspace?"

"I…I think so."

"I'm sure she did," Josh said as he returned. "Did you see that glazed look in her eyes?" He smiled down at her. "You just wait. Give me a few weeks to keep you feeling that good, you won't want to leave."

"What?"

"Let's move to Mark's room," Ted said. "He's got a king-size bed."

They helped her walk, Ted keeping a steadying arm around her as they gathered on Mark's bed.

"Let's talk for a few minutes, okay?" Ted suggested.

She nodded.

"Don't know how you feel about it, but if you're open to it, we would love to have a relationship with you. Long-term, not just a fling."

"How do you even know you'd like me long-term?"

Ted stroked her cheek. "How do you know you'd like us? But maybe a better term is a closed relationship. The three of us and you. No one else. Not for play, not for dating, not for sex. It's the four of us. We're not saying you need to move in here tomorrow. But at least give us a chance to show you how good this could be, all of us together."

"Move back to Florida?"

Mark nodded. "That would be ideal. Long distance would suck, but if that's the only way we could see you at first, we'd do it."

This was a lot coming at her very quickly. "You all are so sure?"

"We are," Josh said. "But we also know it takes time to build something that will last. And we're willing to take the time we need to earn your trust if it means you'll give us a chance." He captured her hand and brought it up to his lips, kissing it. "Give us a chance. That's all we ask."

Before she could think about, she nodded. "Yes."

It was close to midnight when she realized she'd dozed off in the middle of them. Josh and Ted were also snoozing, Mark awake and propped up on one arm, watching her sleep and the TV at the same time.

He smiled. "Hey, Sleeping Beauty."

"Sorry."

"No, it's fine, really." He nudged Ted and Josh. "She's awake, guys."

They both sat up, and her heart wanted to break with how cute they looked, rubbing their faces, smiling when they spotted her.

"I think we need to take her home instead of frying her brain a second time. I'll drive her in her car if you guys want to follow us."

"It's okay," she said. "I can make it."

She'd started to sit up when Mark hooked an arm around her and pulled her to him. "You don't understand," he said, his voice dropping into *that* tone again. "We aren't asking you. We're telling you."

She looked up into his smiling face. "Yes, Sir," she said.

He grinned before leaning in to kiss her. "Such a good girl. *Our* good girl."

Chapter Eighteen

Wednesday morning, Essie had a hard time climbing out of bed. Places on and in her body ached in ways they never had before. Pleasant aches, but aches nonetheless.

The men had driven her home, where she'd fallen into bed without even undressing. She'd just kicked off her shoes and face-planted into her pillow until the alarm on her phone rudely woke her up.

It was only the thought that she'd be seeing her guys again shortly that cheered her up and got her ass moving.

Her guys.

She smiled as she looked at her ass in the mirror. There was the faint imprint of a hand there, but nothing bad.

It had felt good.

Another truth from some of the books she'd read.

I get it. I really get it.

And they'd made plans for her to come back to their house that night at seven for dinner.

She suspected she was the dessert.

They also promised to be a little more prepared, and hinted that they would do quite a bit of talking before the après-dinner activities.

All during the day the men teased her when they could, out of sight of the camera crews and with either their mics turned off, or silently so no one could hear.

They made her excuses to her mother and to Ross and Loren. "We want to discuss the other case with her," Mark told them. "See if we can work around her schedule, maybe get her back here for more filming for that case."

Her mom definitely bought it.

But after Essie got her shower and was getting ready to go to the men's house, Loren knocked on her bedroom door.

In her hand, she held a small cloth bag.

She handed it to Essie with a smile. "Tell those numbnuts to use these. Unless you like bruises on your wrists."

Essie glanced at her arms. She hadn't noticed them that morning, and wore work gloves most of the day that covered them. But sure enough, faint purple bruises were forming on both wrists.

She felt her face heat.

Loren kindly laughed. "You can borrow those. They're a spare pair. I included a couple of extra snap clips.

Essie opened the bag and found a pair of nice, soft, supple leather cuffs. And, yes, two double-ended snap clips.

"Thank you."

"No thanks necessary. They look happier than I've ever seen them." She hugged Essie. "You can trust them," she whispered in Essie's ear. "They're good guys. They just needed the right woman." She stepped back with a smile and closed the door behind her.

Essie looked into the bag again before putting it in her purse.

After bidding everyone good-bye, she fought the urge to run for her rental car.

She knew she was already growing wet again at the thought of what the men might have in store for her tonight.

After dinner, they led her into the living room, where they sat her on the couch.

"Okay," Ted started. "I should have insisted on this part last night, but I think we all got a little ahead of ourselves." He sent her a playful wink. "We are all clean. We've all been tested as of more than six months ago, and we haven't been with anyone since then. So while I think it'd still be smart to use condoms until you decide for sure you want to move here and be with us, if you're okay with oral, we are, too."

She was trying to figure a way to turn that whole statement around so it didn't seem like he was trying to insinuate she wasn't disease-free and couldn't. "Don't you trust me when I say I'm clean?"

Mark took her hands in his. "Yes, we do trust you. You don't strike us as the kind of person who would lie about something like that. But even with the pill, accidents can and do happen. Last night we sort of got...busy, before we had this conversation. I mean, it would be kind of presumptuous on our parts to say, "Hey, we'll wrap it for fucking you, but we'll dump our cum down your throat without discussion."

Okay, that popped her irritation. She laughed. "Got it. Actually, I was hoping for a little of that kind of action." She licked her lips. "I believe someone mentioned a spit roast last night. I've read about it, but since you guys are my first ménage, it's only been a fantasy."

The men stared at her for a moment. "Holy fuck," Josh whispered. "I think I just came in my shorts."

Ted slapped his shoulder. "Dumbass. Get naked."

They moved to Mark's bed, shedding clothes all the way. Señor Hitachi sat ready on the bedside table, as well as several strips of condoms and a bottle of lube.

"Oh, wait." She returned to the living room and retrieved the bag from her purse, bringing it back to them. "Loren gave me these," she said, heat filling her face. "She noticed bruises forming on my wrists this afternoon."

Mark opened the bag, letting out a laugh as he dumped the cuffs onto the bed. "Remind me to thank her tomorrow." He handed one to Josh while he buckled the other around her left wrist.

"We'll have to buy you a set," Ted said. "Sorry about the bruises."

"I'm not," she said before realizing what she'd said. Then she shrugged. "I kind of like the idea of remembering what happened the night before."

Ted leaned in to kiss her. "So do we, except we'd like them to be where others can't see them. And we should have been more careful last night. It's one thing if someone likes bruises, it's another if they don't and you bruise them anyway."

"I didn't even think about it at the time. It just felt so good."

"Any special requests tonight besides the spit roast?"

"I'm a little sore. Achy," she amended. "Not in a bad way. But just to warn you I might be moving a little slow."

"That's all right." He reached behind him and grabbed the vibrator. "That's what Señor Hitachi is for."

Josh hadn't actually creamed his shorts, but he had a wet spot on them when he pulled them off. He sat at the head of the bed and eagerly guided her mouth onto his cock with a pleased hiss.

"Oh, baby. That's perfect."

They'd clipped her wrists together with one of the snap clips Loren provided. Hobbled like that, on her elbows and knees, Ted rolled a condom on and knelt between her legs. He reached between her legs and slid two fingers deep into her cunt, making her moan around Josh's cock.

"Oh holy fuck!" Josh gasped. "That's fantastic!"

"I'm going to put a gag in *your* mouth in a minute," Ted lightly teased. He finger-fucked her before replacing his fingers with his cock. At that angle, he slid home deep, bottoming out when his thighs pressed against the backs of hers.

"Shit, yeah," Ted muttered. "Mark?"

She heard the vibrator click on. Mark reached under her, the vibrator between her legs, his other hand working back and forth between her nipples, lightly pinching them.

She moaned louder, trying to fuck herself onto Ted's cock.

He slapped her ass, hard, making her whimper but also giving her a surge of pleasure. "I'm driving, baby," he warned.

She whimpered around Josh's cock but stopped moving.

Ted laughed. "Oh, maybe baby wants her ass slapped?" He alternated slapping each side of her ass, pressing his cock even more deeply inside her but still not fucking her the way she wanted. The stinging intensified, making her whine, until he withdrew his cock and then slammed home, shoving her hard onto the vibrator and Josh's cock.

"Come for us, sweetheart," Ted ordered.

She couldn't have resisted him even if she wanted to. Before he'd even finished saying it, her orgasm had started. He started fucking her, hard and fast and alternating with stinging slaps on her ass that made her writhe and moan, doubly impaled between the men.

"Keep coming," Mark coaxed. "You just keep it up until we let you stop."

Josh's fingers dug into her scalp. "I'm about to blow, man, do it quick."

And then his cock hardened along her tongue just as hot streams of his cum exploded into her mouth. She swallowed, keeping up with it, moaning through her orgasm.

"Good girl," Ted grunted, finally climaxing, his cock buried deep inside her cunt.

Mark switched off the vibrator and pulled it away. Essie flopped onto her side, breathless, her cheek pressed against Josh's thigh.

He stroked her hair. "Better, baby?"

She nodded.

Ted pulled out and walked into the master bathroom. "Oh, don't you fall asleep on us yet," he warned. "Mark's still got a turn coming. Heh. Coming."

"And *he's* the counselor," Josh said with mock disgust.

When Ted returned, the men scooched her to the end of the bed, on her back, ass at the edge. Ted and Josh held her legs back and open, pinning her arms down with their bodies. In one hand, Mark held Señor Hitachi. In the other, he stroked his condom-clad cock.

In this position, the men had her spread wide open. Mark held up the vibrator. "You know what happens now, don't you?"

She nodded. "Yes, Sir."

"Tell us."

She swallowed to form spit. "You're going to fuck me and use the vibrator on me, Sir."

"Such a good girl. Do you want me to?"

"Yes, Sir."

His tone deepened, sending another flood of moisture straight to her already well-fucked cunt. "Then ask me."

"Please fuck me and use the vibrator on me, Sir."

"Be more specific." He wore a sadistic grin.

Her face heated. "Please," she managed to whisper, "fuck my pussy and use the vibrator on my clit."

"Good girl!" He fed his cock into her before clicking the vibrator on and pressing it to her clit.

Her back arched, but Josh and Ted held her down with their bodies. "Good girl," Josh said before leaning in and sucking her nipple into his mouth.

Ted did the same on her other side, and now her body totally belonged to them again.

Wave after wave of pleasure washed through her as Mark slowly fucked her, content to watch her with a pleased smile on his face as she writhed between them. "I rubbed one out in the shower this morning," he told her. "And another before you got here tonight. So I can hold it a little while." He chuckled. "And you, poor baby, look at you, so helpless and coming so hard for us."

He took a hard thrust, deep, increasing her pleasure before teasing her again with several shallow strokes. "Ask me to let you keep coming."

She shouldn't have fallen for it, but she did. "Please let me keep coming, Sir."

"Well, of course I'll let you keep coming, you good girl."

Aaaand there was the brain blizzard, back with a delicious vengeance.

Between the pleasant ache of the men pinching her nipples, and the way Mark was fucking her and using the vibrator on her, she felt she could coast for hours like that, blissful, wanting it to both stop and never end, pleasure and the sweet bite of pain all rolled into one mosaic.

She was gasping for air when he finally started fucking her, hard, deep, regular strokes she suspected meant he was near the end of his ability to hang on. "Get ready, sweetheart," he said. "Ask me to come inside you."

"Sir, please come inside my pussy."

"Good girl!" He took a few last, hard strokes before letting out a moan. Then he switched the vibrator off and tossed it onto the bed.

Ted and Josh released her legs while Mark leaned in and kissed her. "Such a good girl," he whispered, his smile twisting her heart into tangled knots.

Chapter Nineteen

Thursday afternoon, Essie was head-down over her phone and sorting through e-mail as she walked. She wanted to call Amy and talk for a few minutes in the relative privacy of the backyard. But before she rounded the corner, she heard voices and stopped at the corner of the house to listen. Purson was having a conversation with what sounded like one of the men from his crew.

"I'm telling you, I heard it," the guy said. "They're involved with her, all three of them. If we use this as part of the show, it'll blast the ratings through the roof."

Horror chilled her, even in the muggy Florida afternoon. The heat suddenly filling her face had nothing to do with the temperature, either.

"You let me handle those kinds of decisions," Purson told him. "Your job is to film."

"So you're not saying no?"

"I'm saying I need to talk to Mark, Josh, and Ted. Until I do that, just keep quiet and keep filming."

Essie made an about-face and ducked into the side garage door, her heart racing as she ran through to the kitchen.

The irony that she could make it in a straight beeline now without winding her way through canyons of garbage didn't escape her. The garage, utility room, kitchen, hallways, dining room, and most of the living room were completely dejunked, even though the carpeting hadn't been removed yet. The bedrooms were also being chipped away at, and the spare bathroom and powder room were both completely cleaned out. A plumber was scheduled to come out the next day to replace the powder room toilet. They'd even been able to downsize the work crew to just a few men now that the worst of the clutter hoard was gone.

The house felt huge, enormous. Larger than she ever remembered it from her childhood. By Mark's best guess, they'd have the rest of the dejunking finished by Friday evening, could get the carpets ripped out, and be able to get rid of one of the large trash containers. The other would stay until Essie and her mom finished sorting the things the cleaning crew had saved for them to go through.

I have to talk to the guys.

The problem was, they wouldn't be back for a while, and she didn't want to have that kind of conversation over the phone.

She was about to turn her microphone off and go have things out with Purson when her mom walked in through the front door. "Oh, there you are! Honey, I need your help going through these boxes, please? Some of the papers are your schoolwork and I don't want to throw it away unless you want it gone."

Dammit. "Sure, Mom."

They were sitting on a tarp going through the boxes, her mom smiling. "You were always such a good student."

Something about the wistful tone of her mom's voice pulled Essie's attention fully to her and away from what she'd overheard earlier.

"He was proud of you," her mom said. "He always told people how smart you were, how you got good grades."

Essie struggled against her irritation. "Would have been nice if he'd told me that himself."

She realized her mom had gone silent. When Essie looked, she spotted the tears rolling down her face.

Essie immediately scooted closer to her and pulled her into her arms. "I'm here, Mom. I'll have to go back to Spokane at some point, but I promise I'm not abandoning you. We can talk on the phone all the time. And…maybe we can talk about me moving back to Florida in a few months."

Her mom's tears became sobs. "I'm so sorry I didn't stand up to him more," she said. "I should have. I should have stood up for you more. I lost you for so many years."

Aaaaand here we go. She suspected this was her mom's long overdue breakdown. "It doesn't matter," Essie said. "We have each other *now*, and nothing's going to change that. I promise, even if I'm not with you, I'm in your life. You won't ever lose me again."

She sat there, gently rocking her mom as she cried, her own tears once again dried up and missing where her father was concerned. She'd deal with that later.

Right now, she wanted to focus on her mom.

It took her a while for her mom to regain her composure. Someone had brought and set a box of tissues close by, even as the film crews unobtrusively recorded what happened.

"I know I'm going to cry a lot," her mom whispered, "but I spent a lot of years crying myself to sleep. Or crying on the way home from work to…this," she said. "I feel like I'm mostly cried out. But I wish he'd reached out to you. I wish he'd made things right with you." She dabbed at the tears in her eyes. "You know, I wonder if he wasn't feeling bad that night. Before I went to bed, he said, 'I love you.' I told him I loved him, too, and gave him a kiss."

Her heart broke for her mom. Essie had barely known the man he was. She could compartmentalize as much as she needed to for right now.

He'd been a daily part of her mom's life. "I love you, Mom."

She smiled and took a deep, hitching breath. "I love you, too, sweetheart."

After a quick trip over to Ross and Loren's to wash her face, her mom returned, ready to finish going through the boxes of paperwork.

And that was where Essie was sitting, outside the storage pod under the shade of one of the picnic tents, sorting papers, when her men returned.

Before she could stand and get their attention, Purson was there, greeting them and leading them off to the backyard.

* * * *

Ted's senses were already on high alert when Purson practically tackled them upon their return and asked them into the backyard for a private discussion.

After making sure the camera crews weren't around, Purson started, keeping his voice low. "Guys, you really need to be more careful. I can control the edits and what gets on the air in the final cuts, but I don't want anyone taking any cell phone videos of you four together."

"What?" Ted asked. "What are you talking about?"

"Essie," Purson said. "Cat's out of the bag. One of my guys overheard something or saw you three with her and now he knows you're a poly item, as it were." He waggled a finger at them. "Congrats, but you need to be more careful unless you don't care who knows. If that's the case, then we can use it to add an extra level of interest."

"No," all three of them said at once. Ted held out a staying hand to his brothers. "No," he repeated. "We don't want our personal lives in focus like that. We certainly don't want Essie being in the limelight."

"Okay, that's what I figured." Purson ran a hand through his hair. His voice returned to its normal tone. "I'll handle my crew member, but you guys be more careful, okay?"

"Thanks."

"While I have you here, I need to talk to you about the case with Lisa Parker's mom. When can we start filming that? And do you think

Essie will let us film her for that case? At least give us an interview about rescuing the dogs?"

Mark and Ted left that up to Josh. Josh rubbed the back of his neck. "I don't know. We can ask her. She was pretty upset about it. It was overwhelming for her. I don't know how she handled it so well."

* * * *

Essie once again stopped at the corner of the house, listening. The film crew had stayed with her mom, the second crew focusing on the cleanout inside, the third crew taking a lunch break.

"I don't know how she handled it so well," she heard Josh say. "She took it like a champ, though. Like she'd been doing it for years. I was worried about her at first, but she had a good cry when we finished, and I think she did okay."

Shocked, she found she couldn't make her feet move. Frozen in place, she listened, horrified at the men's betrayal.

"Well," Purson said, "please talk to her about that. Getting her on film in that situation, it'd be a great thing. Add some depth to her story, too. Show another side of her."

"Let us handle it," Mark said. "We'll talk to her about it. See if we can ease her into the idea."

Ease me into it, my ass. Anger and shame coursed through her, with grief egging those emotions on.

She'd *trusted* them.

Worse, she knew she'd fallen in love with them.

She turned on her heel and headed, practically at a dead run, for Loren and Ross' house.

Once locked inside her room, she ripped off the microphone, making sure it was off before she tossed it onto the bed.

Then she locked the bathroom door going to her mom's room and jumped into the shower, just long enough to hose off the grime and sweat. With adrenaline still coursing through her and making her hands tremble, she quickly packed all her things, searching through the dresser to make sure she hadn't missed anything. She shut her phone off and jammed it and her laptop into her carry-on bag.

Once she was ready to go, she unlocked the doors, took a deep breath, and snuck out the back door and around the side of the house to where her rental was parked on the grass next to the driveway. She threw her suitcases and carry-on into the trunk and darted across the street to where her mom was still sorting stuff.

Before she could start crying, Essie hugged her mom and reached down to shut her mom's mic off. "I have an emergency," she whispered. "I have to go. I love you, and I'll call you when I get back to Spokane. I left my mic on the bed in the guest room. Please tell Ross and Loren thank you for everything for me." She switched her mom's mic back on and, before her mom could protest, Essie was bolting for her rental car.

She had already pulled out of Ross and Loren's driveway when she saw in her rearview mirror that her mom had flagged down the three brothers.

Forcing herself to look forward instead of back, she quickly headed for I-75. It wasn't until she was on the interstate that she glanced in her mirror again, afraid she'd see a pickup truck with her three men in it pursuing her.

And partly afraid she might feel disappointed if they weren't.

Fuck. Them.

As she neared the turn-off for the Skyway, her determination faltered.

I should have had it out with them there.

Then the scared voice fought back. *You haven't doubted yourself for quite a few years. Why would you start doubting yourself now?*

She resisted the urge to pull off into the southern rest area just before the bridge. If she stopped now, she knew her determination might falter. Instead, she pressed on, all the way to Tampa International, where she ditched her rental car.

She didn't have a return ticket. She'd booked the flight one-way, not sure how long she'd be there. As she approached the airline ticket counter she realized she didn't even know when the next flight to Spokane was.

After waiting a few minutes in line, the ticket agent was able to book her on a flight to Denver leaving in two hours. From there she'd have to spend the night before catching an early-morning flight to Spokane that would get her on the ground before eight o'clock local time the next morning.

Essie nodded. "Perfect. That. Give me that." She handed over her photo ID and credit card.

Hell, I can even make it in to work tomorrow.

* * * *

"What the hell?" Mark said, his hands planted on his hips.

He turned on his brothers. "What the *hell* did you guys do?"

"Us?" Ted protested. "We didn't do anything."

Mark and Josh both whipped out their cell phones. Mark assumed Josh was trying Essie's phone, too. "Dude, I'm trying to call her," Mark told him.

"Screw that, *I'm* trying to call her."

"Both of you, stop it. *I'll* call her," Ted ordered as he pulled out his phone.

It went straight to voice mail.

Mindful of the film crew and microphones, he was careful. "Essie, it's Ted. Please call us."

Loren had returned to their house. She emerged from the front door, carrying the mic and battery pack Essie had been using. "All her stuff is gone. This was on the bed." Purson took it from her and headed for the production trailer.

A moment later, he returned, frowning as he walked over. "I think I know what happened." He led just the three men over to the production trailer where their equipment was set up.

Purson ordered everyone out of the trailer except the three brothers. Once they were alone, he motioned to them. "Switch off your mic packs."

They did.

He queued up a feed on a laptop. "This is from Essie's mic." They heard sounds, like she was walking, indistinct voices in the background that came into focus.

It was the conversation between Purson and his film crew member.

"Shit," Ted muttered. "She heard that."

Purson paused it, nodding. "Oh, it gets better. I bet she got the wrong end of the stick on part of our conversation." He queued the feed again and hit play.

From the sound of it, she had approached the backyard right in the middle of Purson's discussion with them.

Ted looked at his brothers. "She only heard the tail end of it. She thought we were talking about—" His mouth snapped shut as he looked at Purson.

Purson held up both hands. "Hey, I don't judge, okay? I'm pretty kinky."

"I was talking about her rescuing the dogs," Josh said. "You guys were there, you know that's what I meant!"

"Yeah, *we* know that," Mark countered, "but she didn't."

Ted ran a hand through his hair. "Mark, keep trying to call her."

"Why can't I call her?" Josh asked.

"Because we all can't keep trying to call her. Text her if you want, but if we all bomb her phone it'll just keep going to voice mail." He turned to leave.

"Where are you going?" Mark asked, his phone already to his ear.

Ted paused. "To call Tracy and have her make us plane reservations for first thing in the morning."

"What?" Mark and Josh echoed.

"Duh. She's going back to Spokane. Obviously, we have to go to Spokane, unless Essie picks up or responds. Which, considering how she left, I sincerely doubt she will."

"Can't we tell her mom?" Josh asked.

Ted and Mark both rounded on him.

"Oh, brilliant," Mark said, pausing only to hit speed dial again on his phone and wait for it to go through. "Yeah, let's tell her mom what we've done and why she left. Because Essie thought we were going to put our *sex* lives on the *fucking* air. *Dumbass.*"

Josh reddened. "I didn't mean it like that."

"Josh," Ted said, yanking off his mic pack, "get our work crew set for tomorrow. Get the foreman up to speed with the schedule, and tell him we've got an emergency consultation or something we have to take care of." He handed the mic pack to Purson. "You can handle it from your end, I take it?"

"Yeah."

Ted stepped in close and jabbed a finger at Purson. "You keep that crew member of yours under tight wraps. I find any *fucking* hint of him putting our private lives out there for the world to see, and I will personally show up in Ryan Ausar's office and give him holy *fucking* hell about it."

Purson snorted. "Well, we wouldn't want *that*," he drawled.

"What?"

"Sorry, I'm just…Sorry. Go after her. My mic was live and caught the whole thing. Lucky for you guys. I'll e-mail you an audio file of the full conversation from my mic feed so you can play it for her and she'll understand what she didn't hear. And I'll take care of the crew. No one will breathe a word."

Purson set the mic pack down. "You just be careful from now on. Show a little more discretion." He reached under his shirt, grabbing his bloodstone amulet as he walked. "I'll go do what I do best," he muttered as he headed out of the trailer.

Chapter Twenty

It was late that evening at a hotel in Denver when Essie finally turned her phone back on. As she'd expected, she faced a barrage of concerned text messages and voice mails from her men.

Well, not *her* men anymore.

She deleted the men's voice mails and texts, unread and unplayed. She was in no mood to deal with them. Once she was back home and settled and feeling stable again, she'd e-mail them and tell them off and make it absolutely clear that she was ending things with them.

And that she didn't want them to contact her again.

It was her mom's plaintive tone in her voice mails, however, that made her break down.

"Sweetheart, please, I don't know what happened, but call me, okay? I love you. I don't want to lose you again. I'm worried about you, and so are the boys."

Essie suppressed a bitter snort at that term. They were no "boys." They were coldhearted assholes concerned only about their image, obviously.

After taking a deep breath to calm herself, she called her mom's cell phone. She answered almost immediately.

"Essie? Sweetie, are you all right?"

"I'm fine, Mom. Couldn't make it all the way to Spokane tonight, but I'll be there in the morning."

"Where are you?"

"Layover in Denver."

"What happened? Why did you leave?"

She couldn't tell her mom about the guys and what she'd done with them. "It's a long story. You didn't do anything wrong, Mom, I promise. Once I get everything situated on my end, I'll let you know when I can come back and visit you again. It won't be long."

"Please, Essie, talk to me. I know I wasn't there for you when you needed me but please don't shut me out like this now."

Essie barely succeeded in holding back her tears. "Mom, I promise, I'm not shutting you out. It's…complicated. Very complicated, and it has nothing to do with you, I swear. I can't get into it."

Maybe the men would talk about what they'd done, but she wouldn't stoop to their level, if nothing else. "I need to get off here, my phone's almost dead. Love you, and I'll call you when I get to Spokane tomorrow."

She hated how sad her mom sounded. "Love you, too, sweetie."

Once Essie ended the call, she shut the phone off again, rolled over, and sobbed into her pillow.

* * * *

The next morning, Essie turned her phone on only long enough to delete texts and voice mails from the men, as well as to text Amy.

Landing 7:46 a.m. Spokane from Denver. Can U get me?

She held her breath, just about to gasp for air when her friend replied.

What happened?

Nearly sobbing in relief, she texted her back.

Can't talk now. Pls?

Amy responded almost immediately. *Ok. Want deets later.*

Will do.

She started to shut her phone off again, but not before another text from Mark arrived.

Will you please call us and talk to us? We're worried. Love you.

She angrily deleted it and turned her phone off.

I'll have to dump that crap off my Kindle, too. I was stupid to think those kinds of fairy tales could really come true. Idiot.

Essie thought Amy would be sitting in the cell phone lot and awaiting her text to pick her up at the terminal, but instead she was standing just outside the security zone inside the terminal, waiting on her and holding two Starbucks cups.

Essie thought she might break down crying right there but somehow struggled to keep it together as she carefully hugged her friend before taking the cup Amy offered her.

"Thank you," Essie said. "For this and especially for the ride."

"Let's go get your bags." She draped an arm around Essie's shoulders and led her toward the baggage claim area. "And then I want to know what the hell happened."

"I want to get home and changed and get into work."

"Work? *Seriously*? After what you've been through? How about a recovery day? And lucky you Pete's on forty-eight. I, however, was planning on sleeping late and enjoying my day off."

"Sorry." Now she felt even worse. Once again, she'd totally upended her friend's life.

"Naw, it's all right." She held Essie's coffee for her while Essie pulled her luggage off the carousel and transferred it to a cart. "But I do want the story."

"I was stupid," she said as she pushed the cart toward the doors. "I trusted not just one guy, but three, and got my heart broken." She stopped and turned to Amy. "I just want to get back into my life as soon as possible. I want to go to work, forget what happened, and resume my routine."

Amy frowned before leaning in for a hug. "When you get home tonight, we'll go out to eat and you'll spill your guts over a bottle of wine and get shit-faced and tell me everything. Okay? I'll be your DD and hold your hair when you puke before you pass out." She smiled.

Essie smiled back. "That sounds like heaven."

Amy blinked, shock evident on her face. "Wow. You really did have something fucking bad happen, huh?"

"No, just something really fucking stupid."

Amy left Essie on the curb while she got her car. Twenty minutes later, they were on the elevator back to their apartment. Opening the door and walking in felt like…

Heaven.

She closed her eyes and inhaled. They both loved the scent of vanilla and had reed oil diffusers scattered around the place.

While it was tempting to fall onto her bed and cry, she knew she needed to get back into her routine as soon as possible. It would be the only thing to keep her sane. And as much as it killed her not to start doing her dirty laundry immediately, she knew there'd be plenty of time for washing as well as telling Amy her personal dirty laundry later.

She changed into work scrubs, grabbed a spare pair for her bag in case of an accident at work, and headed back downstairs after hugging Amy. When she reached her car, she paused only to call her mom and tell her she was there and safe and that she was heading in to work.

Her boss was surprised to see her, but glad she'd come in. They'd had three emergencies arrive already that morning, and they were short-handed because one of the other tech's kids had come down with the flu.

By the time lunch rolled around, Essie knew this had been the right decision. She kept her phone turned off and in her purse, locked in her locker in the back room. She didn't want to look at it.

When two of the other techs asked her to go to lunch with them, she readily accepted, glad for the additional distraction.

I knew it. I needed this. I needed it more than anything else. To get back to where I belong.

It might not be with a Dom, but at least I know what I'm getting.

And she'd keep repeating that to herself until she finally believed it.

Maybe, one day, she would believe it.

* * * *

The men were quiet that morning as they emerged from the terminal a little before noon. They'd gained a couple of hours, but were starving because they hadn't taken time to eat since before they flew out of Tampa.

After getting their rental car, with Josh navigating and Ted driving, they found Essie's apartment building.

"Do we call first?" Josh asked.

"We call Amy," Ted said.

"What?" his brothers asked.

"Amy. Her roommate." He pulled out his phone and found the number he wanted.

"Wait," Mark asked. "How did you get her roommate's number?"

He shrugged. "I asked Corrine." He hit the send button and waited.

A cautious-sounding woman answered. "Hello?"

"Is this Amy?"

"Yes?"

"I don't know if you know who I am, but my name's Ted Collins. I was working with your friend, Essie, on her mom's house."

Now her tone sounded even more guarded. "What do you want?"

"My brothers and I want a chance to talk to Essie, face-to-face. We suspect there was a horrible misunderstanding and now she thinks something about us because she only caught the tail end of a conversation that made us look like assholes instead of the guys who love her with all our hearts."

There was a moment of silence he wasn't sure was her contemplating his words or that she'd hung up on him.

"What do you want from me?" Amy finally asked.

"Is she home?"

"No."

His heart sank.

"Do you believe she had me pick her up early this morning at the airport, and now she's already back at work?" Amy asked, her voice full of disbelief.

Relief filled him. Essie was retreating to her comfort zone and trying to deal with this as best she could. He could deal with that.

Would deal with it. He had the audio file on his phone, ready to play as soon as he could get Essie to stand still and listen to it.

"What time will she be back?"

"Usually by six, unless they have an emergency. Call me on this number when you get here and I'll buzz you up."

"Thank you. Thank you so much, you have no idea how grateful we are."

"Yeah, well, I'm not leaving while you're here. And my boyfriend's a firefighter with a lot of friends and is stationed at a firehouse only three blocks away. I can have some of Spokane's other finest here in less than two minutes and ready to kick some serious ass."

He could already tell he liked her. She was protective of Essie.

"I swear, we just want a chance to talk to her. We won't even come inside the door if you don't want us to."

"Okay. Let me see what I can get out of her in the way of intel. Be here by six and wait. I'll text you when she gets here and buzz you up when it's safe to come upstairs."

He thanked her before ending the call. Then he closed his eyes and laid his head back against the seat.

"Well?" they asked.

He told them. "She made it perfectly clear we'll get our asses beat by a bunch of firefighters if we make any trouble."

"I don't want trouble," Mark said, his tone a mirror of what Ted felt in his heart. "I just want a chance to make things right with her."

"Hey, you're preaching to the choir," Ted told him.

"So what do we do until six thirty?" Josh asked.

Ted opened his eyes and sat up. "First, we find a damn restaurant and eat something before we all keel over from hunger."

"Then we need to find a jewelry store," Mark said.

His brothers looked at him.

"Hey, I'm not showing up there empty-handed," he told them. "I'm going to propose to her for us."

"She can't marry all of us, dumbass," Josh said.

"No, but she can marry one of us and we can figure out the rest."

"Why you?" Ted asked.

"Because I wanted her first." He smiled. "I'll be her vanilla beard. In private, she'll be all ours."

Ted smiled. "That's the best idea I've heard out of your mouth in years."

They turned to Josh. "I'm fine with it," he said. "As long as she comes back to Florida with us. That's all I care about."

* * * *

Essie never thought she'd ever feel grateful for an insane day at work. By the time she walked out the door a little after six o'clock Friday evening, she was more than ready for the evening Amy had promised her earlier.

It's good to be home.

She'd keep saying it until she felt it, believed it. She already missed her mom.

She wouldn't stoop to admitting she missed the men.

Fuck them.

Actually, that was the problem, that she *had* let them fuck her. That, and other things she never thought she had a snowball's chance of ever checking off her sexual bucket list.

Amy was lounging on the couch with her Kindle when Essie got home shortly after six thirty. She hugged her friend. "Thanks again for this morning. Sorry I got you up early."

"Hey, it's what friends do."

Essie headed for the bedroom. "I'll get my shower and then we can go."

"Okay."

She'd just emerged from her room a couple of minutes later when their doorbell rang.

"Who the hell is that?" Essie asked. Pete had his own key. He always let himself in.

"I'm getting ready," Amy called from behind her closed door.

Essie dumped her stuff in the bathroom and went to answer the door. She was shocked to see Mark, Josh, and Ted standing in front of her door when she looked through the peephole.

Anger mixed with longing as she threw the door open.

Before she could order them gone, the men pressed in through the door. Ted held up his phone. "Just listen before you say anything. Purson pulled up your mic feed so we figured out what happened. You only heard the last half of our conversation. This is from the mic Purson was wearing." He had an app opened and hit a button.

She froze as she heard the men's and Purson's voices on the recording.

She was well aware of all three men staring at her while she listened.

A combination of relief and shame filled her as she realized exactly what had happened.

They hadn't betrayed her.

But *she* had acted like an utter dumbass.

I don't deserve them. I'm obviously not mature enough to handle this kind of relationship.

Essie was aware of Amy walking into the living room. "Want to give me the 411, girlfriend?"

Essie didn't even know where to start.

"We love her," Mark said, filling the silence. "All three of us. And there was a big misunderstanding. She thought she heard something when she only caught the tail end of a conversation and totally out of context."

"You love me?" she whispered.

They nodded. "We do," Josh said.

"With all our hearts," Ted added.

"You're Mark, Josh, and Ted?" Amy asked.

The men nodded.

"I can't do this," Essie said. "I'm sorry you flew all the way out here, but I can't do this. Please, just go."

The men stared at her, the sad looks on their faces nearly breaking her heart, but she knew this was for the best. She was far too broken for them.

They needed—deserved—someone better than her.

Finally, Ted slowly nodded. "Is that what you really want, sweetheart?"

The endearment almost shattered her reserve. She nodded, stepping back and turning away from them. "Please. Just go."

* * * *

They silently filed out of the apartment as Amy mouthed, "Wait downstairs," at them before closing the door.

Josh had felt certain that once they played the audio for Essie that she would understand, they would kiss and make up, and she'd be ready to return to Florida with them.

He never imagined…this.

At the elevator bank he stopped. "We can't be seriously just going to leave, are we?"

Ted punched the button, his face an expressionless mask. "Let's see what Amy meant. She told us to wait downstairs. That's what we'll do. If she or Essie don't come down after a while, I'll call Amy back."

They rode downstairs in silence. In the lobby, they waited near the front entrance for what felt like the longest minutes of Josh's life.

Chapter Twenty-One

Essie sank to the couch as Amy closed the door and turned to her, confusion on her face.

"I'm sorry, I couldn't help but overhear what happened," Amy finally started. "So let me get this straight. All three of those guys are into you? And you're into them? Like, what, out of one of those kinky books we read?"

Essie nodded, her face heating.

"They're the guys who are helping your mom save her house, right? From the TV show?"

Essie nodded again, unable to meet her friend's heavy gaze.

"And they explained whatever it was that made you leave Florida so suddenly?"

Another nod.

"And it turns out they're innocent, that you went off half-cocked and were wrong about what you thought you heard?"

She nodded and closed her eyes to blink back the tears wanting to fall.

Amy's no-nonsense nurse tone bit into Essie's soul. "Okay, so tell me if I'm wrong. Three hot hunks, who are gainfully employed, and who I'm assuming aren't homicidal maniacs, probably want you to move back to Florida, where they want to spend the rest of their lives with you?"

Essie nodded, finally opening her eyes again to look at her friend.

Amy stood there with her hands planted on her hips. "What the *fuck's* wrong with you, girl?"

"I know, I can't—"

"*Why* did you throw them out?"

Essie's mouth snapped closed. "What?" she eventually managed to whisper.

"I asked what the fuck's wrong with you!" She crossed the living room until she stood in front of Essie. "They're gorgeous! They're apparently self-sufficient in terms of income, and they've already proven they're good guys."

She stared at Amy. "What?"

Amy rolled her eyes. "Do *not* start with me." She pointed at the door. "They flew across the damn *country*. For you. *You!*" She jabbed her finger at Essie. "Not for my ass, not for your mother. For you. That means something in my book."

"But...all three of them?"

"Oh. My. God. Do you have any idea how many women secretly wish they could find three hot brothers who only have eyes for them?"

"But...I just...The apartment," she lamely finished.

"So? Pete and I have been talking about moving in together anyway. This makes it that much simpler. He can take over your part of the bills. I've been putting off talking to you about it, and then when your dad died, Pete and I agreed to wait until you were back and you had your feet under you again to bring it up."

"My job."

Amy frowned. "*Seriously*? They have vet clinics in Florida, do they not?"

She stood in front of Essie and grabbed her hands. "I love you like a sister, I really do. But while you were gone, any time you talked to me on the phone about those guys, it's like a light started shining inside you, a light I've never seen you have before. I could hear it in your voice and see it when we FaceTimed. *Ever*. About *any* guy you ever dated. Not that you do much of that to start with."

She squeezed Essie's hands. "You're young. I want you to be happy. They have these things called airplanes that can magically move someone from one end of the freaking country to the other in a few hours. And we can FaceTime and Skype." She shrugged. "And who's to say Pete and I won't be coming to visit you a lot in the winters to get in some beach time?"

Essie's mind still swam, even as Amy pulled her to her feet and led her to the front door, which she opened. "Go after them. Hopefully you can catch up with them."

Then Amy gave her a good hard shove out the door, closing it and locking it behind her.

"I don't have my keys!" Essie yelled through the door.

"I'm not letting you back in unless they're with you anyway!" Amy yelled back. "So move your ass before they leave."

Dammit!

She stared down the hallway at the elevator.

Empty.

Finally, she forced her feet forward, at a full run when she hit the door and punched the button. It felt like forever for it to make it back up, but then she was in it and heading down to the lobby.

The men were still standing there in the lobby, talking near the door, when she stepped out of the elevator.

She couldn't see them very clearly, though, because tears blurred her vision. And then they were all heading toward her, their arms outstretched. Essie sobbed as she let them engulf her, holding her, kissing her.

"Please don't leave," she finally managed.

Mark smiled down at her as he cradled her face in his hands. "Does this mean you'll at least listen to us?"

"We love you," Ted said. "We mean it."

"Yeah," Josh said. "Look, if you want us to give up the BDSM—"

"No," she said. "I don't want that."

The men stared at her, waiting for her to speak again. She sniffled back more tears and finally forced the words out of her mouth. "I'm sorry. I was scared, and then what I thought I heard, I panicked. I love you guys, too."

"Please come back with us," Mark softly begged. "It's pitiful to see three grown Doms cry, but we swear we will if you don't."

That managed to draw a smile from her.

We can rent a truck and move your stuff for you," Ted said.

"Please?" Josh added. "I'm great at groveling. I don't mind being the first to do it. I'm not too proud to grovel if it means you'll come back with us. I'll drop to my knees and do it right here in the middle of this lobby."

Ted and Mark nodded their agreement with their brother's statement.

"I don't know if I'll make a good slave or whatever," she said, glad they were alone in the lobby. "I'm too used to being in control."

"Then you can be whatever it is you want to be for us," Mark said. "We're not asking you to give over every part of yourself to us. Just your heart and your love and your trust. That's enough for us. Anything else is a blessing."

"You'd be okay with me just doing it for fun? I thought you guys wanted someone to be like that full time."

"We love you," Ted said. "That comes first. What's more important to us is that you know who we are, and can you accept us the way we are?"

"We're not going to boss you around all the time," Josh said. "Not unless you want us to. But you've seen the dark side of us already. It's who we are, it's part of us. We're not looking for a doormat. We want you to be who you are, and yet still love us and want to be with us and want to submit to us. That's the most important thing."

"We'll never be able to just be vanilla," Mark said. "But you've seen us in full-on Dom mode. It's like anything else in life, the average is somewhere in the middle between our public personas at work and what you see in a dungeon. Can you accept that?"

She stared at all three of them. She'd spent almost half of her life standing on her own, not leaning on anyone else for support.

Not *having* anyone else for support, other than Amy, and that was only as a friend.

Isn't it time I think about what I really want *for a change?*

"What will people say?" she softly asked.

Really? You're going to go there*?*

She couldn't help it. Giving in was something totally alien to her.

Mark smiled and dropped to one knee in front of her, something in his hand. She realized it was a jewelry box. "The three of us already talked," he said. "Will you please marry me? Our kinky friends won't care that we're poly. And it's not like we'll be doing any of that in front of your mom. So we all live together? Big deal. We're brothers. The only people who will know more than that won't give a damn."

"You barely know me," she whispered, the *yes* she wanted to scream locked in her throat.

"And you barely know us," Mark said. "But we know we love you. Come back to Florida with us. We don't have to get married tomorrow. Move in with us. If…" It sounded like he choked up a little. "If you decide it's not working, we promise, we'll move you wherever you want to move and make sure you're on your feet. Please?"

Ted, who had her right hand, laced his fingers through hers. "We'll put it in writing if you want."

Josh held her left and also laced fingers with her. "Anything you want."

Her brain raced. "How can you be so sure?" she whispered.

Mark still knelt in front of her. "Because we already know what *didn't* work. We went through the bad end of things. All three of us agree there's no way in hell we won't do whatever we have to do to get another chance with you. Because we also agree nothing has ever felt as right as being with you. Instead of trying to figure out why this won't work, how about letting us show you that it can and will?"

She felt herself nodding, tears welling in her eyes again. Ted squeezed her right hand while Josh maneuvered her left so that Mark could slip the ring on her finger.

"Essline Barrone, will you please marry me? *Us?*" Mark asked again.

It felt like someone else speaking. "Yes."

A beaming smile broke across Mark's face, the same one she found herself helpless against in the dungeon or in bed or in the kitchen or any-damn-where. He stood and kissed her.

Behind her, she heard the elevator open. Then Amy's voice called out. "Please tell me you guys got through to her?"

They all turned. Amy wore a smile and carried her purse and an overnight bag as she walked across the lobby toward them.

"I hope so," Ted said. "Otherwise, the building manager might call the cops on us for camping out here."

Amy stopped in front of her. "Well?"

Essie smiled, nodding and holding up her left hand to show her.

Amy caught her hand. "Oooh, nice!" She grinned. "I called Pete and told him I'm spending the night at his place. So it's all yours." She held up Essie's key ring by the apartment door key. "Which of you guys wants it?"

Josh grabbed it. "Thanks, Amy."

"Wait, how did you know her name?" Essie asked.

"Well, for starters, you told us about her," Mark said.

"And secondly," Amy said, "they called me earlier and asked if you were there and I told them I'd text them when you got home."

"How'd they get your number?"

"Your mom," all three men said together.

They way they'd said it made her laugh. "I guess it'd be stupid to keep fighting this, huh?"

Amy giggled. "Duh. Listen, on the off chance this blows up, you're always welcomed back with me and Pete. I promise. But I suspect that won't be necessary." She hugged Essie. "So go upstairs and let them suck up to you. I'll be back around ten tomorrow morning. I don't have to go to work until the day after, but I have stuff I need to get done tomorrow. It's a little after six now. I'm guessing in oh, sixteen hours or so, you four can figure stuff out, right?"

"Sure can," Mark said.

Amy shook hands with the men. "Good luck, gents. She's a stubborn cuss. But if anyone can persuade her, I suspect the three of you can."

Amy gave them a wave and headed for the front door, leaving Essie standing there and surrounded.

"Your call, sweetheart," Mark softly said.

* * * *

Not that Essie didn't want to jump into bed with them, because she did, but she wanted to slow things down just a hair.

"Look, I just got home from work. Can I grab a shower and then you can take me out to eat and we can talk before we come back here?"

The men exchanged a glance and smiled. "I think we can manage that," Mark joked.

Ted grabbed their overnight bags from their rental car before rejoining them in the lobby. Back upstairs, she didn't know if it was good or bad that the bathroom didn't have a shower big enough for all four of them to climb into. She left them sitting in her living room while she grabbed clean clothes and locked herself into the bathroom.

All *three* of them? Of course, at the time it had seemed like a perfectly acceptable idea. Then she'd bolted, scared she'd made a horrible mistake in judgment.

Now that all three of them were here in front of her again…

She stood under the spray and let hot water sluice over her. Opening her eyes, she spotted the ring on her finger.

It was a very nice ring.

Why *couldn't* it work? The books made it work out, happily ever after, the end. And in real life she'd met people who'd made it work.

Happily ever after.

Why couldn't *she* have a happy ending for a change?

She could keep making excuses all she wanted for why it couldn't work.

Then again, she could take a chance that it might.

She had a safety net. She knew Amy had meant what she'd said. And if this was a really bad idea, Amy would have been the first to voice her concerns and put the brakes on the whole thing.

But Amy had encouraged her.

And she had been the one who looked at this whole thing as a chance to reconnect with her mom. Kind of hard to do a couple of thousand miles away in Spokane.

Ted drove while Essie sat in the back with Mark. They asked for a nice restaurant to take her to. She gave Ted directions to an upscale Italian restaurant downtown that she didn't treat herself to enough.

Once they were seated in a corner booth, with her between Mark and Josh, she glanced at her left hand again.

Even in the dim light the ring sparkled, brilliant.

"That was Mark's idea," Ted said from his place on the other side of Josh. He wore a playful smile as he templed his fingers together in his best impression of an evil scientist. "To go for the jugular and be as pitiful as possible so you'd be merciful."

She giggled. The way he'd said it came off playful, now knowing him the way she did.

"You can even rearrange the house however you want," Josh said. "We'd like to remodel, make the master bedroom larger. Or we can move, if you want. Build a new house."

"We'll live in an empty cardboard box," Mark said, "as long as you're with us."

"I'm sorry I bolted," she said, now feeling ashamed of how she'd reacted. *Over*reacted. "I should have confronted you guys."

"Understood and forgiven," Ted assured her. "Hey, we've seen you at your worst, and we can honestly say we understand what you were going through. You were overwhelmed, still dealing with your dad's death—"

"And we should have been honest sooner about our feelings for you," Mark added. "We just didn't want to scare you off by coming on too strong too soon."

"Didn't work so well for us, turns out," Josh teased.

"I don't want to just up and quit," Essie said. "I would like to give them two week's notice. They've been good to me."

"Understood," Mark said. "And in those two weeks, we can get you packed."

"There's not a lot I need to take. I'll leave furniture and stuff for Amy and Pete. Besides, you guys have to get back to work."

"We're the bosses," Mark said. "Tracy's got everything under control. In fact, she sort of made it clear that if we came back to Florida without you, she might go all nuclear on our asses."

Josh added, "She mentioned something about how damned pitiful we were and that we were depressing the hell out of her."

"I'm not afraid to admit she scares me a little," Ted said. "So if nothing else, come home with us to protect us from the big, bad administrative assistant." He grinned. "Hey, she was your friend in high school. You've technically known her longer than we have."

"You guys are too much."

"And we're all yours," Mark said with a smile. "Lucky you."

It felt good to smile again. "Lucky me, indeed."

"And don't worry if you can't find a job right away," Ted assured her. "It's okay."

"I want to sign a prenup," she said.

When the men all went silent, she realized they might have misunderstood her intent. "I remember what you guys said about the

Kraken," Essie said. "I don't want you to ever worry about me like that."

"We won't," Josh said. "I promise, we don't think that about you."

"Never will," Ted said. "You're a vastly different and better woman than the Kraken ever could be."

"I appreciate that, but I want it in writing."

"I was thinking something different," Josh said.

From the way his brothers looked at him, she suspected this was news to them. "What?" she asked.

"Why don't you come work with us?" Josh said. "Purson is right. You looked great on camera. You've got firsthand experience both as the child of a hoarder and dealing with the aftermath. You are great with handling clients because you really do know what they're going through." He glanced at his brothers before returning his focus to her. "And when we have to deal with animals, your expertise will be invaluable. Please, think about it."

She hadn't really considered it before.

"You'll get paid a salary just like we do," Ted said.

"You could do a lot of good," Josh added. "Help a lot of people." He smiled. "Get to boss us around on camera."

Okay, that made her laugh. "While you three boss me around in bed?"

Ted's sexy smile made her wet, she wouldn't deny it. "Oooh, that sounds like a winner of a plan to me."

Chapter Twenty-Two

Her worry about the logistics of trying to fit four of them in a two-person bed was solved when she remembered the pullout couch.

"Do you mind sleeping on the floor?" she asked.

Ted grinned. "We didn't have sleep in mind, sweetheart."

She laughed. "It's a queen-size sleeper sofa, but I don't think all of us on it is a good idea. It's for guests. I'll get the sheets if you guys will take the mattress out and put it on the floor."

"Ah. Now I'm tracking." He pointed at the coffee table. "You guys move that. I'll get this."

Josh and Mark sprang into action as Ted started pulling the cushions off the couch and opened it. By the time she returned with the sheets for it, they had the couch closed up again and the mattress in the middle of the living room floor.

Ted took the sheets from her and gently caught her by the chin with his other hand. "I think there's someone who needs to drop to their knees and apologize for scaring the crap out of us."

"Apologize? I—" She swallowed hard. She had gone off half-cocked. "I'm sorry."

His blue gaze burned through her, but he didn't move, didn't answer.

She remembered. "I'm sorry, Sir."

A wide grin curled his lips. "Such a good girl."

When he released her, she dropped to her knees, her insides already melting as Josh and Mark moved to stand next to Ted. Looking up at them, she realized this was exactly where she wanted to be.

With them.

"Rule number one," Ted said. "If you have a problem with us, you handle it immediately, or as soon as possible if we're around other people and we can't discuss it. You do not run away from us. If you ever decide you want to leave, it'll break our hearts, but you will have to face us and tell us you want to leave. We won't force you to stay with us. We only want you to stay because you want to be with us. If you run without telling us why, we will follow you and make you talk to us. Understand?"

She nodded. "Yes, Sir."

"Rule number two," Josh said. "If you do run, and you don't tell us you want out of this relationship, you will get a spanking from all three of us. Including this time. You have the option to protest this one, but I'm in a mood to give you a spanking for having a year of my life scared out of me when I thought I'd lost you."

She swallowed back tears. She'd been so caught up in her anger and outrage and fear that she hadn't stopped to consider their feelings. She nodded. "Yes, Sir. I'll take the spanking."

He reached out and stroked her hair. "Such a good girl."

She kissed his palm, nuzzling his hand.

"Rule number three," Mark said. "When we call you, unless you're in a situation where you cannot talk or answer, like driving or on a plane or something, you never ignore a call from us. We'll work out a code later, maybe a D for driving or B for busy or something, that you can text us. But if we call you and you can take the call, you will take the call. You will not ignore voice mails or texts. If you do, that's a spanking. You also will never hang up on us in a conversation. I'm not talking a dropped call, either. That's different. Understand?"

"Yes, Sir."

"And yeah, I want to give you a spanking for that now."

Fear set in. He must have sensed it, because he quickly added, "We'll condense all the spankings into one, not separate ones. *This time.*" His expression hardened. "We're not saying this is one-sided, either. We won't ignore your calls or texts, and we will never hang up on you."

"We won't run away from you, either," Josh said.

"And we promise we will always talk with you," Ted said. "Open communication, good or bad."

"What if you order me not to talk?"

All three of their expressions softened. Ted caught her hands and pulled her to her feet and into his arms. "We will never do that, sweetheart. I promise." He kissed her, slowly, sweetly, taking her breath away. "You want to talk, you just say so and we sit down and talk as equals. You might belong to us, but you aren't without a voice or a vote. Just because we make rules doesn't mean we don't respect your opinion or won't listen to you. You get to make rules, too."

She looked at Mark and Josh. "No other women. No play partners but me. I might be legally marrying him, but all three of you are my husbands."

They nodded. "We only want you, sweetheart," Mark said.

"I will need alone time sometimes."

"Then you say that," Ted assured her. "There will be times we each need alone time. Or we might want alone time with you."

"That's not alone time," she teased.

"You know what I mean, sweetie."

"Any other rules?" she asked.

The men exchanged a glance. "Come back with us to Florida," Josh said. "We'll go with you tomorrow to talk to your boss for you, if you want. Maybe he'll let you get by without the two weeks. If he looks like he really wants that, then one of us will stay here with you and help you pack. But we need to get your mom's house finished. The McAdams house has to get started. All three of us can't be gone for a whole two weeks."

It was tempting. *Soooo* tempting. Then reality hit. "You all three can't go in as my men. You'll scare the 'nillas."

Ted laughed. "We'll let Mark take point and we'll use the excuse that the production company wants to film you. We'll even offer to give his office free promo on the show in exchange for letting you go sooner."

All three of them looked hopeful.

They wanted her. It'd be stupid to prolong their agony and hers. "All right."

They surrounded her, taking turns kissing her until she felt like she was ready to crawl out of her mind with need.

After several minutes, Ted stepped back and handed the sheets to her. "Get the bed ready, sweetheart. You need your spanking before you can have your reward."

She was still gasping for air as she clutched the sheets against her. "Spanking?"

"You agreed," Ted told her. "*Red* is your safeword. If you want to stop and renegotiate, you have to speak up. Otherwise, you will get your spanking."

This is what I wanted. And she knew what a reward entailed. Already her pussy betrayed her, growing wet, her clit throbbing.

She nodded before she realized what she was doing. "Yes, Sir," she said.

They grinned. "Then get busy, sweetheart," Josh told her, his tone dropping to that thick, deep honey voice he used on her in a scene.

She spun around and dropped to her knees again, hands trembling as she got the fitted sheet onto the mattress. When she finished, she sat there and looked up at them. Mark was rooting through his carry-on bag and produced the Hitachi and a bottle of lube, as well as a box of condoms.

She snickered. "What'd TSA say to you at the airport?"

"The agent said it looked like I was getting ready for a party. I told him he had no idea, that I was going to see my fiancée. He congratulated me."

"And here I thought he'd be embarrassed when I stuck those in his bag," Josh said. "Dammit."

"You're mean." She waggled a finger at him. "No getting each other in trouble," she warned. "With me or the TSA. Especially the TSA. If you want a free body cavity search, I'm sure we could arrange for Landry to give you one."

At that, all three men looked queasy. "Uh, no thanks," Josh said. "I'm not too proud to admit that I like him as a friend, but he scares me a little. I'm not sure how Tilly controls him, but that must mean she's scarier than him. Cris is a better man than I am to take what he does in a scene."

That clarified in her mind how she knew she could do this. The men might "punish" her, but they were sadists on the more sensual end of the scale, preferring to express it sexually, not with impact play.

They weren't interested in giving her more than she could take. But they would drive the point home to her that they were men of their word.

"Get naked," Ted said.

She pulled her blouse off. "Why aren't you getting naked?"

"We will," he assured her. "But first you get spanked."

Dammit, that made her clit throb even more. She tossed her blouse to the floor, successfully resisting the urge to grab it, neatly fold it, and put it on the coffee table.

Her bra, jeans, and panties followed, leaving her standing, naked, in the middle of the mattress.

"Turn on the TV or music or something," Mark said. "Background noise."

"I didn't pack a gag," Josh said.

"I'll get a towel." Ted headed for the bathroom and returned with a hand towel while she put the TV on gO! Network, where an episode of *Otherworlds* was currently playing.

All three men arched an eyebrow at her.

"Really?" Mark asked.

She set the remote down. "Why not?" Purson was actually in the frame, doing a ghost investigation with Will Hellenboek.

"Fine," Ted said. "Me, first." He sat on the edge of the mattress and patted his lap. "Head to my left."

Her stomach twisted even as her clit throbbed. Her nipples peaked in the cool air, only adding to her discomfort. She crawled into his lap, the warmth from his legs washing through the coarse denim of his jeans and into her flesh.

He handed her the towel. "Bite down on that. Don't want to scare the neighbors."

She did, closing her eyes when he stroked her ass with his right hand. His left settled between her shoulder blades. "Oh, you will wear a day collar, once we decide what to get you. You'll have a play collar, too. We'll set up specifics for that when we get home. A spanking if we catch you without one or the other on, unless it's a predetermined circumstance or an emergency. Understand?"

She nodded and mumbled, "Yes, Sir," around the towel.

His right hand fell still. "Good girl." She felt the stiff outline of his cock straining against the front of his jeans. The wait was killing her.

Then he lifted his hand and she didn't have time to tense before he began spanking her. It wasn't just a fun spanking, either. Each stroke was hard and designed to impart a message. Tears sprang into her eyes and she started crying, biting down on the towel, when he suddenly stopped.

She gasped as he soothed her stinging flesh with his hand, gently rubbing. "Ten from me. That's all I'm giving you. Josh's turn."

She'd felt the first eddies of subspace working their way into her brain when the men helped her sit up. Josh took Ted's place and she stretched out across his lap.

He used his left hand to grab and hold her ponytail. "Need to remind our girl who owns her," he said, his sensual tone drawing a soft moan from her. "Going to remind you that we love you and worry about you and want to protect you." Then he started spanking her, every bit as hard as his brother had, but apparently only ten strokes.

She felt her juices already running down her legs despite the stinging in her ass as they helped her sit up again.

Mark smiled as he grabbed her by the back of the neck and guided her into position across her lap. "You're going to be a well-loved, well-fucked, well-cummed slave. Because all good girls get rewards."

She barely had time to bite down on the towel again as he spanked her. He used more strokes than his brothers, not stopping until she'd started crying.

That was when his hand slipped between her legs without soothing her stinging ass.

Of their own volition her legs parted for him.

"Good girl," he cooed, his fingers finding and sliding into her wet cunt. "Oh, she liked getting spanked."

"Did she?" Ted asked.

"Yes." He slowly finger-fucked her, making her moan, her hips involuntarily flexing in time with his strokes. "She's wet."

"Hmm. Should we spank her for that?" Ted asked.

She'd started to whine but Josh laughed. "Even I'm not that evil." She heard a click and a hum, and then the feel of the Hitachi being worked between her legs, under Mark's hand and against her clit.

This time, she was glad she had the towel in her mouth because it felt like her pussy exploded. She screamed into the towel as the orgasm slammed into her hard and fast. Mark slipped a third finger inside her and finger-fucked her.

"Oh, yeah," he said. "She likes that. Look at our good girl all spread out and fucking my hand."

"Should I mention the no-panties rule now?" Josh teased.

"No," Ted said. "That's not fair. She'd probably agree to anything right now."

Hell, yeah, she would. Her fingers curled into fists as she rode each orgasmic wave, her hips flexing and fucking back against the vibrator and Mark's hand.

"Okay, she's going to leave a wet spot on my jeans," Mark joked. "And frankly, I want my cock in her."

"Okay." Josh switched the vibrator off and pulled it away.

She let out a gasp of protest that made all three men chuckle.

"Oh, that's just the warm-up," Ted assured her. She looked up and both Ted and Josh had gotten naked. They helped her sit up and Mark slid out from under her.

He examined his jeans. "Lucky for you, no wet spot." He leaned in and kissed her. "That would have been another five." He touched his fingers to her lips. "Open. Clean my hand."

She needed no prodding. She sucked Mark's fingers into her mouth and laved her tongue over them, sucking her juices off his fingers like she would his cock.

"Oh, such a good girl." He pulled his hand from her mouth and quickly unfastened his belt and jeans, freeing his cock from his briefs. "Now that."

She engulfed Mark's cock, holding on to his legs as she sucked him all the way down to the base, his scent filling her lungs as she moaned around his rigid shaft.

He grabbed her hair and took over. "I wanted to fuck my first load into your pussy," he said, his voice sounding strained, "but I can't wait. Suck me dry, baby. You'll get me hard again real fast and I'll be able to last longer when I fuck you."

Hands reached around her, grabbing her arms and gently pulling them behind her back and holding them there. One of the men nudged her legs apart and she heard the click of the Hitachi again.

She moaned around his cock, another orgasm rolling through her as the vibrator pressed against her swollen, sensitive clit.

"That's it," Mark said, his tone low and breathless. "That's it, baby. You keep using my cock as a gag while we make you come."

Now he was slowly fucking her mouth, Essie unable to move between his hands on her head and the hands pinning her wrists behind her back.

Fingers grabbed and pinched her nipples, making her moan again and triggering another orgasm.

She'd always chalked up the erotic books she'd read as being pure fantasy.

Nope. Multiple orgasms goooood.

She didn't know how long she knelt there, Mark taking his time, slowing down when she felt him growing harder and hotter against her tongue, each orgasm washing into the next from the vibrator against her clit. Her jaw was starting to get a little sore when he finally took pity on her.

"Ready to swallow?" he gasped.

"Mmm-hmm!"

His fingers pleasantly dug into her scalp. "Every drop, baby. Every last drop, or you'll get spanked."

That kind of rule she could live with. He let out a grunt as the first jet shot into her mouth. Then her moans mixed with his as she eagerly swallowed, glad to be used like this, to know that she belonged to all of them.

His grip eased on her head as his cock grew soft. "Good girl," he whispered. He finally made her let go and leaned in to kiss her. "Such a good girl."

They pulled the vibrator away and shut it off. Mark stepped away and started stripping as Ted turned her around and pushed her down onto the mattress on her hands and knees.

Josh knelt in front of her, fingers around the base of his cock, his other hand grabbing her ponytail. "Open, baby," he hoarsely said. "My turn."

Behind her, Ted nudged her legs apart and knelt between them. "And me," he said. She felt him swipe the head of his cock between her pussy lips before centering on her cunt. He grabbed her hips and slammed home, hard, driving her deeper onto Josh's cock.

"Oh, yeah," Ted said. "I think another rule we're going to have is that, unless you don't feel good, you will get fucked at least once a day. With three of us, I'm sure at least one of us will be in the mood to take care of you. And even if we aren't in the mood, we'll use our backup, Señor Hitachi, to pinch hit."

"Or give a blow job," Josh said. "Fucked or a blow job."

"I like that." It sounded like Mark had moved into the kitchen. Then she heard the tap run.

She didn't have time to think about that, however, because the Hitachi powered up again. "Or a blow job," Ted agreed. "There will be many mornings we start the day with you giving all three of us blow jobs. Maybe we'll wait to make you come until later that night, keep you horny all day."

She let out a growl of dissent around Josh's cock at the last part of Ted's statement.

Josh laughed. "Nix that plan, brother."

"Fair enough. I take it she was objecting to the making-her-wait part?"

She whined.

"That would appear to be a yes," Josh interpreted.

"All right. Morning blow jobs for us, and maybe morning sessions with Señor Hitachi for her." He reached around her and held the vibrator against her clit as he started fucking her, hard and fast.

Her whine turned into a moan as the combination of his cock and the vibrator sent her over the edge again.

"Oh, I like that sound," Mark said. It sounded like he had returned to the mattress. "Keep her doing *that*." Then he reached under her, found her nipples, and started tweaking them with his fingers.

"I can't keep her doing it for long," Ted said, "because I'm about to fill...her...up." He thrust one last time before burying his cock inside her pussy.

Still, he didn't pull the vibrator away.

"You keep coming until Josh comes," Ted told her.

"Ooh, I like that plan," Josh said, beginning to fuck her mouth. "I love the way it feels when she moans around my cock."

It felt like she had no energy, no will. Her existence had shrunk to a small bubble encasing her and her men and the pleasure they were giving her.

Heaven help anyone who interrupted them now.

She sucked and licked as he fucked her mouth, both wanting a respite from the intense pleasure and yet never wanting it to stop. It was a form of torture, the best kind ever. Finally, she felt his cock grow harder, hotter.

"Good girl," he moaned before his balls drew up and emptied his load into her mouth. He let out a content sigh. "Give her a rest."

Ted clicked the vibrator off and pulled it away. The men eased her down onto the mattress, where she felt like every bone in her body had turned to jelly.

The three men smiled down at her. "How do you feel, sweetheart?"

She managed a weak smile before giving them a thumbs-up.

Mark helped her sit up enough to get a drink of water from the glass he held. "Such a good girl," he said in *that* tone, the one that melted her. "We'll give you a few minutes to recover, and then you're going to get round two."

She looked up at Mark, his playful smile.

"Oh, I'm fucking that sweet ass of yours," he said. "Why do you think we have condoms? We're going to fill every hole, baby. More than once. By tomorrow morning, we might have to carry you into work."

Ted picked up one of her feet and started rubbing it, drawing another moan out of her. "I think she should get morning spankings while she's still working here," he said. "Just because."

All three men looked at her, waiting.

"What?" she asked.

"You didn't say red," Ted noted.

No, but she felt her face grow red.

How had she gone from being totally independent to enjoying being the object of love and lust to these three men?

She didn't know, and right now, her still-buzzing clit didn't care. "Yes, Sir," she softly said.

Now she got it. She understood what they'd meant that very first night. That sometimes they'd challenge her, give her orders that would force her to decide to submit or safeword.

The corners of Ted's eyes crinkled. "So you're agreeing to morning spankings for every morning you still work here?"

She nodded. "Yes, Sir."

"Well, Mark, now I don't know if I want to talk her boss out of the two weeks' notice or not. That could be fun, conditioning her for morning spankings."

"Who says we can't do that when we get her moved back to Florida?" Josh countered. "I've been having a lot of great talks with Tony and Bill. Give me six weeks, I'll have her begging for morning spankings. Maybe sooner than that." He waggled his eyebrows at her, a grin on his face.

The little whimper she let out wasn't because she objected to that idea. It was because the idea made her clit throb again, made her pussy clench.

Maybe this is exactly *who I was meant to be.*

She wasn't about to complain.

* * * *

The next morning, Essie let the men drive her to work after they woke her up early enough to give her not only a morning spanking and to give them morning blowjobs, but to make her endure Señor Hitachi the entire. Fucking. Time.

She was more ready to go back to bed and sleep for the day than to work, but the tingles in her ass and clit were reminders the men weren't through with her yet.

Not by a long shot.

They'd promised her more of the same that night, even if they had to go to a hotel to do it.

And it warmed not just her ass, but her heart, too, when they pitched in without asking to put the living room back together again.

They really *get me.*

She'd given them a spare key to the apartment so they could go back there and wait while she was at work. They had informed her that she would text them an advance warning so they could come get her for lunch, and they would be picking her up after work.

Okay, these kinds of rules I can easily live with. They didn't feel the least bit confining.

If anything, it felt freeing to know she had them to lean on. They might want her to do things their way, but she knew if she asked it of them, they'd twist themselves inside out to make her happy.

And that's what sealed the deal for her.

She introduced Mark to her boss and coworkers as her fiancé, and his brothers. Several of her coworkers recognized them from the TV show and asked to take selfies with them, which they happily obliged.

When they gathered in her boss' office to talk with him, he smiled. "I'm guessing you're here to give me notice?"

She tried not to blush and failed. "Yes. I'm sorry, I've loved working here, and I'll work two weeks if you want me to, but it's my mom. I really miss her. And now…" She clung to Mark's arm. "Can you believe we first met in high school? It's no secret now, I guess. My dad was a hoarder. I broke up with Mark then because I was afraid of my secret getting out."

The vet took his glasses off and rubbed at his eyes. "My brother-in-law is a hoarder. Ex-brother-in-law, I should say. He's a lonely, miserable man. His own kids don't want anything to do with him." He addressed his next comment to Mark. "She's worked for me ever since she graduated. You going to take good care of her?"

His broad smile warmed her heart and set her clit to tingling again. "You'd better believe it, sir." He stared down into her eyes. "We've actually asked if she'd come to work with us on the show. She helped us with another hoarding case involving animals. She single-handedly rounded up the owner's dogs from the house. She was great."

"I can imagine. She's the best tech I got." He jabbed a finger at her. "I'd better be invited to the wedding."

"Everyone will be. We'll do it here, in Spokane."

"Good." He extended his hand across the desk and shook with Mark, then with Josh and Ted. "Well, I hate to see her go, but I'm not going to force her to work two weeks. And if you need a reference, you have them call me. Or if something happens, you're welcome back."

She walked around the desk to hug him. Dr. Channing had been like an uncle to her, and she'd learned a lot from him. "Thanks, Doc," she said, fighting back happy tears. "I will work today. It's Saturday and I know we're busy."

"Good. I'm just glad you finally found a guy. I don't mean that to sound the wrong way, but you look like a different, happier person now. You're glowing."

Somehow her men managed not to burst into laughter. She knew her ass had been glowing red earlier. Ted had made sure to comment on it.

"I finally figured out who I need to be, and who I need to be me with."

Chapter Twenty-Three

Essie stood in front of the full-length mirror hanging on the back of the door of what had once been her bedroom. Her mom sat on the end of the bed. "You look beautiful, sweetheart."

Essie turned to her. "You're not upset we're doing the wedding out here, are you?" The past twelve years of her life had been spent in Spokane. Her friends and coworkers and Amy's family were all out there.

The past eight weeks had been beautifully brutal, with her move, her men helping Pete move, flying back and forth from Spokane to Florida to film and then coming back for wedding preparations.

Her mom's house had been completely cleaned out, and their friend Seth had personally overseen the repairs. Her mom was ecstatic over her new flooring and furniture.

Her mom had also celebrated by having everyone over and cooking dinner for them in her beautifully cleaned kitchen.

Essie knew they both had some grieving to do over the loss of her father, but the joy in her mother's face, the youth that seemed to have returned to her, would be worth all the bittersweet tears.

Meanwhile, Essie had agreed to help with Lisa Parker's mom's case, and had to film scenes for that episode as well.

And then the wedding arrangements took over Essie's life.

It had all finally culminated with this day.

A few of their friends had flown out for the occasion, Loren and Ross, Seth and Leah, and Tony and Shayla, but most of their friends would attend the collaring ceremony her men were planning to have for her at Venture the next weekend. She'd come to think of the club almost as a second home, where she'd met and made dozens of new friends since moving back to Florida. They'd also become regulars at the Suncoast Society munches, where she'd met even more people who'd quickly become friends.

This weekend, however, was all about the 'nillas. Her men's parents had also flown out for the ceremony. Amy would be her maid of honor, with Amy's younger sister, Susan, as a bridesmaid. Ted would stand as best man and Josh the groomsman. Ross would give her away.

"No, I'm not upset. This is *your* day." Her mom rose from the bed and walked over to her, taking her hands. "I also want you to know that I know there's more to what's going on than what you four are saying."

Essie felt heat fill her face and started to protest, but her mom squeezed her hands. "Listen, life is short. Follow your heart. Chase happiness down and don't let go of it. I can see how you are with them. Ross and Loren said they're good men, and I know Ross and Loren are good people." She gave a curt nod. "That's good enough for me. I'll keep your secret for you, but I don't expect you four to put on an act in front of me. I want you to be yourselves. You spent too many years having to hide things. It wouldn't be fair of me to judge or make you keep hiding things that don't need to be hid."

Essie really didn't want to cry, because she wasn't sure if the makeup Amy had insisted she wear was waterproof. "Thanks, Mom."

Corrine hugged her. "I can see the way they look at you. I remember what it felt like to be in love. I choose to remember the good times, even though they were so long ago and so few years. I want you to have that happiness. That fairy-tale ending."

"Thanks, Mom." She fanned her face with her hands, trying to stave off her tears. "We weren't sure how to tell you."

"I could see it. I might have spent most of my adult life held hostage in a house full of junk, but I'm not an idiot." She smiled. "They make you happy. That's good enough for me."

Amy knocked before opening the door. "Ready? The limo's here."

"Ready." She clasped her mom's hand. "Let's go."

Amy, of course, knew her secret. Essie couldn't have kept it from her if she wanted to after the way Amy had first met the men. In front of the rest of the guests, however, the men would be careful.

Although Josh and Ted made sure to send her plenty of playful winks as they gathered together in Riverfront Park downtown, one of her favorite places in the city.

The ceremony would be short, the dress business casual, and they'd chosen to hold it on a Sunday so her coworkers and Dr. Channing could attend. They were holding their reception at a nearby restaurant.

The sister of one of her coworkers was a notary and performing the ceremony. As Essie hooked her arm through Ross' and he walked her toward where the rest of the wedding party waited, he leaned in close.

"Blink twice if you want rescuing," he softly teased.

She didn't bother suppressing her giggle. "You try to rescue me, I'll fight you tooth and nail."

"Atta girl. They're crazy about you. This is the happiest any of us have seen them since we've known them."

"I'm crazy about them, too."

"Good." They reached the front of the gathered group.

The notary asked, "Who gives this woman?"

"Her mother does," Ross said as he handed her off to Mark after placing a fatherly kiss on her forehead.

One of the things she loved about her men was they didn't try to change her. When she'd told them she didn't want a large wedding and all the associated expenses—and clutter—they'd agreed without argument. She'd also asked the men to let her keep this ceremony short and sweet. What mattered more to her than becoming Mark's wife was the collaring ceremony they'd have back in Florida, when she could publicly acknowledge in front of the rest of their friends her true relationship with all three men.

After exchanging rings and vows, Mark leaned in to kiss her. Then he whispered in her ear.

"I hope you're prepared for tonight, Mrs. Collins. Because you've got three husbands who are looking to make sure you know who that ass belongs to."

She didn't know how they did it, but they managed to yank her equilibrium out from under her in a good way.

She loved it and wouldn't trade it for anything.

"Uh-huh."

He nipped her earlobe. "What was that?" he whispered.

She swallowed, sure that everyone could see how red her face was. "Yes, Sir."

"Good girl."

Oh, she was wet now. And she knew from the evilly playful looks on Josh's and Ted's faces that they would keep her wet all afternoon, until they got to the hotel.

Then the fun would begin in earnest.

Starting with her being able to put Ted's and Josh's rings on them, since she couldn't very well do it in front of the wedding guests.

Must not scare the 'nillas.

Time both dragged and blurred for her. When they finally made it to the restaurant for the reception, it was a flurry of congratulations and hugs and handshaking and dancing and eating.

During the dancing, Ted and Josh took turns with her on the floor, making sure to whisper their own little teasing comments in her ears until she wasn't sure she could even stand to stay for the cutting of the cake.

It felt like forever until Mark finally took pity on her and directed her over to the table where the cake sat.

In this way, she'd let the men help choose. She didn't mind spending more money for an ornate cake, because it wasn't like there would be much, if any, left over at the end.

And the beautiful ceramic cake topper, made up of four white doves, would look beautiful on the shelf in their living room. Josh had already found a domed glass display case for it to protect it from dust.

Her men knew her so well.

It still took almost an hour more for her and Mark to get out of there. Ted and Josh would hang around a little longer and then join them at the hotel.

This time, her men had prepared for their trip to Spokane, although it was Ted's suitcase that had received TSA scrutiny. When he'd opened it to unpack, he'd found they'd left him a note.

Josh theorized it was the butt plug, dildo, and vibrator that had triggered it, although he'd had leather cuffs, a collar, bit gag, lube and condoms in his suitcase.

Mark had brought the rope and a riding crop.

Upon reaching the suite, Mark scooped her up into his arms with a grin after handing her his key card. "Mrs. Collins, let's get you inside and properly attired."

She found out that by that he meant naked, collared, cuffed, gagged, and tied facedown and spread wide open over the end of the bed, feet on the floor, when Josh and Ted arrived.

"Not starting without us, are you?" Ted joked as he unfastened his tie.

"Nope." Mark sat, still dressed, in a chair next to the bed. He'd laid the riding crop, butt plug, dildo, vibrator, condoms, and lube out on the bed. "Just getting her ready. But I think she wants to do something first."

"Blow jobs?" Josh joked.

Mark produced the ring box with the men's wedding bands in it and took it over to the bed. He held it so she could reach it with her right hand. She took out the slightly larger one, which she knew was Ted's.

Ted knelt next to the bed and held his left hand out to her. "'Til death do us part, sweetheart," he said.

She smiled and mumbled around the gag. "'Til death do us part." She slipped the ring on his left finger.

He leaned in and kissed her over the gag, amused when she tried to kiss him back.

"Who's our good girl?" he asked.

She felt her juices flow even more. "Me, Sir," she mumbled.

"Yes you are."

He stepped out of the way so Josh could take his place. She got the other ring out of the box and Mark put it on the bedside table. Josh knelt next to her, repeating what Ted had done.

"'Til death do us part, sweetheart."

"'Til death do us part, Sir." She slid the ring onto his hand and he also leaned in to kiss her.

Mark clapped his hands together, rubbing them eagerly. "I'm thinking time to stripe her ass. To remind her who this ass belongs to."

They didn't use a crop on her very often, but she'd take it over a cane any day. They'd given her the choice of ten hard strokes each with a paddle, five each, hard, with a riding crop, or ten total, hard, with a cane.

"First things first," Ted said. "She needs those toys stuffed in her. And I want to be using the Hitachi on her."

The men quickly stripped. Mark lubed up the butt plug while Josh grabbed the Hitachi. Josh started teasing her with the vibrator, keeping it on low and not leaving it in place long enough to let her come. Meanwhile, Mark worked lube into her ass with his fingers before sliding the butt plug home.

She moaned as it slid into place. They'd worked her up two sizes in the past eight weeks, enjoying taking her all three at the same time, loving the way it totally unhinged her mind and nervous system and turned her into a satiated puddle of happy.

Now her morning spankings consisted of being stuffed with a dildo and butt plug before they used the vibrator on her while they each spanked her.

It was the rare morning, unless she was on her period and didn't feel up to it, that she didn't look forward to their morning ritual. In fact, the men were delighted when they realized a couple of weeks earlier that just the mention of a butt plug made her wet.

She'd thought they might order her to wear it during the wedding. She would have, even if she hadn't wanted to.

She'd quickly come to learn what Loren and her other friends meant, that sometimes it was fun to submit even when she didn't really feel like it. Because her men could tell when she made that active choice, and always rewarded her for it.

Which reinforced that submitting was fun. Which made them challenge her more.

Which made her want to submit more.

And the wheels on the bus go round and round...

Ted slipped two fingers into her pussy. "Yep, she's ready." He withdrew his fingers and slowly worked the dildo inside her ready cunt.

Josh pulled the Hitachi away and she heard it change from low to high.

"These are going to sting, sweetheart," Ted warned. "Okay?"

She closed her eyes and bit down on the flexible gag. "Yes, Sir," she mumbled.

"You still want them?"

"Yes, Sir."

"Good girl." She felt Josh switch places with Ted, and now Josh was holding the dildo inside her. Ted stood next to her, his left hand resting on the small of her back.

"Hold her down, Mark."

"She's tied down."

"She likes to be held down."

"Oh, duh. Sorry."

She felt him climb onto the bed, one hand in her hair, the other firmly gripping her by the soft leather play collar she wore.

The gauzy haze of subspace sank into her. It always did during their morning ritual, and especially so now when she knew they'd take their time with her.

"Okay, Josh."

He pressed the vibrator against her clit as she heard the *whish* of the crop slicing through the air before it struck her squarely across both ass cheeks.

Her back arched as she let out a howl, the pleasure and pain mixing, merging, becoming indecipherable from each other as her orgasm tempered and masked the pain of the impact.

He drew it out, four more really hard ones, harder than she normally took. But with the feel of the dildo and butt plug inside her, her body clamping down on them, and the vibrator forcing wave after wave of pleasure out of her, she barely felt the other four strokes.

The men switched places. Josh pulled the vibrator away only long enough to give her a breather while the men got into position. Ted held her down while Mark stood next to her.

"My turn," Mark said. Josh timed it so he got her clit with the vibrator at the same time the first stoke sliced into her ass.

Her body arched against the ropes and Ted, subspace sending her blissfully soaring as Mark striped her.

She got another brief respite while the men swapped places again, this time Josh and Mark changing position. Josh rubbed the crop over her upper thighs. "I think I'm going to put my marks here."

"Just don't whack me in the head," Mark snarked.

Mark pressed the Hitachi against her clit in time for her to howl over the pain of Josh landing the riding crop directly in the crease between her ass and upper thighs.

It was one of his favorite targets.

He left his five stripes up and down her thighs, and when he finished, Mark switched off the vibrator.

"Gentlemen," Ted joked. "Time for round two." They untied her ropes and removed the gag, dildo, and butt plug from her. With Josh at her head, Ted underneath her, and Mark with a condom on ready to fuck her ass from behind, they hesitated.

Ted's tone deepened. "Tell us what you want, baby."

"I want all your cocks in me at once, Sir," she said, subspace making it feel like she could barely form words and force them out her mouth.

They loved it when she asked.

"That didn't sound very convincing," Ted teased.

"Please, Sir. Please fuck me at the same time."

Mark swatted her stinging ass. "You know what we want to hear."

She licked her lips. "Please, Sir, I want to be sucking Josh's cock while Ted fucks my pussy with his cock and you fuck my ass with your cock."

All three men drew in sharp breaths.

"I don't care how many times she says that," Josh said, "but it fucking makes my dick hard every time she does."

She let out a moan as Ted and Mark filled her pussy and ass with their cocks. They held still while Josh got a comfortable hold on her head. Then Ted grabbed the vibrator. "Ready?"

"Ready," Josh and Mark said.

He turned on the Hitachi while Mark made her arch her back. This was another familiar routine. They'd get at least one more out of her before they'd finish.

She closed her eyes, the men in complete control of her body as the vibrator hit her clit and sent her over the edge again.

"There we go," Ted cooed. "Such a good girl for us." He waited until he was sure she'd finished before turning the Hitachi off and setting it aside. "And here we go."

They found their rhythm, Essie along for the ride, being ridden, Ted and Mark seesawing inside her ass and pussy while Josh's strokes into her mouth only served to drive her harder onto his brothers' cocks.

It didn't take long. Mark came first, followed by Ted, and then that left Josh being deep-throated by her.

"Look at me, baby," he hoarsely ordered. She forced her eyes open and managed to peer up at him.

He smiled. "Such a good girl. Swallow every drop."

He came, but then something in her brain switched over. She swallowed.

Mostly.

She looked up at him as she let a little of his cum escape past her lips down the corner of her mouth.

A slow grin spread across his face. "Oh, baby. You disobeyed me."

She knew he knew she did it on purpose. She nodded, his softening cock still between her lips.

"She missed some?" Ted asked.

"Yep," Josh said.

Mark pulled out and headed to the bathroom to clean up. Before she could react, Josh had pulled her up and off of Ted and pinned her facedown on the bed again.

Arms held her wrists over her head as Josh straddled her back, holding her down. Then Mark returned, forcing her legs apart.

The Hitachi turned on. "That's twenty, baby." Josh pressed the vibrator between her legs as he started spanking her with his bare hand.

Ted leaned in and whispered into her ear. "And you'll get twenty more from me next."

A full body shudder rippled through her as another orgasm pulled her deep into subspace again.

Yes, she knew.

And twenty more from Mark.

And when they all recovered from that round, she'd do it again.

And again.

As long as they promised to never stop loving her the way they were now.

Chapter Twenty-Four

They rented a condo on Siesta Key for the week following the wedding, and pretty much stayed there the whole time, until Loren and Tilly arrived Saturday afternoon to pick Essie up.

Ted handed Tilly a garment bag that Essie hadn't been allowed to look in. "There's her outfit."

"Has she seen it yet?" Tilly asked.

"I'm right here."

"No," Ted said with a grin. "Don't let her see it until she puts it on."

Tilly nodded. "Will do."

"Hey, whose side are you on?" Essie asked.

Loren laughed. "She's in full-on Domme mode right now, honey. Landry likely wouldn't argue with her if his life depended on it and you know what a hardheaded sadist that man is."

"Damn," Essie's men muttered.

After the three kissed Essie, they sent her on her way with her friends.

"Where to first?" Essie asked from the backseat of Tilly's SUV.

"Hair, then to Shayla and Tony's to get dressed. We have to take her to the club because Tony's going to help the guys set up."

"I thought you all were doing that?" The men had compromised with Essie. She got total control of the wedding and reception.

They had total control of the collaring ceremony.

"I'm officiating the ceremony," Loren said, "but your guys assured us they have everything under control."

When they reached Shayla's later, Tilly unzipped the garment bag. "Oooh, sweetheart, this is gorgeous!"

The iridescent black dress looked like something from another era, long and flowing, with draped sleeves and a low bodice. There were also a pair of black ballet flats in the bottom of the bag.

"No underwear?" Essie asked.

Tilly snorted. "Nope, but there is this." Pinched between her thumb and index finger, she drew out a zipper-top baggy. Inside, a butt plug and a tube of lube.

She held it out to Essie, who finally took it. "Um, no offense, but I'm supposed to make sure you wear what's in this bag. Don't make me check you for *that*, 'kay? I love ya as a friend, but girls are *not* my thing."

Loren and Shayla burst out laughing as heat filled Essie's face. "Oh, honey," Shayla said, "get used to it. Because your guys know you love it and them, and they know that you aren't about to safeword for sex."

Essie stared at the butt plug. No, she wasn't going to safeword for this. Hell, it wasn't even the largest size they'd used on her.

"Dammit," she muttered.

"We'll let you get that put in first," Loren said. "We'll be back in a few minutes."

"I'd better do it in the bathroom."

"Recommended," Tilly said.

Essie wasn't sure if she should be aggravated or turned on by the fact that getting the butt plug inside her made her fricking horny.

Whatever her men were up to at that moment, they were no doubt getting a giggle out of knowing she would be very horny by the time she arrived at the club.

Her friends helped her get the dress on over her updo so she didn't muss it up, the hairstyle another directive by her men, relayed by Tilly and Loren at the salon.

"Hey, at least they didn't make you put the butt plug in before the hair appointment," Shayla said with a grin.

"Are ya *helpin'*?" Tilly asked.

Shayla shrugged. "I thought I was."

Tilly drove them to the club and timed it so they arrived just before seven o'clock, the time for the ceremony. Several dozen cars filled the parking lot, unusual for this early hour.

In the lobby, Ross met up with them, giving Loren a kiss. "They're ready for you inside," he said. "Go on in and find Ted."

He handed Tilly a roll of duct tape, which Essie realized had Hello Kitty printed all over it. "What's this for?" she asked.

"Gilo."

"Goddammit," she muttered before she stormed through the door and into the playspace.

Shayla hugged Essie. "I'm sure I'm wanted inside, too. See you in a few." She followed the other women inside.

Ross smiled down at her. "Nervous?"

"Yeah. Which is weird because I'm married to them. Well, one of them."

He offered her his arm. "My instructions are to wait for the music to start before I bring you in. And that should be any minute now that you're here."

Sure enough, less than a minute later, she heard the strains of violins start.

"That's our cue."

He escorted her through the door and into the space. The lights had been dimmed, candlelight illuminating the large room in a soft, flickering glow.

Loren stood under an arbor that had been decorated with gauzy, light blue fabric. Mark, Josh, and Ted stood there, dressed in formal tuxes and smiling so widely she thought their faces might break.

They get their wedding.

On the floor in front of the men was a large, black satin pillow. Essie held on to Ross all the way down the center aisle formed by chairs on either side. She noticed Tilly was actually standing with a couple of people, off to the side, an angry look on her face and the roll of duct tape around her wrist like a funky bracelet as she seemed to scan the gathered audience.

When Essie and Ross reached where her men were standing, Ross patted her on the arm before helping her kneel on the pillow and then taking his seat in the front row next to Tony and Shayla.

Loren gave everyone a big smile. "Welcome, friends and adopted family. We're here tonight for a celebration, as witnesses to a collaring. The men have written their vows and will read them as they pledge their bond to their woman. Sometimes, we get hung up on labels when all that matters is the people they're stuck on. Master, Dom, slave, submissive, just labels people pick for themselves. Labels, like—"

"Dry-clean only!" someone called out, making people laugh.

"God*dammit*, Gilo!" Tilly yelled as she bolted through the audience, practically climbing over people. "That's it. I fucking warned you the last time."

Now everyone roared in laughter as, on the other side of the room, Landry and Cris stepped in front of the escapee, blocking his path while the distinctive *riiiip* of duct tape being pulled off the roll followed as Tilly closed in.

Loren, as well as Essie's men, seemed unphazed. Mark leaned in and whispered, "It's not his first offense."

"Oh."

Once Loren got the room settled and Tilly apparently had the offender bound in a Hello Kitty duct tape hog-tie, Loren continued. "Labels, like lover and loved above all, are all that matters. In this case, one husband, but they all have the last name, so who cares? And now, these men shall state their cases as to why they want this woman to wear their collar."

Mark stepped forward first, a smile on his face. "I've known you since high school. We parted ways, but I never forgot you in my heart. Maybe it was better this way, for me to find out more about myself, for you to learn who you were. Maybe this was the greater plan of whatever universal powers there might be, that we grow and learn before we finally come together."

There was a muffled comment off to the side from the audience, followed by the sound of a slap as Tilly belted Gilo.

"Ow," the duct-taped offender clearly said even through his gag.

"Warned you," Tilly darkly muttered.

Essie closed her eyes and tried not to laugh, failing miserably, as did most of the room.

When it settled again, Mark continued. "I know who I am now, and what I want. More importantly, I know *who* I want. I want you. Regardless of how you want to label yourself, even if at some point you only want the title of wife and lover, I'm okay with that. As long as you're by my side and we keep growing, together, as a couple. In front of all these people, I ask if you will please take and wear our collar, as a symbol of our love, our oath to you, and our promise to always walk by your side."

"Do you accept?" Loren asked her.

Now Essie had to blink away tears. She nodded. "Yes, I accept."

Josh went next. "I know this happened fast, but I also know how right it felt from the very beginning. To find someone so perfect not just for me, but for us, is like it was really meant to be. I swear to you, I will always be faithful, will always have faith in you, will never lie to you. I will walk beside you for the rest of our lives together. And I ask in front of all these people, will you please take and wear our collar, as a symbol of our love and faith, our hopes and dreams, our future and forever together."

"Do you accept?" Loren asked her.

Essie nodded. "Yes, I accept."

Ted smiled down at her. "I've been lonely a long time. I didn't know how lonely I was until I met you. And then I realized that if I thought I was lonely before I met you, it'd be a thousand times worse if I ever lost you. I swear to you I will live the rest of my life proving to you that your faith in me, and in all a three of us, is not misplaced. And in front of all these people, I ask if you will please take and wear our collar, as a symbol of that never-ending vow we make to you today to never do anything to make you lose faith in us."

"Do you accept?" Loren asked.

"Yes, I accept."

Loren handed Ted a pink velvet bag. He and Josh took out a shiny stainless collar, a piece of metal joined by a smooth hinge at the side. On the front, a ring was fastened to it. Josh used a thin rod to push a magnetic pin out of the side of the collar, opening it so Ted could place it around her neck.

"We get to do this since he got the ring," Josh teased.

The metal felt cool at first, quickly warming to her flesh.

"This is your formal collar," Ted said. "We don't expect you to wear this every day. However, your day collar is something you will wear every day."

Loren handed Josh a jeweler's box. From it, he withdrew a gold necklace with a heart-shaped locket hanging from it. On the back they'd had all four of their initials engraved, theirs surrounding hers.

Josh carefully fastened it around her neck. "This is your day collar. Unless you're in the shower or in a situation where it could get lost, you will wear it unless we've said otherwise. Understand?"

"Yes, Sir."

Mark smiled down at her. "And lastly, as your owners, we want to mark that pretty ass of yours in front of everyone so they can see who you belong to. Three strokes each from a cane. Do you accept?"

Of course she was going to accept, because she was already so horny she could barely see straight due to the butt plug. "Yes, Sir."

"Ask for it," Ted prompted.

"Sir, please mark my ass in front of everyone so they can see who owns me."

Mark held out a hand to her and helped her stand. "Such a good girl," he said. "Bend over."

She'd thought they were going to take her over to one of the benches.

She'd thought wrong.

Loren handed a rattan cane to Ted, who passed it to Josh. "You get first honors."

Mark and Ted steadied her while Josh lifted the hem of her dress and draped it over her back. "Good girl," he said. "You did put it in. Ted owes me ten bucks. He said he bet you wouldn't."

"Dammit, sweetheart, you cost me ten bucks," Ted joked. "That's an extra cane stroke for you."

She laughed. "Yes, Sir." She was in a no-win situation with them.

And she wouldn't change a thing about it. She knew she could safeword at any time and they'd stop.

So far, they hadn't given her a reason to want to make them stop.

Josh kept one hand on her back as he gave her three quick and actually not-too-painful cane strokes. She wasn't sure if he was holding back or her ass had toughened from her morning spankings.

Then they switched places, Ted taking his turn—including the extra stroke—while Josh and Mark steadied her.

And then Mark.

When Mark finished, he lowered the hem of her dress and they helped her straighten.

Loren smiled. "Everyone, except Gilo, who's now hogtied for the evening, is welcomed to enjoy refreshments before playing." She started clapping for them, which got the audience clapping.

Her men gathered close, sexy evil gleams in their eyes. "Ready to eat, sweetheart?" Mark asked.

"Ready to be eaten, Sir."

Josh laughed. "That's our girl."

* * * *

She was afraid they might tie her down to a bench and do orgasm play on her there after the ceremony, but they didn't.

It wasn't that she didn't want them to do it to her, but a few days earlier she'd sneezed while they were playing with her and the butt plug shot out and smacked Josh in the thigh.

Once the men had stopped laughing about it and helped her clean up, Josh had playfully given her five swats with his bare hand in return.

She really didn't want a repeat of that here tonight in front of witnesses.

Once they got her home, however, and in the master bedroom they all now shared, it was clear what their plan was.

Good hard fucking.

They used rope to tie her up on the bed, on her back, knees to her chest, butt plug still in place.

Señor Hitachi was called into action. As Mark knelt between her legs first, he smiled and held up the vibrator. "Olé."

She'd started to laugh, but then he switched it on high and pressed it between her legs as he buried his cock inside her pussy.

Her laughter turned to moans.

"Good girl," he said. "Just let it happen."

Josh and Ted stretched out next to her, playing with her nipples. "I think nipple clamps are in your future," Ted told her. "The kind we can adjust. So when you get used to them, we can tighten them."

She whimpered, jolts of pleasure washing through her, her orgasm rapidly approaching.

"That's it, baby," Mark encouraged. "Come on my cock."

Aaaand there it was. She let out a moan as he fucked her, hard and fast to find his own release and fill her with his cum.

Breathless, he passed the vibrator to Josh and switched places. "Next."

She'd barely caught her breath. "My pleasure." Josh held the vibrator against her clit, smiling as she started whining immediately. "What's wrong, baby?"

"Please make me come again, Sir."

"Of course." He slid his cock into her, deep, hard, fast. They knew the week had worn her out and weren't going to drag tonight out. It didn't take Josh long to add his load of cum to her pussy.

Then it was Ted's turn. He held the buzzing vibrator just above her swollen clit. "Last one of the night, baby. Then you can go take that butt plug out." He pressed it against her flesh, grinning when she let out a loud moan as her orgasm swept through her.

"There you go." He fed his cock into her cunt, following suit, a quick, hard, deep fuck she knew would get him off fast, his balls slapping against her ass with every thrust. Once he'd come, he switched the vibrator off and she was finally able to catch her breath. She closed her eyes as they untied her, and, one by one, kissed her.

"Love you," Mark told her. "Always, baby."

"Love you, too."

Josh stroked her cheek, a sated smile curving his lips. "Love you, too, baby."

"Love you."

Ted was last, helping her sit up before kissing her. "Love you always."

"Love you, too."

They helped her into the bathroom, helped her clean up, and then they all collapsed into bed together.

Snuggled tightly between Mark and Ted since Josh had been next to her the night before, she began quickly drifting to sleep.

A stray, random thought made her snort with laughter.

"What's so funny, sweetheart?" Ted mumbled, his voice already thick with sleep.

"Dry-clean only," she said, snickering. "That *was* pretty funny."

Chapter Twenty-Five

Essie held out the box of tissues toward the tearful woman, who gratefully took two of them. "Just start wherever you want," Essie gently said.

Roberta Foss nodded as she blew her nose. "I couldn't take it anymore. I kicked him out and filed for divorce. Then the next morning, I've got an inspector at my front door threatening to take my kids."

The woman looked angry. Rightfully so. "I caught the bastard cheating on me. It's *his* mess I have to clean up, and he calls the state on *me*? Bastard." She blew her nose again. "He always threatened if I tried to leave him that he'd take the kids from me. I guess this was always his plan. Asshole. I was trying to wait until my youngest was eighteen, but I can't stand it anymore. I want my life back."

Essie glanced over at Mark and Ted, who stood in the doorway and nodded encouragingly at her to go on. "Where are your children now?" Essie asked.

This was her sixth case with the men, but the first one she'd dealt with where child custody issues came into play.

"With my mom. We're staying there, so they said I can keep the girls with me. But I have to get that shit out of my house! He was always the one who brought it in. He'd yell at me any time I tried to get rid of it or clean. And between the divorce attorney and everything else, I don't have a lot of money."

"It's okay. We'll worry about that part later. And if you want to let the production company film this, we can have them underwrite part of the expenses."

She stared at Essie for a moment. "They'd be around all the time, right? If he tries something, it'd be on camera?" The woman sounded almost hopeful.

"Well, yes. He'd have to sign a waiver to appear on camera, but if you've got a court order keeping him off the property, he couldn't come onto it anyway."

"I want that bastard on film. If he says anything, I could use it as evidence against him in the divorce to prove what he tried, couldn't I?"

This was over her head. She sent Ted a pleading look. He stepped into the room.

"Mrs. Foss, we're not a mediation firm. We can assure you our people will keep you safe during filming, and if he does try to get violent with you, you'll have plenty of witnesses to it. We can also arrange for security during filming. But I would ask that you keep your children away from the property while we're doing the cleanout as a safety precaution."

"Oh, believe me, they will be. They've been scared of their father for years. They're sixteen and fifteen." She turned back to Essie. "They told the judge at the emergency hearing my lawyer got for us that they're afraid of their father and that they didn't want him around any longer. I feel horrible I stayed as long as I did. I should have gotten out of there. But that house was mine before I met him. Why should I have left it? And then he basically trashed it. I never should have put up with it."

Roberta blew her nose yet again. Essie suspected they were the first people she'd really been able to discuss her problems with other than her attorney. "I just want a clean sweep," she softly told them. "I want it gone. Me and my kids, we deserve a chance to be happy. Is that too much to ask?"

Essie reached out and touched her hand. "No, it's not too much to ask. And we're going to help you. I promise."

Essie shifted a little in her seat, the butt plug the men had ordered her to wear that morning digging in.

Ted caught her eye and winked, knowing exactly what she was doing. Heat flooded her face. Ten months since the wedding, and she had no regrets.

None whatsoever.

THE END

WWW.TYMBERDALTON.COM